I0672763

Resistance

STRATAGEM BOOK TWO

CHRISTINA HAGMANN

www.ten16press.com - Waukesha, WI

Resistance: Stratagem Book Two
Copyrighted © 2023 Christina Hagmann
ISBN 9781645384748

Resistance: Stratagem Book Two
by Christina Hagmann

For information, please contact:

www.ten16press.com
Waukesha, WI

Cover Designer: Josh McFarlane
Art Director: Kaeley Dunteman
Edited by Jenna Zerbel

Dedication

To all the friends and family I ditched to write this book.

"Supreme excellence consists of breaking the enemy's resistance without fighting."

Sun Tzu, The Art of War

Chapter 1

The paint-chipped wood cooled my bare feet as I stepped out onto the porch to survey my surroundings. Happiness couldn't last forever. I should have learned that by now. Not that I thought at seventeen my life would be without troubles, but it seemed possible with Brody by my side, especially because there were no Isi or Agency members around.

One week had passed since the incident at the White House, but the pain of the events leading up to the mission wasn't really behind us. I could see the moments of grief in Brody's eyes as he stared off in the distance, and I thought of poor Dan, who had died helping me. Aaron's family. My mother. All gone because of my actions, like a pebble thrown into the water, the casualties rippled and flowed out to sea with far-reaching effects. I'd foiled the Agency's assassination attempt on the president by eliminating my mother, and I implicated the vice president in the press conference that followed. As a reward, they whisked me off to the wilderness to go into hiding with Brody.

The sun blazed in the sky, but the days grew shorter. In this cozy cabin in the woods, protected by tall trees that had stood like guardians for decades, it was easy to forget the problems in the world.

While Brody was off in town, picking up a few supplies, I sat on the deck drinking lemonade. The familiar rumble of an approaching vehicle, the gravel crunching under tires, alerted me to an incoming presence. My body tensed with anticipation, but it was just Brody, driving the nondescript sedan that had been gifted to us by the Opposition for helping them with the mission. The Opposition didn't have the funding that the Agency did, but they were strategic in how they used their money, and they would do anything to keep me, a mimic, out of the hands of the Agency.

He put the vehicle in park, and the trunk popped open as he stepped out of the car. He disappeared around the back and, after some rustling, reappeared carrying two reusable grocery bags.

"Hey, there." I smiled at him, my stomach fluttering with the sudden shyness that popped up at the oddest of times around him. I wasn't used to the freedom of living without someone giving me orders or watching over me, but I also wasn't used to sharing a space with anyone, let alone a boy. But Brody was not just any boy, as he had proven time and time again. He was intuitive and gentle, and after everything we'd been through, we both needed time to recover, so we made sure to give each other space and privacy.

He climbed the porch steps with a smile stretching across his face. As he reached the top, he bent over and placed the groceries on the deck. Then with that same smile plastered on his face, he stood and studied me.

"What?" My cheeks burned hot as I pulled at the hem of my sweater.

"Nothing, you just look…" he tilted his head, "happy."

A wind whispered a warning through the trees, but I ignored it. I waited for Brody to come over and plant a kiss on my cheek, but he held up one finger. He bent over and rifled through the grocery bag before standing and taking the two steps over to where I sat.

He held out a paperback book. It was *Little Women*. My favorite.

I shook my head in surprise. It was a minor detail from my life from before the Agency took me and forced me to be an operative, but it meant a lot to me that he remembered. Although I felt like I didn't know myself because I was never allowed to be myself, Brody knew me through and through. I counted myself lucky that the Agency assigned him to kidnap me that day. Who knows what would have happened if they'd assigned Aaron alone? He'd held me solely responsible for the death of his entire family and believed I was to blame, but all I did was impersonate his father and make him look capable of killing his loved ones. It was no wonder that Aaron had hated me when he first helped kidnap me and shoved me into the trunk of his car.

"Do you need help with supper?" The chair creaked under my shifting weight.

He put his hand up. "Let me, Meda. Read. Relax. Do what you want. I got this." He scooped up the groceries and disappeared through the door.

I flipped my legs over the arm of the chair and opened the book. Jo lamented on holidays without their father in the first few lines. It made me think of my father. Not my biological dad, but my dad who raised me. I'd need to check with Brody to see if it was okay if I called him soon. Maybe tomorrow. I hoped he and my sisters were okay. The Opposition looked after them, but we couldn't be together. Being anywhere near a mimic like me was dangerous. It seemed like a lifetime had passed since I had lived under the same roof as them.

After we ate, I took my book to bed, and as I was reading, Brody crawled in beside me. I placed my book down on my chest and looked at him.

When we had first arrived, he offered to sleep on the couch, but that night, he checked on me four times in the first hour, worried about the guilt that gnawed at me. The fifth time he tiptoed into the room, I invited him to sleep by my side. He'd propped pillows between us, acting as a barrier to comfort me. I'd removed the *Great Pillow Wall* sometime near the early morning hours and pulled his arm over me. He'd asked if I was okay, and I assured him I slept better with him near me.

Now, he was staring at me, and I wondered if he remembered that first night the same way I did. "What is it?" I reached over and folded my hand over his.

"I was thinking about us." He brought my hand to his lips. Then he pressed his other hand on my cheek and drew me in for a kiss. I leaned into it, letting the comfort of our touch wash over me like ocean waves as our lips dissolved into one another. I didn't want to worry about my family or the future. I just wanted to be in the present.

I kissed him back, and he pushed his fingers through my hair, gently pulling me closer. I parted my lips, and his tongue grazed mine.

He broke away from our kiss, whispering, "I love you." Brody looked at me with wide eyes. "I love this face. Your face. I love being with you. Here."

"I love you too," I whispered, surprised by the ease of those words.

"I also love watching you read." He touched the tip of my nose with his finger before settling back against his pillow.

I let out a laugh. "How boring."

He nodded like he agreed. "Yes, boring and normal. And real." He smiled but kept his eyes on me.

I reached over and patted his hand. There was a strange flash of light and a stabbing pain in my temple, and suddenly, I saw myself lying down on the bed. It was like I was looking at myself from his perspective.

I let go of his hand, gasping. Confusion wrinkled Brody's forehead as I rolled over so he couldn't see my face. Meanwhile, my mind raced, working to run down the list of all the things that could be wrong with me. I focused on staying still so as not to make a noise or draw his attention.

"Are you okay?" Brody asked.

I took a deep breath and rolled back to face him. "I'm fine." I felt guilty for lying, but I didn't want to worry him.

I grabbed my book and pretended to read, but the words swam in front of me. I couldn't concentrate, and my head felt funny, like it was wrapped in a fuzzy blanket.

I felt his gaze as he dozed off. The fuzzy sensation in my head spread like a warmth through my body, making everything heavy and tired. When my eyelids were too weighty to hold up, I turned the lamp off and curled into Brody. My brain flashed a faded signal that something was wrong, but I lost it in the fog of sleep that enveloped my thoughts.

Chapter 2

In my dream, my mother, Ava, glared at me across the vast room. The smug look of disappointment masked her face. "You aren't cut out for this life. Just think how much easier it would be for your father and sisters if you were gone. Meda, I know you wanted the dream. The family. But it isn't in the cards for us." She shook her head. Ava, my mother, was now a complete stranger. But I never really knew her, and her hateful words made it easier.

She had worn an oversized suit that fit her when she shifted into the president, having been snuck in by the Agency to take his place. It was a job they had originally intended for me to do before Brody, Aaron, and Dan kidnapped me. If either of us had been successful, the Agency would rule the United States now.

But she aimed her gun at Isi, not me. And when I saw her grip tighten, I understood what I had to do.

Squeezing the trigger, I flinched awake.

When I opened my eyes, I momentarily searched the room to figure out where I was. There was a plaid curtain and wood paneling on the walls. I looked to my right, saw a brown-haired boy lying next to me, and I remembered.

I blinked my eyes slowly and then closed them, trying to go back to sleep. This time, the dream ended the way it had played out in real life, but sometimes there were variations: my mother killing me, or Isi, or sometimes even Dan. This time it was a memory, the one I tried to block out when I was awake but came to me in my sleep. I still pictured her blank eyes looking up at the ceiling after I'd pulled the trigger. I had done it out of pure reflex. She was about to kill Isi, who had already stopped my mother from killing me once but only because she was ordered to bring me back to the Agency. I'd surprised myself that day.

Brody breathed softly, his mouth open just a hint as warm air passed through his lips. It would take longer than a week to put the Agency, the Opposition, my mother, and Isi behind me. It would probably take a lifetime. I chalked the dream up to effects of post-traumatic stress and tried to set it aside. I didn't want to worry Brody about what was going on in my head. He had enough to worry about.

An owl called in the night, and I wondered if that was what had awoken me in the first place. I slid out of bed, walked out of the bedroom and into the living room–kitchen area of the modest cabin. The curtains were drawn. Behind them, the windows were locked tight. Brody double-checked them every night. I proceeded to the door, seeking fresh air. My slip-on boots sat on the mat to the right of the door. I stuck my right foot in and nearly stumbled as I slipped my left into place.

I slowly pulled the door open, the knob clicking as the invisible mechanisms did their work. I planted one foot on the weathered deck, holding the door open. The night breeze smelled of rain. There was a storm on the horizon, and bursts of lightning flashed in the distance.

I fixed my other foot out on the deck when something moved off to the side of the porch where the shrubs met the forest. Chills broke out on my arm as I squinted in the blackness. I leaned back on my heels, ready to retreat into the cabin. Probably just a deer, but I didn't plan on leaving the porch to check it out.

"Meda," someone whispered. It was a man's voice. My neck stiffened and tensed as a tingling sensation spread throughout my body. I turned to retreat, seizing the knob to pull the door shut behind me, but the voice called out again. "Meda, wait. It's me, Aaron."

I froze. My hand remained on the doorknob. I closed my eyes. It could be anyone, including Isi. The breeze grazed my face, and I opened my eyes, searching in the darkness.

Aaron started toward me, his arms sweeping away the foliage so I could look at him. He held his hands in the air. He was unarmed. "Meda, we have to talk." His voice was low, barely above a whisper.

I surveyed him, though no matter how closely I looked, I couldn't be sure of his identity. A mimic can take the exact form of anyone. I knew that better than most. "Aaron would have called Brody. Aaron wouldn't be lurking in the dark, trying to lure me out."

I stepped back, just on the threshold of the doorway.

"Brody can't know I'm here." *"Aaron"* proceeded deliberately. The porch creaked under his weight.

I leaned back toward the door, still gripping the handle but not opening it. "Why can't Brody know you're here?"

He kept his hands up to show that he meant no harm, but why would I think Aaron wanted to hurt me? I mean, Aaron *used to* want to hurt me because of what had happened to his family. And that was my fault, so I couldn't blame him. But Aaron and I were friends now, or so I thought. Then I thought again about what Dan said. *Trust no one.*

"Because I promised I'd leave you alone. That I'd make sure the Opposition didn't try to use you for anything." He took another step closer, and there was concern in his eyes. I softened a little. It would be like Brody to protect me, even from the Opposition, who had helped to free me from the Agency.

"Leave me alone? What is it, Aaron? What do you need?" I leaned closer, so I could pick up every word.

"Meda, I need you to be quiet." His face was void of all emotion. He stood a couple of feet from me. The night fell mute.

What would he tell me? I scanned his eyes for a clue. "Brody will be fine no matter what you tell me. If you need me, I'm here, and Brody knows that. He knows I can make my own decisions."

Aaron's mouth twisted in a manner I had never seen before. He looked away. "Because Brody wouldn't be happy with what I'm about to do." Then he lunged at me.

I couldn't pull the door back fast enough before he grabbed me, clamping one hand on my mouth and the other around the back of my neck. His forceful grip knocked the breath out of me, and I lost balance as he dragged me off the porch and into the grass.

I let out a muffled scream and tried biting at his hand. He didn't even flinch. He was strong. Stronger than I remembered. I tore at the hand latched onto my mouth, but he jerked my head back again, violently, and a sharp pain pinched a nerve in my neck as I staggered along with him. The night was quiet but for the twittering of tiny insects and Aaron's harsh breathing as he struggled to haul me deeper into the woods. I watched as the cabin disappeared into the darkness behind us.

"Meda, don't worry, it'll all be okay. You aren't in danger." He said it between breaths, and then I knew for sure he wasn't Aaron. No matter who asked him to do something, he would never sneak around. Brody was Aaron's best friend, and no matter what happened between him and me, he would never betray Brody that way.

My mind flew to Isi because she was the only other mimic I

knew besides my mom, who was dead. Isi and I had parted on good terms, but she was still with the Agency, and she was an excellent agent — a ruthless one, too. She would do what they asked of her. She had no loyalty to me. And who knew what standing she was in with the Agency, now that Ava was gone?

I fought for every inch as I dug my heels into the grass and dirt, but I couldn't anchor myself. And Aaron, or whoever this was, had momentum. He dragged me from behind, so I couldn't see where we were going. When we halted in the darkness, I wasn't ready to react.

The mimic continued to grip my mouth, but I felt his weight transfer as he reached up. When he was off balance, I grabbed at the fingers that clutched my mouth and twisted my body around. I spun free and faced him, tugging down the door of a moving truck. I crouched, ready to run.

"Wait," he called. He grabbed at his waistband and pulled out something shiny tucked into his jeans. "I promised I wouldn't use this."

Even in the dim of the night, I saw the gun in his hand. If I still had any doubt that this might be Aaron, the gun made it certain. He'd never pull a gun on me. "Isi?" I squinted through the dark, searching the face for a sign.

With the gun, he gestured for me to get in the back of the truck. I shook my head. I knew I was a goner if I got in there. He motioned again, then pointed the gun at me. "Get in."

I let out a huff of air. "At least tell me who you are."

The imposter stared blankly at me. I shook my head as I walked past him and hoisted myself into the back of the truck. He motioned for me to move back, and I stepped away from the door, rubbing my neck.

He reached up to close the door but paused. "I hope I didn't hurt you." He looked at me with Aaron's eyes.

"Who are you?" I asked, once again squinting in the moonlight. "Who do you work for?" My brain toyed with the idea that maybe the Opposition sent someone in to use me again, but *they* had placed me here, so why wouldn't they just ask?

He took a deep breath and closed the door. Blackness enveloped me. A metal bolt slid into place, and I knew I was locked in.

Through the door, a muffled voice said, "I'm your brother."

Chapter 3

My brother? I thought to myself. *How could he be my brother?* I had no brothers. Only Ginger and Georgia, my twin sisters.

The truck's rumble drowned out all other sounds. Exhaust fumes funneled into the enclosed space, making me want to gag. I got up and moved to the door, trying to pry it open. I slammed on it with my open palm and then kicked it for good measure. Nothing. I was trapped. I plopped back down on the bench.

The Aaron impostor told me he was my brother.

My mother had a history I didn't know about. She'd been an agent before she had me, and she was an agent again after she mysteriously disappeared from our lives. It was only before I killed her that I realized she had been "playing" Mom for a bit with me and my sisters. But there was no way she'd had another kid. I'd forced her to be a mom, and that was why she'd resented me.

Then I thought about my dad. Not my dad growing up — George the librarian, who had watched after me and first told me about mimics — but my biological father, Chayton, head of the Agency. I knew nothing about him, except that he wanted me working at the Agency and didn't want me dead when my mom was all too eager to off me. I had never considered that I could have other siblings. The prospect excited me, but, of course, being related to someone really meant nothing. Look at how my mom had treated me. She had to pretend to be a doting mother when George took her in because she'd had nothing when she ran from the Agency. And when she grew tired of that, she abandoned us and returned to the Agency, swearing loyalty and begging for forgiveness.

As the truck began moving, branches scraped against the sides. Maybe Brody would hear the rumbling in the darkness and follow us. But, of course, we hadn't heard it when it first arrived, so there wasn't much hope in that. I slumped into a corner of the flatbed. Resting my head on the side, I thought about Brody.

What would he think when he awoke and found me gone? Would he think I left? *No,* I thought to myself. *He knows I have nowhere else to go. No one else to turn to.* He would suspect the Agency came for me. At least, that was my suspicion.

The drone of the engine and rocking of the vehicle lulled me into a sort of trance. I shouldn't have been so careless. I should have been on alert. The White House incident had occurred only days ago, and the Agency was bound to be angry and on the hunt for me.

I sat up, my back rigid, when the vehicle came to a full stop. I listened as the cab door opened and closed and waited to see what would happen next.

Someone tapped on the back gate. "Meda," he called through the door. "We have a ways to go, and I'd rather not have you locked in the back the entire trip. I only wanted to get you away from the cabin without alerting anyone."

Don't trust anyone, I told myself. I lifted myself from the bed of the truck but stayed toward the back. "Then why'd you put me here in the first place?" I waited for an answer.

"I was told you wouldn't go easily, not without your boy toy."

I glowered at the door. *Boy toy?* It sounded like something Isi would say. Who was this guy? And who had told him about me?

I didn't respond.

"Meda, I'm going to open the door. Don't force me to use the gun. I don't want to, but if I have to, I will."

"I thought you were my brother?" I yelled across the empty space.

The door opened inches at a time. Aaron's face looked in at me.

"Yeah, but I don't know you, and you don't know me."

He stopped, waiting to see what I would do.

I stepped halfway to the door, squinting at him. "Why don't you show me your real face, and then maybe I'll have reason to believe you." I peered down at him.

"Oh, sorry," he called.

In front of me, his face began to shift. I expected the familiar face of Isi. Instead, before me stood a young man with long, dark hair and a deep tan. He was shorter than Aaron by half a foot. His eyes were deep blackish-green, and his bushy eyebrows rose as if waiting for me to react.

When I said nothing, he spoke, "So, will you be good?" He dipped his head at me, as though speaking to a child.

I crossed my arms. "Will you be condescending?" I asked, unable to help myself. I'd put up with a lot over the last few weeks, starting with my kidnapping and ending with being forced to murder my mother in order to save the country from nuclear disaster. I had earned the right to be irritated.

"I'll try not to be." He smirked, opening up the door the rest of the way. "But sometimes I can't help myself." He stood in the dark parking lot wayside. Trees congregated on one side of the parking lot along with the bathrooms, and a highway with little traffic stretched out on the other side. He had been smart not to stop at a gas station, in case I ran. His hand rested on the revolver tucked in his waistband.

"Then I need you to give me a little more information before I decide to cooperate." I stayed planted on the spot.

He studied me. "Well, I don't 'need' to give you information in order for you to cooperate. You need to cooperate. But I'll answer a few questions if it will make you feel better." He took a few steps back.

An owl called from somewhere, and the choir of crickets quieted. "Okay. How are you my brother?"

"Oh, that one's easy. I'm your half-brother. We have the same father: Chayton. Head of the Agency?" I remained silent, searching for signs that he was lying. "I mean, I know you don't really know him, but you've heard of him. That much I'm sure of."

"And your name?" I leaned forward.

"Elan." He offered no last name. I moved closer.

"And… Elan. What is it you need from me?" I stopped again, crossing my arms over my chest.

"Well, it's not what I need. It's what *we* need. We need you to return to work for the Agency." My jaw fell, and so did my arms. My brain struggled to process his words. "Come on." He motioned for me to move out of the back of the truck. "I'll tell you more on the way."

I looked at him and then glanced over his shoulder at the empty parking lot. I could run, flag down a ride, call Brody, and be free of this madness once again.

Elan shook his head at me. "Meda, don't run. It'll do no good. Chayton sent me for a reason. Anyone else wouldn't have stopped to talk to you. Anyone else wouldn't have offered to let you ride in the cab to explain what's going on." He stepped back, as though he trusted that I wouldn't run. "Chayton told me about you. He told me you'd try to do the right thing as long as you recognized what that was. I'm here to tell you that going back in will save many people. It will save people from being forced into the life you have."

I felt the corner of my lip turn up in a sneer. Save people from having the life I have? Save mimics from being used by the Agency to imitate, deceive, and kill for their political connections and monetary gain? Or save innocent people, like Aaron's family, who found out about mimics and were murdered because of what they knew? It sounded like, once again, I was being forced to surrender my freedom for someone else's. Last time, they held my family against me. This time, I was supposed to do it for strangers? I stood at the edge of the flatbed and looked again at the woods.

"Meda, somewhere out there is a girl like you. She's just learning that she's a mimic. She is learning to control her shifts. And somewhere, a database is tracking all the mimic bloodlines. They will find her. They'll find us all. Then no one will be safe, mimics *or* regular people — like your boyfriend, Brody."

I studied him, trying to determine if he was lying or not. His smooth face maintained an air of innocence. He hadn't seen what I had seen, hadn't been through what I'd been through. "Have you seen this database?"

"No. I don't work for the Agency." He crossed his arms. "I'm a free mimic. I live, well… it's best if I don't tell you."

I glared at him, confused.

"There are more of us than you think. My father has been hiding us. But he knows there are people out there who have plans for us."

All around us, crickets chirped again, and night birds cooed. If what Elan said was true, then maybe they really needed my help. I sighed and jumped out of the flatbed onto the blacktop. Elan stepped back as though ready to chase me if I ran. I looked into the woods once more, longing to run back to the little cabin.

"Your father…" I corrected myself, "*My* father, the head of the Agency, is trying to stop the use of mimics? That makes no sense. It's what he does. It's his job."

"It will make sense when you learn the entire story."

"If I do this, then you have to let me contact Brody, so he knows I'm safe." I waited as Elan considered it.

"Deal," Elan said. "But you have to wait until we get to the meeting spot." He reached his hand out.

I realized what he was doing. They didn't want me to talk to Brody for fear that he'd change my mind. I was aware I shouldn't be trusting Elan, because someone could have carefully crafted everything he was saying to deceive me — *if* what he was saying was even true. I needed to learn more about him, about my father, and about what I really was.

I extended my hand. He clutched it, looking into my eyes.

"All right. Let's get going. We're already running late." He let go of my hand and wandered around to the front of the vehicle. I glanced out into the woods once more before proceeding to the passenger side of the cab and clambering in. It was better than riding in the back. At least I could keep an eye out for an opportunity to escape.

Chapter 4

The sound of the radio filled the stuffy cab of the van. Elan had it tuned to a classic rock station. I realized then that I had listened to little music in the last year, but I recognized these songs. My mom loved classic rock, so my dad had always played me her favorite songs. I thought back to my dad, George, telling me which songs my mom loved. Blinking, I wondered if any of it was true. I wondered if my mom loved those songs or if it was just part of the persona she was portraying.

I studied Elan's face for traits we shared, trying to imagine how Chayton looked. When I closed my eyes, though, I couldn't envision him. I'd never met my real father.

"So, where exactly are we going?" I asked.

Elan looked at me, as though weighing whether it was safe to give me that information or not. He didn't answer. As I searched the side of the road for signs, I sensed him staring at me. When I looked over, he looked away, but I wasn't about to let him off the hook.

"So, tell me more about the others. The mimics." It was strange hearing myself say those words. My entire life, I had hidden what I was. *Mimic* was always a dirty word. My identity fascinated Brody, but I really couldn't talk with him about it. It reminded me too much of the awful things I had done.

Elan turned to me. "What do you know about mimics?" The corner of his mouth hitched up into a scoff.

I glanced up, examining the ceiling and thinking about what my father had told me. "I'm afraid my father, George, told me a story, but he was no mimic, so I don't know how accurate it was." I bit my lip.

"Let me guess." Elan smiled to himself. "Native American lore? Skin-walkers?"

"Yes." I nodded.

He laughed a little. "I mean, that's one way of explaining it. But it's not completely accurate." He looked in the side mirror before braking and pulling the vehicle to a stop on the side of the road.

I looked around, trying to figure out why he stopped. I wasn't sure what he was looking for. The roads were empty.

He gestured to me. "Listen carefully, Meda. What they did to us was not a part of 'our culture' as everyone wants us mimics to believe. They tested on us, like animals. They manipulated our DNA." He continued to stare at the mirror.

"What?" I asked, confused.

"Our ancestors, who happened to be of Native American descent, volunteered to be test subjects during World War II. Higher-ups in the military rounded up members from different tribes. Some think they did it because of the lore. Others say it was because we were expendable." Elan raised his voice, his eyebrows furrowed in anger. "Those men were just trying to help beat the Nazis. We know better than anyone what can happen when someone comes into your home and tries to push their ideals down your throat. We know better than anyone about the massacre that comes with war."

He slammed his fist on the steering wheel, making me flinch. He took a few slow breaths while putting his head down. I didn't know what to do. He spoke as though the wounds were fresh, and perhaps they were for him. Maybe he had a history like I did. Maybe he'd lost someone he loved. I hadn't learned enough to comfort him.

He let out a big puff of air and turned to me. "Sorry. It just pisses me off." I studied him as he proceeded. "Anyway, it worked. The project was code-named *Mimic*. So here we are." He gestured at both of us.

"What happened to the men?" I asked, needing to learn more of the story.

Elan looked off into the distance and put the vehicle in drive. "After the war, I guess they tried to let the men live in peace. They wanted to reward them for their help. One scientist tried to remove any trace of the project. They even burned the lab down. Over the years, most of the scientists turned up dead."

"Then how did you get this information? How do you know this?" I asked.

He continued to watch out the window in his mirror as he spoke, "I guess someone told. Could've been the mimics, unable to control or contain their ability, or someone connected to the project. Who can say?" His phone on the dashboard revealed a map, like he'd pulled up some kind of GPS. I looked at it out of the corner of my eye, trying to make out the location of our next stop. The dot on the screen continued traveling.

"What's going on? What are we doing?" I hoped he felt like I deserved an answer. I didn't know where I stood with him.

"We're being followed." He said it like it wasn't a big deal.

I tried to squint at the phone, but he jerked it out of the holder so I couldn't see it.

He glared at me.

"What?" I asked.

Elan sighed. "Looks like your boy didn't trust you as much as you thought."

"Brody?" I asked.

Elan pressed down on the gas, pushing the limits of the van's engine.

My mind went back to when we'd first arrived at the cabin, struggling to remember if Brody had given me something that would send out a signal. I looked at my hands and my clothes, considering whether I should be mad that he planted a tracking device on me.

In the beginning, when we first met, we hadn't been honest with each other, but we couldn't be. We were on two different sides. I had hoped we'd gotten through all that. Now Elan was telling me I was being tracked by Brody. Again. The intrusion of my privacy should have upset me, but if Brody was tracking me, he must have had a good reason. He always had my best interests in mind, but I couldn't fight the nagging feeling that he knew something.

And then I saw the lights in the mirror. I sat up in my seat, straining against the seatbelt to get a glimpse of Brody behind the steering wheel. In the distance, I saw another set of lights gaining on the vehicle behind us.

"What's going on?" I looked back and forth between Elan and the two sets of lights trailing us. "Who's in the other vehicle?"

Elan put the phone up to his face. "Voice command," he said. The phone beeped. "Send a message to Raven. Get rid of him."

"Wait, what?" I reached over to seize Elan's hand. "What are you doing?"

Elan shook me off.

I looked out my mirror as a set of headlights sped up and were side by side with the vehicle that tailed us. I realized why Elan had pulled over. He'd known we were being followed. With an abrupt jolt, the approaching vehicle swerved and smashed into Brody's car.

I let out a scream, my hand clutching my jaw. I couldn't breathe as I watched Brody try to right the car. But the new car hit him again, and Brody didn't stand a chance. His car caught the gravel on the shoulder and lost control, being pulled down into the ditch.

"No!" I called out. I looked over at Elan, who glanced in the rearview mirror but continued driving. I screamed in his face. "No!" I punched him in the shoulder. When he didn't react, I hit him again and again. He reached over with one hand to deflect my blows, but he kept his eye on the road. That made things even worse. I growled as I grabbed at his neck.

"Meda, stop." His voice was intense. "You can wreck us, but it won't help anything." His statement was patronizing, but it was enough to make me stop.

Tears spilled down my face. "Why would you do that? I don't understand. I came with you." I wiped my face to prevent myself from hitting him.

"I didn't do anything," he stated. "You know how this works. It's way bigger than all of us." He gripped the steering wheel with both hands, as though convinced that I was done hitting him.

"Bigger than Chayton?" I asked. I still couldn't bring myself to say "our father" because, at the moment, I didn't trust Elan.

He shook his head. "If you thought that Chayton was the head of the Agency, you were sorely mistaken. No way a mimic is in charge. No. Dad plays the game and gets certain perks because of it."

"Yeah," I didn't believe him, "but he sent you."

"His thugs have no clue. They do what's necessary."

Tears streamed down my face. Was Brody okay? He had to be. We couldn't have gone through all that we had been through to have it end like this. "But I came with you. I'm cooperating." I turned and looked back.

"Again, big picture." He glanced in my direction. "It's easier for everyone if you cooperate, but don't be mistaken. Yes, you are my half-sister, but I have a whole other family to protect, and I'd give you up in a heartbeat to save them. You know what that's like."

When the corner of his mouth lifted in a smirk, I couldn't control myself. I brought my hand back to slap him, but before I could connect, he clutched my wrist, and something locked in place. I looked down. It was a bracelet, a silver one — thin, but enough to do the trick.

"You son of a bitch." I growled, reaching down to pull it off, but there appeared to be a locking mechanism on it.

"No, *your* mom was a bitch. You know nothing about me." Before I had time to react, he drew his elbow back and slammed it into my face. A curtain of darkness fell.

Chapter 5

I awoke to an intense twinge in my temple and a cramp in my neck. My head slumped over on the passenger side door. As I straightened myself out, I grimaced with each fresh jolt. I reached up and touched my temple. Fresh blood had coagulated over a dried wound, but the spot remained tender to the touch. I looked up at Elan with a puffy eye.

"Where are we?" I felt groggy.

He didn't answer, and I knew he wouldn't. What I really wanted to do was punch him in his smug face, though that wouldn't help anything.

The vehicle stopped, and the light of early morning revealed what looked like a factory. As he slipped out the door, I watched him stride around to the front of the vehicle, keeping his eye on me the entire time. My stomach heaved when images of Brody and his car running into the ditch popped into my head. What had happened to him?

I tried to convince myself that he was okay, and I made a vow to myself that if he wasn't, I'd kill Elan, brother or not.

Elan jerked the door open, and he took me by the elbow. I ripped my arm away, but he grabbed for it again. "Meda, don't make this difficult."

"Why would I make it easy?" My words were daggers, but he

wrenched me from the cab of the truck. He was much stronger than me. Even with my small stature, I could be strong if I drew on the strength of the people I had once shifted into, but not with this bracelet locked on my wrist. Still, Elan overpowered me by a lot, and he could do the same.

I glowered at him as he hauled me along, his fingers gouging into my skin. I pulled my arm away again, but he spun and glared at me.

"Meda, I'll let go of your arm if you walk with me. Don't try anything else because there's nowhere for you to go."

I clenched my jaw. I'd heard that one before, not that long ago.

He raised one eyebrow, a question. I dropped my arms to my side and balled my hands into fists, nodding at him. Reaching down, he unhitched the hidden latch on the silver bracelet and removed it from my red and itching wrist. Not only did silver prevent me from shifting, but I also had severe allergic reactions when I came into contact with it, causing me to black out, and when I awoke, I would find an itchy reminder of where the silver once had been.

I walked a couple of feet behind him as he led me through the checkpoint at the gate where a guard sat on duty. We walked up to large doors with tinted glass. Elan motioned at someone we couldn't see behind the glass. The door buzzed, and the lock clicked, opening the gate. I mentally kept track of all security measures, knowing that the info might come in handy at some point.

I pretended to keep my head down as Elan led me through the blank, white hallways that reminded me of a hospital. The halls were empty; the only sound was the light tapping of the soles of our shoes on the shiny white tiles.

As Elan brought me to a metal door with a security panel, I took a deep breath of sterile air and lifted my chin. He pulled a swipe card out of his pocket and ran it through the machine. After, he punched in a number. The locking mechanism clicked open. Elan pushed me forward. I stumbled a little.

Looking up to glare at him, I noticed someone else standing in the center of the room.

He had a dark complexion, and I recognized my own bright green eyes mirrored in his. I searched his face for signs of recognition.

"Hello, Meda." This was Chayton.

My father — my biological father — wore a black suit with a white button-up shirt that had no collar. I watched as he lifted his right hand and straightened his shirt cuff with his left hand. Breaking eye contact to watch his footing, he walked around his desk chair and grasped the back of it.

"Funny, I always loved the name Meda. It was the name of my sister, who was separated from me when we were young…" His voice trailed off as he looked at me. "Ava must have remembered that." He looked over my shoulder at Elan, still standing just inside the door. What was he saying? My mother named me after my father's sister? What did that even mean? My mom did everything for a reason, usually to get her own way. So why this?

I stared at him. "Well, if she remembered, I'm sure she had some plan to use it against you." I straightened my spine, trying to keep my composure, but thousands of questions prowled through my mind.

Chayton stepped out from behind his chair. "Meda, I know it's been hard for you."

I put my hand up, checking him. "No. That's unnecessary."

He put his hand back on his chair, holding himself to his spot. "Did Elan tell you why you're here?" He looked back and forth between my brother and me.

"Oh, do you mean before or after he kidnapped me, ran my boyfriend off the road, and punched me in the face?" I lay my hand on my hip to stop my hand from visibly shaking. This was my first real meeting with my father, and it wasn't because he wanted to know me. It was because he wanted to use me.

Chayton looked at Elan from under his brow. Elan smirked and shrugged.

"I'm sorry. It wasn't supposed to be like that. Elan isn't used to this kind of thing." His voice came out low and soothing.

Elan opened his mouth to speak, but Chayton put his hand up, stopping him.

"I'm sorry, Meda. We'll get confirmation that Brody is okay. But in the meantime, I'm going to be direct, and I know you're not used to that."

I shook my head, breathing hot air out of my nose. I couldn't believe he was talking to me this way. Not after my last experience with the Agency.

"We need you. Your people need you."

"Ha!" I laughed. "*My* people? I don't have people. My family — my real family — *they're* my people, and you know what I learned about that? Anyone I know and love is in danger, because you'll use them against me." I looked between him and Elan.

Chayton shook his head and moved to step forward, then corrected himself. "I shouldn't have said that. I mean, there are people who need you. You know what this life is like. Would you wish it on anyone else?" His eyes shimmered as if wet.

I shot him an icy gaze. He didn't know what my life was like. I didn't choose the Agency like he did. I didn't choose to shift into innocent people and lie and steal from others or make them look mentally unstable. But he was right in saying I wouldn't wish it on anyone. "What are you trying to say, Chayton?"

"Meda, we need you to become a member of the Agency. We

need you to operate as a loyal member." He looked around the room, as though concerned that someone was listening in, before leaning forward and continuing. "Then we need you to destroy the database that houses the name of every mimic in the US."

I froze as my brain processed what he'd said. There was a database tracking mimics? I shouldn't have been so surprised, but my thoughts traveled to my sisters. They had shown no signs of being mimics, but what if one day they did? "Wait, why can't *you* just do it?" I asked.

"Because we don't run the database. The Opposition does." Chayton crossed his arms and watched me. The Opposition had helped to rescue me from the hands of the Agency after they'd taken me and forced me to work for them by threatening my family. Brody and Aaron were part of the Opposition.

"Oh, sure. I'm not an idiot. I'm not going to give you access to their intel." The lights in this white room were hot, and a bead of sweat trickled down the side of my face.

"You saw firsthand how they feel about mimics. You were at the safe house. The Opposition sees mimics as evil. We need to make sure all mimics can disappear."

I remembered how the men looked at me, like I was a curiosity or curse, and in both those cases, less than human. I motioned to Elan. "They see us as evil because of you, forcing mimics to work for the Agency. And what about him?" Then I turned to face my brother. "Why aren't *you* going in? Why can't you do this?"

Chayton interrupted. "Elan is staying off the radar. The Agency doesn't know that he exists, and I'd like to keep it that way."

A flower of jealousy blossomed in my chest. Chayton was protecting Elan, his son. Yet, I was his daughter, and he had never protected me. Sure, he had visited me under the guise of someone else when the Agency held me as a prisoner. But he didn't get me out. He never revealed himself to me. I had spent almost my entire life thinking George was my dad.

Elan spoke, "They weren't aware you existed until your mom came back. It's why Chayton stayed in place to help hide the rest of us, including me."

"Oh, so it's my fault," I sneered at Elan. "Because of my mom." An image of her lying dead flashed in my brain. I pushed it back into the recesses of my mind and continued. "Besides, Chayton had this whole Agency gig going on before my mom ever joined the game. He was the one who got her involved."

Chayton interrupted. "That's not what he's saying. I'm not innocent here, and I know that, but I'm trying to make things right. I'm trying to atone for the mistakes of my past. When I was younger, I wanted to move up the ranks, but now I see the error of my ways. There are many people in danger. They'll become slaves, but you can stop this." I imagined little kids around seven or eight, as young as my sisters — Ginger and Georgia — or even younger. Being trained like Isi, to be an assassin. At least I'd been old enough to refuse to kill, but what about the younger kids who would be more susceptible to brainwashing?

I took two steps closer to him. It was a great planned speech, but I wasn't buying the midlife reformation act. "And why do I care?" I looked at him.

"Well, think of how powerful the Agency will become with dozens of mimics at their disposal." Chayton looked down at me.

"But sending me in does just that. It puts the database in the hands of the Agency."

"The Agency is sending someone either way. But you can get in and destroy it before anyone can use it against us."

My mouth drew into a thin line, hating the way he used the word "us" like we were the same, as he sat in his cushy office.

The Agency was already a powerful invisible entity, snaking through the government and making deals with politicians and terrorists alike, using the mimics at their disposal to imitate, intimidate, and eliminate anyone in their way. Their last plan would have cost thousands of human lives. I was willing to work with Brody and Aaron to bring them down, but this sounded like camping out on top of the hornet's nest.

Crossing my arms, I mirrored my father. "I still don't understand why this is my problem. I didn't want to be a part of this. You brought me into this." I thrust my chin at Chayton. "Along with my mom. This was never something I wanted. I never wanted any of this." I threw my arms up.

"But it is what it is." Elan shrugged. "Will you help or not?"

I stared at him, trying to imagine what he would be like as a brother. Probably just as annoying.

"Oh, now you're asking?" I shook my head at him. The way Chayton looked at me made my stomach explode. I didn't understand it. It was almost like I wanted him to be proud of me, but that promptly made me sick to my stomach.

I couldn't believe they were asking me to do this. I shouldn't feel any guilt about the Agency and what their plans were with mimics. It wasn't my obligation to mankind or whatever to help people like me. I was just one teenage girl. I wasn't strong enough to hold the weight of all other mimics on my shoulders.

Chapter 6

Chayton took a phone call, presumably to give me time to think about the situation. Glancing at the cream-colored walls, I attempted to appear bored. The central room in Chayton's office was high-ceilinged and vast. Bookshelves covered the wall to my left, and a mahogany door led outside to my right. I sat in a white leather chair, watching Chayton as he spoke with someone on the phone.

I'd never been here before, in Chayton's inner sanctum. In fact, the last time the Agency held me captive, they'd locked me in a room until they needed me. Though that had happened only a little over a week ago, I wasn't even sure this was the same place because I'd only seen my cell and empty hallways. Now that I thought about it, I never really had time to consider how I stayed sane when they held me captive. I guess the threat of killing my sisters and my dad kept me compliant, so I had to give them credit.

Warm air blew from the vents above me. I had an uneasy feeling in my stomach, and my palms were sweaty. I rubbed them against the fabric of my leggings, trying to rid myself of the nervousness.

"Okay. Thank you." He pushed the end call button and slid the phone into his pocket.

Chayton grabbed a stack of papers from his desk and arranged himself in the matching chair next to mine in front of his desk. He leaned forward with his elbows on his knees. A few moments passed before he said anything else.

"I just received confirmation that Brody's okay." He crossed his legs and leaned back in his chair.

Thankfully, Elan had left. I thought about what I'd do to him the next time I saw him. I would never forgive him for what he had done to Brody. Chayton added, "We're still tracking him. His friend picked him up."

I turned to face him. "Aaron? Wait, how are you tracking him?"

"The same way we were tracking you." He leveled his eyes with mine.

I waited for a second, but he would not give away all his secrets. "You people and your tracking devices. If I never hear the word *tracker* again, I might live a happy life."

He ignored me and handed me the papers. "Here is intel on one of the known mimics."

"Isn't this some kind of breach? Like top-secret intel? How did you get these?" I held the papers in my hand, afraid that if I looked at them, I was committing to help.

"What are you going to do, Meda? Go find the mimic on your own? It's just a name and a family tree. Per security protocol, only one name is authorized for retrieval at a time. One of our people inside exposed themselves just getting these few sheets." Though his words sounded like a joke, he wasn't smiling. He stared at me, a puzzled expression on his face.

"What is it?" The confusion in my voice surprised me. I squirmed under his stare.

"You just… You seem different." He studied me.

I couldn't mask the bewilderment on my face, but then I remembered.

After I'd killed my mother and Isi took my place so I could get away with Brody, she told me that John, my security guard from when I was being held at the Agency, had never existed. John had been the first one to tell me about Isi, the ruthless assassin mimic. I wasn't sure why. He was also the only one who was kind to me at that place. He even brought me books after I'd told him my father was a librarian. But if John had never existed, and if it wasn't my mother or Isi posing as John, then it must have been Chayton who visited.

"So, it *was* you." My voice was flat at his confirmation. I remembered when Isi had told me and I hoped that Chayton, my biological father, had visited because he cared. Because he wanted to get to know me. And now he sat here in front of me, talking about saving mimics. I wondered if any of it was true, but I was too afraid to ask. I didn't want to lose hope. I'd lost enough already.

He tilted his head, his green eyes sparkling in the bright white of the room. "How did you..." he asked, his voice trailing off as an expression of understanding came across his face. "Isi." He nodded.

I didn't know what to say, so I waited for him to speak.

"Meda, I'm sorry we had to keep you locked up, but I didn't think you needed to learn the truth. They forced my hand in taking you in. If your mother hadn't come back, they never would have known about you. You might not appreciate this, but they did not welcome her with open arms. She was a high-risk security breach, and they forced us to use extreme tactics to extricate information from her." There was pride in his words, and the thought of him being proud of her for enduring torture made my stomach churn. "That's why I came to check on you. It was my fault as much as your mother's." He reached over and tapped the papers in my hand. "You know, it's the same for them." He dipped his head at me. "You don't know them, but you could. Imagine a girl, younger than you, being forced to do the same work that you did. Imagine your sisters."

"Don't." I closed my eyes, my hand clenching the papers. I had already thought of them. "Do not bring up my sisters. I never want to hear anything about them from you or anyone else at the Agency."

"They're in the database. Under your name."

I felt rage bubble up inside me. "No. No." I shook my head.

"You can help them be erased —"

I held up a hand. "Don't use my sisters to justify this."

Chayton put his hands up, halting me. "Fair enough. I just needed you to understand the gravity of the situation. Think of how much harm the Agency can do with dozens of mimics. They've done enough with the few they have."

I gestured to myself. "I still don't understand, why me? Why can't you do it? They trust you, right?"

"There is a plan, and I'm part of it. When the time comes, I'll let you know. But first, I need to know if you'll do it." He scrutinized my face, trying to anticipate my answer.

I thought about what he'd said. What if this was all a trap to get me back in the Agency? Then again, I was probably more of a hassle than an asset. As long as the people I loved were okay, then I would do some good, which might atone for the bad I'd done. My brain bounced back and forth between complete refusal and forced compliance. I sighed, knowing I had to take the job, but we'd need some ground rules.

I nodded. "I'll do it. But you have to promise me that everyone I love will be safe. My dad. My sisters. Brody and Aaron. They are off-limits to you and the Agency."

"I don't know that I'm able to make promises, but I'll do what I can, Meda. Of course, I'll protect them at all costs." Chayton stood and waited for me to follow.

I looked up at him, unsure of what he wanted. Maybe a handshake?

"Now, that's done. Let me show you where your accommodations are." He gestured to the door.

"Oh, not a cell like the old days?" I couldn't help myself.

"No, you'll have regular accommodation. Much like your friend, Isi, when she's stationed here."

I nearly scoffed. My *friend*. I stood anyway, and he took the documents from my hands.

"I'll need to shred this printout."

"Why shred it?" I asked. I hadn't even looked at the printouts, but it seemed like a waste if they'd lost a double agent just getting one name.

"It is top secret. And I don't want it in the wrong hands. I just needed to show you proof." Chayton walked over to the desk and set the papers on the corner.

I shook my head and clenched my jaw. I still didn't understand why he was dragging me into this.

Chayton beckoned for me to follow, and he didn't glance back. I jogged to catch up. He led me through the door and out into the hallways. We wound through the maze of halls that all looked the same before he stopped at a room with a metal door. He swiped his card, and it beeped green. The door swung open with a clank as the lock released.

I studied the door, remembering my previous stay at the Agency. "Does it lock from the outside?" I asked. Unlike my old room, there was no window to look in.

He opened the door to a fully furnished room. "I told you, this isn't a cell. Although, a camera monitors the entire corridor. No sound, though." It looked more like a hotel room, with a desk, an area to watch tv, and a bed. There was another door in the back.

Chayton pointed to the door. "That's the bathroom. It's the only place without cameras."

"Well, that's nice." I brushed past him and entered the room. "I actually get my own bathroom this time?"

He stood planted at the doorway, looking like he wanted to say something.

I stopped inspecting my room and turned to watch him. "What?" I asked.

He took one step forward, just on the threshold. "You don't know how many times I've thought about how life would have been different had I known about you. I think it worked out for the best. I'm no father, and you got to have that. You got a normal upbringing. You deserved it."

He stood like he was waiting for me to say something back. Did he want me to thank him for his kind words? Thank him for letting me grow up without understanding who or what I was?

I turned my back to him. His words were a cop-out, and that was okay. I wouldn't trade my fake life for anything. My dad and sisters meant the world to me, and even though I recognized that she was pretending, I still loved the faded memories my mom left behind. It didn't mean I couldn't keep those memories close to my heart.

I heard him still breathing behind me, expecting me to respond. My chest tightened, and I clenched my hands, my fingers digging into the palms. Long moments passed before he moved away, his dress shoes tapping down the hallway. The hush of Chayton leaving filled the room like a vacuum sucking up silence.

I walked over and shut the door before making my way to the

bed and collapsing on it. My head hurt, and my heart raced. My body ached like I was fighting a losing battle. I stared at the ceiling as my mind whirled through everything that had happened today. It seemed so long ago that I was kissing Brody.

What had I gotten myself into? Even more importantly, what trouble would Brody get into trying to get me out of this? Worry washed over me as I fell into a restless slumber.

Chapter 7

A metallic click sounded, and my eyes peeled open. While I struggled to lift my heavy lids, I heard the hinges of the door squeak. I rolled over on the bed to see who'd entered the room. If they weren't going to knock, then it really was like a prison.

My eyes flicked up from the white tile floor and caught sight of a familiar figure standing at the foot of my bed with one leg propped against it. I blinked my eyes. She stood there, watching me. My mother.

I rolled out of the twin-size bed, recoiled, and lurched. Though, with the down blanket wrapped around my legs, I landed in a squat. I got up and looked at the door after I staggered a bit. There was no one there.

"She's gone." I mouthed the words to myself. My brain was still processing what had happened a week earlier, still seeking to make sense of the twists and turns. I couldn't shake the nagging feeling that there was something wrong with me, and I needed more time to rest. More time to process my feelings. But time was something I never had.

A tap came from the door, followed by silence. I stared for a moment. Words finally came to me. "Hello?" Who of the few unwanted visitors might knock on my door?

No one answered. I stepped closer, listening. After my dream,

I still wasn't sure if I'd really heard a knock. "Hello?" I asked again. Another light-knuckled tap came from the other side of the door. "Come in," I murmured, but I backed away from the door, bracing myself for another vision of my mother.

The door swung open, and this time, the squeak was real. A person appeared on the other side of the door. Elan. I would have preferred it to be Isi.

I clenched my jaw, then let a thin line of words escape. "What do you want?" I asked. "Shouldn't you be gone by now?" I turned my back to him and walked over to the bed, letting myself drop.

He ignored me and walked over to the desk in the corner. He pulled out the chair and sat in it backward, resting his arms on the backrest as he gazed at me.

"I thought you should know," Elan cleared his throat, "that your boyfriend is all right."

I sat up, even though I didn't want to give him the satisfaction of seeing a reaction. "I knew that already. Chayton told me." I glanced at him and then quickly back down at my lap. I could see him smirking out of the corner of my eye.

"No, I mean he's really all right. I know that with Chayton, it's best to get information from multiple sources." His eyes blinked slowly, and I watched as he tucked his long, dark hair behind his ears.

I leaned forward. "Why would I even believe you?" My words had sharp edges. The air between us was stuffy.

Elan leaned forward as well, and my eyes flickered to his fingertips. His nails were jagged and chewed at the edges. "You don't need to, but I have no reason to lie." He let out a sigh. "We got off on the wrong foot. I'm not saying this because I care to get to know you. My dad may have protected me, but Chayton has never been a father to me, either." He placed a biting accent on the word "father."

I folded my arms over my chest, my lips pursed, waiting.

He sagged in the chair, an unnatural posture for his muscular physique. I noticed Elan had useful muscles — not the kind that you get in the gym, the kind you get from living life and working hard.

He let out a sigh. "I'm sorry, Meda. I just want to say, I appreciate what you're going to do. Even if you don't accomplish it. I'm telling you that your boyfriend is okay because I have no reason to lie to you anymore, and I want you to focus on the job you need to do."

He reached down into his pocket.

I flinched, unsure of what he would pull out.

A photo materialized in his hand. He hesitated before holding it out to show me. "This is Briar." The picture was of a beautiful young girl with glossy, deep brown hair and her head tilted back in a laugh.

I squinted at the photo and then back at Elan.

"I've known Briar since we were kids. She's the most kindhearted girl, I mean, young woman, that I've ever met." He pulled the picture back and looked at it. A hint of a smile played on his lips. "She's a free spirit, but also stubborn."

I saw the love in his eyes when he looked at that picture.

"Meda, if you do the job that they have asked you to do, Briar will live the life she was meant to. She won't be taken and forced to shift into others. She won't be forced to kill people. She couldn't live with that." He stared at me from under a heavy brow. I had been the same way, so the Agency assigned me different duties, to observe and steal. His words softened me toward Briar. I didn't believe the Agency would give her a choice, like they'd done with me.

Elan said, "I know you don't know Briar, and I know that I don't know what you've gone through." He studied my face. "But from what I've heard, it's been a lot. Something only someone strong could get through. Please, don't let what happened to you happen to anyone else."

I looked away from him, shaking my head. I was aware of what he was doing. He was trying to get me to care because someone, somewhere, told him I did. I shot back. "You show me a picture of someone you love because you think I'll care, yet you were willing to risk the life of someone I love just to bring me here."

He clutched the photo in both hands. "I'm sorry. I wasn't thinking. I knew you were an agent. Chayton told me what you did to your mom, so in my head, it prepared me to encounter a ruthless…" He didn't finish when he saw my eyes grow wide at the mention of my mother. "I was… I get angry sometimes." He shook his head. "We needed you, and I couldn't let anyone stand in the way of that. You have to understand. You would do the same thing, right? Especially if it was a stranger." His eyes were pleading.

My mind traveled back to the risks I'd taken to keep my sisters and father safe. My thoughts traveled back to when I let my mom wreck the vehicle with the agents in it, risking their lives, just so that I could see her again. Be with her again. I knew I'd do the same thing.

He sat up straight. "I can see it in your eyes. You would do it, too. But I am sorry, honestly. I don't want anyone to get hurt." He brought the picture up to his face one more time. "Besides," his voice quieted, "I know I shouldn't have been thinking it, but you're not like the rest of us."

I stared at him, not understanding what he was getting at.

He wouldn't make eye contact with me. "You're born of two mimics. You're different."

I knew the theories, but I still didn't understand what he was trying to say. "So, that makes me more of a monster?" I searched his face for confirmation.

"I didn't mean that. Forget what I said. I'm sorry, and it was stupid. I wasn't thinking." He looked back up.

I cleared my throat. "It doesn't change the fact that you nearly killed someone I love. And I won't forget that." My gaze leveled with his.

He stood and pushed the chair back in. "I don't expect you to. I wouldn't either." He looked down at me like he was waiting for something.

"What?" I asked, looking around the room. The fluorescent lights hummed as though they were alive. Everything was cold and metallic. If I could decorate a room, this was the exact opposite of what I would pick.

He gestured for me to follow him. "Come on. I'll show you where the food is in this place."

"But you're not supposed to be here." As soon as the words left my mouth, I watched him shift into someone I didn't know, but I assumed he was an agent. He was around the same height, with perfectly coiffed hair and a neatly trimmed beard.

"Come on." He motioned again and walked to the door, waiting for me. I followed my brother out the door and down the hallway. He pushed through a set of double doors. I stayed a few feet behind.

Chapter 8

I followed my brother, cloaked in the body of a stranger but wearing the same clothes as when we first met. He made his way down the deserted hall, which had no windows and was impossibly white. My feet tapped across the glossy tiled floor, and I realized I didn't know what time of day it was.

I thought about what he'd said, about me being different. I kept my face expressionless, eager to discover what my brother would do next. We passed several doors before he turned to the right, and I followed him into a room with tall cabinets on the back wall. It appeared to be a former conference room, with stiff, crunchy carpeting and gray tables with thin metal chairs, but on the same wall with the cabinets was a basic black refrigerator and stove. A microwave was tucked under the cabinet.

I glanced around, struggling to imagine agents sitting and gossiping while eating their lunches like they were on a television sitcom. This wasn't the Agency I remembered, but then again, last time I was here, I wasn't an official agent.

I hissed to Elan. "Isn't it still dangerous for you to be here?" Catching myself, I wondered why I cared.

"Nah," Elan said. "No one's around right now. Chayton made sure they were all off. He didn't want them staring at you when you got here." I was going to say I could have just shifted, but I didn't know who to shift into. Elan was probably introduced to the agent he was mimicking and was therefore safe to go undetected. I briefly thought about Aaron and wondered when Elan was able to touch him in order to shift into him.

"When did you meet Aaron?" I asked.

He walked over to the refrigerator, ignoring my question.

I remained silent as he opened the door and snatched out some premade sub sandwiches and turned to hand me one labeled *turkey sub*.

I looked down at it as he rummaged back in the fridge and grabbed out some water bottles. I took the bottle, turning it in my hand. After a minute of silence, I looked up at him and found his eyes narrowed on me, as if trying to figure something out.

"What?" I asked. He said nothing but motioned for me to follow him.

I spun and slammed into someone without looking up. The damp water bottle slipped out of my hand. I fumbled for it, crushing my sandwich. When I looked up to see what I'd bumped into, I stared into the eyes of Isi.

Elan walked around us and continued moving, probably unaware of our history.

"Hey," I greeted her breathlessly, but Isi's eyes didn't look friendly. Not surprising. She looked like she'd just woken up, her short hair fluffy and mussed, but she wore a black tank top and black cargo pants like she'd just come from a training exercise.

Her lips were a thin line as she stared at me. I waited for her to acknowledge me, but she didn't say a word. Several seconds passed before I realized she was waiting for me to get out of her way.

"Sorry." I backed away.

"Come on." Elan looked back from the entryway. He still mimicked someone else, and I wondered if Isi had identified who he was. I tried to walk by her, but she took one step, blocking my path.

"Meda!" Elan called. Tension filled his voice.

I stared at Isi, wondering if she'd let me by. She was younger than me and smaller than me, but she was ruthless. The thing that confused me was that we'd left each other on good terms. She'd even helped the Opposition by getting caught after my mother shot her. She showed up when I called the press conference to clear Aaron's dad's name. I wondered if the Agency punished her or if she was mad that I'd allowed her to take the fall, even though she'd insisted. Then again, Isi only did things she benefited from, and it was to her benefit to get me out of the hands of the Agency. Less competition for her.

Isi's face went blank, and she stepped around me. I watched her make a path toward the fridge and didn't stick around to see what she was doing. I chased Elan down the hallway, looking back to see if Isi followed, but the hall remained empty.

We arrived back at my room, and I observed in surprise as he entered and had a seat back at the desk. I walked in and stood over him, not sure what to do with my food and drink.

"Do you mind if I eat with you?" he asked.

I sighed and let out a huff of breath. First, he'd tried to hurt my boyfriend, and now he was trying to befriend me so I could help his friends. I wanted to say no to him, to send him away, but I also was lonely. I told myself I'd done this to get more information, but that wasn't true.

"Sure. Have at it." I walked back over to my bed and sat down, crossing my legs and opening my sandwich across my lap. I watched Elan as he unwrapped his.

"I met Aaron two days ago. I don't know how Chayton knew where he'd be, but he sent me to meet him at a coffee shop he'd been staking out. I posed as one of the baristas and was able to get his imprint."

I wondered what Aaron was up to. Was he doing a job for the Opposition?

"Can I ask you a question?" He took a bite of his sandwich.

I chewed, not answering but giving him my attention.

"I know what happened to your mom. I mean, with you. How are you?" He fumbled for words as he spoke while chewing. "I mean, how did you do it?" I froze mid-bite, studying his face. He put his sandwich down and eyed me. "I didn't mean that. I meant..." His voice trailed off.

I held my hand up, stopping him. My stomach dropped. "Do you mean, how did I kill my mother?"

"No, no." His cheeks flushed red. "I meant, how did you train to become people? How did you so successfully mimic others?"

Dry bread caught in my throat as I struggled to choke down the sandwich. The word "successfully" echoed in my head as I pictured Aaron's family. I lost my appetite.

"I'm sorry, Meda. I shouldn't have asked." He picked up his sandwich and began nibbling it again. I realized, no matter how tough Elan seemed, he'd never lived through what I had. They didn't force him into a life of indentured servitude. He'd never taken someone's life.

We finished our meals without speaking. Elan got up and brushed the bread crumbs from his lap and tossed his wrapper into the garbage.

"Well, I better get going." He walked over to the bed and reached out his hand. I stared at it, unsure what he wanted before realizing, and we gave an awkward handshake. He nodded at me and turned to leave.

Even though I barely knew him, I dreaded the thought of being alone again. "Do you know what happens next?" I asked as he reached for the door handle.

He turned back around, his lips pursing in thought before answering, "I'm assuming you wait for further instructions. Chayton said you'll have to do some work for the Agency first before he can get you access to the database."

I nodded like I understood, but once again I felt like I was someone in the audience, unaware of what went on behind the curtain. Elan waited for a minute more before nodding and leaving me alone and in my little room.

My brain ticked through the events of the night as I sat at the desk, staring at the white wall. I couldn't believe I was back... After all we'd done to get me out of here. After all we had sacrificed. After Dan had given his life to help me get my dad and sisters away from the Agency.

I reminded myself that it was for the greater good. The Agency would come back stronger if we didn't do it. I still didn't understand why they needed me when they still had Chayton. I didn't understand why Chayton couldn't bring the Agency down from inside. It made me wonder just how far-reaching the Agency was.

I considered what Elan said about me being different. Isi had said the same thing. My thoughts lingered around Isi. I had known that I'd be seeing her again; I just didn't think it would be so soon. And she wasn't happy to see me. That could make this even more difficult. I would have to be careful. With Isi, I never knew where I stood.

Chapter 9

"Meda?"

Someone knocked on my door as I sat at the desk, paging through a book — another one of my favorites, *The Handmaid's Tale* — but I couldn't grasp anything. There was a stack of books planted in my room, many of my favorites, and I knew this was Chayton's doing. He was trying to win me over.

There was another knock. It hadn't been long since Elan left, so I thought maybe he'd returned to tell me something he forgot. I closed the book and placed it on the desk before standing and taking a few strides over to the door. I opened the door, and an older man with cloud-white hair and pale skin stood in front of me. He wore a suit and a thin tie. I didn't recognize him from my time before when I was kept here, but it was possible that he'd been there the entire time. Last time the Agency had held me captive, I had very limited contact with the rest of the agents.

I didn't greet him with a "hello." Instead, I waited for him to state what he was doing there.

He stood with his legs spread wide open and arms behind his back, probably with hands clasped, secret service style. All he needed was a pair of sunglasses to cover his blue eyes. "I need you to come with me."

"Who are you?" I asked, scrutinizing his face.

He ignored the question. "Chayton needs to see you." His face remained blank.

"Okay." I glanced around the room. "Do I need anything?"

The man looked above my head, like he didn't want to look me in the eye. "No," he said and turned his back, waiting for me to follow him.

He led me down the hallway, back toward Chayton's... Headquarters? Office? It was more like a wing of the entire building.

The man took long strides, as though in a hurry. I stared at the back of his head, wondering if this could be Isi in disguise. I didn't think so — there would be more disdain in his eyes — but as I continued watching him, I thought I detected something, like a hazy aura around his head. Blinking a few times, I wondered if there was something in my eyes. When I opened them again, the aura disappeared, but a strange sensation settled in my brain. This man wasn't a mimic.

I didn't know how I perceived that. It was like seeing through him. I could sense his thoughts. The man was transparent, like a fence with slats.

I realized I needed to touch him, not only to record his info in case I would need to shift into him at some point, but also so that I might learn more. I quickened my pace, stumbled, and fell forward, reaching for his shoulder and letting out a yelp. He swung, his reflexes sharp, and caught me. I grasped at his hand to help right myself.

"Oops." I smiled, still holding his hand. My skin prickled with pins and needles, but I pushed down that feeling, so I wouldn't shift. That was when something unusual happened. My world tilted, and I couldn't see straight.

I'm looking at myself through someone's eyes, looking down at my hand, but it's not my hand, and it's still grasping my actual hand. I'm disoriented, and I imagine what it feels like to all those people I've shifted in front of. It is disorienting to see yourself outside of your body. Images flash across my brain. I see a teenage boy holding a teenage girl in a passionate embrace. I see a man meeting a tall and lean businesslike woman. The name Abbott flashes in my mind. I see a man — this man, whose hand I'm holding — standing next to Chayton, and he's thinking that Chayton isn't really a man, and he knows Chayton isn't really in charge. My mind travels deeper, and I understand what he thinks of Isi and what he thinks of mimics, that we're only dogs. Then I learn what he's thinking of me, and I'm able to loosen my grip when a wave of nausea hits me.

My hand fell to my side, and the world righted itself. I was staring at the man again, but I was seeing with my own eyes.

The man froze, staring at me with a wide-eyed expression of wonder. His mouth dropped open. "What did you…" His voice trailed off. He brought his hand to his hair and smoothed it down, collecting himself.

"Don't we have somewhere to be?"

He blinked a few times and shook his head from side to side, as if trying to get something out of his brain. Trying to get *me* out of his brain.

He turned and stumbled but corrected himself. He seemed disoriented but tried to straighten himself up as he continued walking down the hallway, looking back once to determine if I still followed. His pace slowed from when we'd first started our little stroll.

When we got to the hallway leading to Chayton's wing, the man nodded to a door off to the right. As I moved toward it, he walked away from me, back down the hallway from where we'd come. He was in a hurry to get away from me, and I watched him walk away. I had no idea what he'd perceived or felt, as his thoughts had rushed through my mind so quickly.

I thought of Brody — the last time I touched his hand. I saw myself, but it didn't occur to me that maybe I was actually in Brody's head. I didn't want to consider the implications of that for the moment, as I entered what looked like a private lounge.

This wasn't the original room where I'd met Chayton. The room was empty but for the furniture. It had bright white chaise loungers and the same white tiled floor as the rest of the place. The walls looked to be some kind of cushy soundproof substance. I made myself comfortable in a chair as I waited for further instructions.

Shoes clicked across the tiles. I looked up to find Isi glaring at me. She wore leggings and a leather jacket, all black, with her hair slicked down to her scalp. She came with quick, fluid strides until she stood over me.

"What?" I asked. After our reunion in the kitchen, I wasn't even going to play nice. If she wanted to be angry at me, fine.

She held up her hand and opened her mouth, but she didn't say a word. Her jaw tightened as she clenched her teeth together. She closed her mouth and opened it again. "I thought you were going to disappear with your boyfriend." Her voice remained flat.

I raised one eyebrow. "I got bored," I shot back.

Her eyes were slits, and I could tell she didn't trust me. Her brain was working out why I would come back. The last time I was with her, she'd quoted something from a book. Something about stratagem or war strategies. She tried to make out my angle, and it was my job to make sure she trusted me or at least believed that I had no angle.

"So, you're just back." She crossed her arms, cocking one hip at me.

"Well, I'm not *back,* back," I tried to explain.

"Meda, don't be stupid. If you're here, you're *back,* back. There's no halfway. We don't get to choose."

I studied her. She was right. No matter what Chayton said, there would be no halfway. Whatever mission they assigned me, I'd be in it. "So, I guess I'm back." I got up from my chair and stood face to face with her. I had the advantage of being a little taller and a little older. She had the advantage of being a lot scarier.

"Well, you better be. Because, for some stupid reason, Chayton trusts you. And, unfortunately for me, I'm the sucker tasked with working with you, babysitting you, and picking up the mess you leave behind after you find whatever it is you're looking for." She picked an imaginary something off her leather jacket.

This would make things harder. Isi would watch my every move. I couldn't fake it with her. That meant I'd actually have to do the assignments. But I had to be sure that the assignment wouldn't hurt anyone — not after what I'd done to Aaron's family. This was another one of those times that judgment would be difficult. Do you sacrifice one life to save the lives of many? I never knew the right answer to this question. If even one person had to die, it shouldn't be worth it, but I also felt that the more lives saved would be the better option.

I reached my hand out to Isi. "Partners?" I asked.

Isi looked at my hand and rolled her eyes. "Yeah, right." She turned her back on me. "Come on. Chayton needs to see us. Normally he wouldn't waste his time giving individual assignments, but you're *special.*" She put an extra emphasis on the word "special."

It was funny. Isi was a complete badass, but at that moment, she sounded like a jealous child. I had to remind myself that it would be dangerous to underestimate her.

We left the lounge and made our way to Chayton's office. I was getting a feel for where things were in this facility. My room was somewhere near the gate, whereas Chayton's wing was in the back corner, probably so that intruders had to get through everyone before they got to him.

Isi led the way into Chayton's office. He sat behind his desk, doing something on his laptop. She didn't wait for him to wave us in. She took the long strides to the chairs seated in front of his desk and perched herself on the edge of one. I didn't follow, and she didn't glance back. I stood at the doorway, mesmerized by Chayton in his natural state. He looked like a regular guy on a computer.

Finally, he cleared his throat and looked over the top of his laptop monitor. "Would you care to join us, Meda?"

Isi looked back at me and raised an eyebrow. This had to be a peculiar situation for her. She'd known Chayton since she was a little girl. He had taken her in, but he'd never treated her as a daughter, which was probably what she had hoped for. Ava had been the closest thing Isi had to a parental figure, and she was a deceitful narcissist.

"Sorry." I walked over and took a seat next to Isi.

Isi folded her hands in her lap and waited for Chayton to speak. She actually looked obedient. I'd never seen this side of her, even with my mother.

Chayton closed his laptop and leaned forward on his desk. "We have a quick assignment. No training or shifting is necessary." He folded his hands. "Isi, I know you're familiar with Meda and her history. You probably don't trust her, but we need her, and she has offered her services." He continued to stare at Isi. "It appears young Meda finally understands that she will never be left in peace. She's rejoined the side she knows and has agreed to cooperate, understanding that we will make sure her family is safe."

Isi leaned back a few inches. "I don't care. You know I'll do whatever you ask me to." She was formal, yet she had a bite to her tone. She knew better than to cross the line with Chayton.

Chayton stood and walked around his desk to Isi. He planted his hand on her shoulder. "I know that, Isi. You are our number-one asset here. I just wanted you to know that you can trust Meda to do the assignment."

Isi looked up at Chayton. "While I respect that, sir, you're the one who taught me never to trust anyone."

Chayton's mouth hitched up in a half grin. "Touché, young lady." He gave her shoulder a squeeze before walking over and grabbing a file off his desk. He handed it over to Isi. "Here you go. Review this, and then give Meda her orders. Report back to me when you complete the job."

Isi took the file from him but didn't open it. She stood as Chayton walked back around and seated himself behind his desk, eyes focused on his computer as he went back to work, picking up where we'd interrupted him.

Isi walked over to the door. She turned back when I wasn't following and nodded at the door. I got up and followed her. Before the door closed behind me, I turned back to Chayton, but he didn't bother to look up.

"So that's it?" I asked as we walked down the hall. Isi ignored me while reviewing whatever she had in her hands. I wanted to know what was in those files, wondering if they'd tell me everything or just reveal parts of the mission bit by bit.

My mind traveled back to the agent and how I could see in his head when I touched him. I stumbled a little and reached out, grabbing at Isi's shoulder. She shrugged me off right away and turned to glare at me.

"What the hell was that?" she asked, the file clenched in her fist and straightening her shoulders, her jacket falling back into place.

"Sorry, I tripped." I shot my eyes down at the floor as we continued toward the exit.

"I can't believe Chayton is making me do this." Isi spoke as though she were talking to herself but loud enough so I could hear. "What a loser." She took a deep breath and continued, this time speaking to me. "This is a quick job," she said, not stopping. "I'll brief you along the way." I was silent as Isi led me to a large door at the end of the hall that unlocked when she swiped her access card.

Either I hadn't touched Isi long enough, or whatever was happening to me didn't work on mimics.

Chapter 10

I followed Isi down the corridor toward the front of the building. "If you need to change, do that now. I'll meet you at the vehicle."

"Wait, we're going now?" I asked. "Where are we going? What do I need?" I looked around and glanced down at what I wore: leggings and a hoodie. Missions required studying the targets and looking the part, but Chayton had said there would be no shifting.

Isi spun around, and I halted in my spot. She leaned in. "Calm down. Act like you've done this before."

My heart slowed as I took a breath. "I have, but..." I sputtered, attempting to find the words to express how I felt. I didn't want to reveal how uneasy I was, or how much I didn't want to do this. "I mean, I just don't want to mess up."

Isi inhaled in through her nostrils and held the air in her chest. She exhaled deeply. "Just do what I say and don't use your own judgment. We both know that doesn't work."

I considered her, trying to determine what she was getting at.

"Oh, and dress like a teenager." She finished and turned to walk away, leaving me standing alone in the hallway.

I swung right and made my way to my room to change my clothes, selecting a sweater and a jacket.

After my wardrobe switch, I walked out the front of the

building. Beyond the gate, a van was running and a man with a stern jaw sat behind the wheel. I pulled up my hood to ward off the chill and tucked my hands into the pockets of my jacket as I walked over to the side of the vehicle.

The door opened on my approach, and as I ducked into the back, Isi was perched on a bench seat. She didn't glance up as I slid next to her without a word. The driver eased out of the parking lot.

We were being transported to an unknown location, and Isi was supposed to brief me on the way, but instead, she just played with her gun. I didn't have a gun, not that I would need one. Even though I didn't need to shift in this case, it was clear that in our partnership, I would be the shifter, and Isi would act as my backup.

She turned her gun in her hand and rubbed a slight blemish on the side. I cleared my throat to say something, but Isi put up her hand, cutting me off.

"Don't feel the need to make small talk." Isi didn't look at me.

"I'm not going to make small talk. I want to know why I'm the primary shifter and you're the backup. You've been doing this longer than I have."

She didn't bother looking at me, and I watched her pull up the hem of her shirt and clean her gun with it. I was never comfortable with guns, and a gun in the hands of Isi made me especially nervous. "I'm not good at being other people. I'm better at being me." She dropped the edge of her shirt and rested the gun on her thigh.

The van rumbled, taking a sharp turn and sliding me down the bench seat we were planted on. Isi barely moved.

"Was that what my mom was like?" My voice was quiet. It would annoy Isi that I was asking about Ava. She had made it clear after I killed Ava that she was done with her.

Isi let out a dramatic sigh. "No one knew your mom. Chayton

didn't even know your mom. He knew Ava, the Agency's top agent, a ruthless killer with a selfish streak a mile long. That's all she would show him." She finally looked up at me. "You think you don't know who *you* are? Ava was a chameleon."

Now she had my attention. One of my biggest insecurities was that I didn't know who I was. I knew who I was with Brody, but I didn't know who I was supposed to be without him.

"I thought you were done with this crap? Ava was crazy, yet you're still trying to understand who she is? Get over it." Isi put her gun on the bench next to her and loosely crossed her legs. "You're never gonna find the answers you're looking for. There's no mimic manual." She continued, "See, the problem with being a mimic is that it's difficult to understand who you are when you can be anyone."

I knew what she meant. I hated the feeling of shifting into someone else, when their thoughts flooded my brain and the initial confusion hit like a tidal wave, threatening to drown me in their memories.

"What's your deal? Why are you so confident?" I asked.

Isi uncrossed her legs and turned to me and squared her shoulders, making direct eye contact. She seemed years older than me. "I never had to hide what I was. Chayton found me when I was just transitioning. I experienced my first change at a younger age than you did."

I fought an eye roll. She was always so competitive.

"Chayton nurtured me and helped me develop my skills." She looked away at the back wall. "Don't get me wrong, I knew it was for the job. He let me know from the beginning that changing into other people was a life skill to be honed and used. Ava had to hide it and wonder what was wrong with her," she motioned at me, "probably a lot like you. So, there you go. You have something in common with your mom. End of story."

"Yeah." I sat up straighter. "I don't need to have anything in common with her." Even when I said it, I was aware it sounded like a lie. My mind replayed the memory killing her.

Isi shrugged. "Either way, she was bonkers. She changed her mind like that." Isi snapped her fingers to show me what she meant. Once again, it appeared as though Isi was catering to me, and it had to be for a reason. No matter how much I wanted to learn about my mom, what I *needed* to learn about was my real dad, Chayton, and how much I could trust him.

The van slowed to a stop, the brakes squeaking. "Let's do this. The quicker we get out, the better." Isi looked at her smart-watch. "We're on." She nodded.

"So, now will you tell me what we're doing?" I fidgeted in my seat. There were no windows to look out of, and I felt like I was trapped in a tin can.

"This one's easy. We're going to go into an office building. Check in with the secretary. We're high-schoolers looking for some local business owners to donate to our charity. All we're doing is shaking hands with the guy."

"So, we're storing his info?"

"Yep." Isi stood up and reached over to grab the gun. She tucked it in her purse and zipped it shut.

"But we're going in as ourselves? That seems dangerous." I stood, pushing my hands down deep in the pockets of my jacket.

"Why? No one knows us." Isi pulled the purse up to her shoulder and gripped it with two hands. She inched over to the door and crouched, ready to exit the van.

I eyed up Isi. "You seem to be more likely to steal from a charity than to raise money for it. Also, why do you have a gun?"

"Don't be dense. Since that little stunt with your boyfriend, we're all required to have a gun. The only reason you don't is that everyone knows you won't use it." I looked between her and her purse, containing the hidden gun. I thought about my mom. Her words were a lie.

"I mean, you won't use it unless they forced you to." Isi averted her eyes but not before I glimpsed sympathy.

I looked away because it wasn't anything I wanted to see from Isi. I didn't need to consider her as a real person with feelings.

"Come on." She seized my arm and yanked me along with her. "Let's finish this little test so we can get back."

Chapter 11

The van door opened to an alley, which made sense because it would look odd if a couple of teenagers came rolling out of the back of a cube van. We jumped out of the vehicle, Isi first and me following. I walked across the uneven alley around the corner to the front of a floral shop. There was no one in the shop's window, and Isi got my attention and motioned across the road to a tall industrial building.

"What do they do here?" I eyed the twelve-story building.

"Yeah, I'm not sure. Apparently, this guy, the owner, has some serious stock that the Agency needs. Once we've stored his info, either of us will be able to sign over his shares. It's pretty simple." Isi adjusted her purse, which I didn't expect her to need.

And just like that, I didn't want to go. My brain told me to turn around and go back to the van. I didn't want to do any more missions. I didn't want to follow orders anymore. But I knew it was too late for that kind of thinking. "Why do they have both of us doing it?" I asked.

"Uh, backup. Did you not get the point I was making about how the Agency learned from your brief vacation?" I followed as Isi walked to the crosswalk and waited for the light to change.

I reached out and grabbed her by the arm, pulling her back. "Wait, what will happen if he signs over his shares? Does he have a family? Will they lose their business?"

Isi turned and looked at me like I was being ridiculous. "It's just the stocks from the business they're worried about. They aren't cleaning him out, but why would you care?" She studied my eyes, searching for the truth.

"It's nothing." I shook my head and pointed to the walk sign.

I followed Isi across the street.

I was using this time to gather intel, but I had a job that I had to do. A deep guilt weighed me down in the pit of my stomach. All I could think about was Aaron and how I had destroyed his entire family, including the legacy of his father, who was a good man until I mimicked him and led people to believe he had gone mad. Mad enough to kill his family except Aaron, who wasn't at home that night. I considered all the different ways this mission might play out and the ramifications if I went through with it. But I had to go through with it. I needed to think about the bigger goal — earning their trust back to destroy the database.

We walked into the building through the double glass doors. A receptionist waited at the front desk. Isi walked forward and gave our names, and after speaking to the woman, she ushered me over to the waiting area.

We were waiting for a couple of minutes when the receptionist called out two names. "Bella and Jessica?" I looked up when the receptionist spoke and then looked at Isi, who shot me a half smile and got to her feet. The woman directed us to the elevator and told us to go to the third floor.

When we disappeared inside the elevator, I raised my eyebrows at Isi. "Bella and Jessica?"

"What?" Isi shrugged. "I thought they sounded like normal teenage names. Much better than Isi and Meda."

"Is that from *Twilight*?" I asked, fighting off a grin.

"How would I know?" Isi looked up as the panel lit up the second floor and then the third. "Do I look like I read *Twilight*?"

I saw the side of her mouth twitch, and I thought that she probably did. Before I could ask her another question about it, the elevator stopped moving and the doors opened. I followed her out and onto the floor, where we would find our mark.

A young man in his early twenties sat behind a desk to the right of the elevators. Isi approached him. I stayed back and scanned the floor. There were office cubbies with partitions in the middle of the wide-open space, and around the perimeter, some of the office doors were open. Most of the doors had names on them, but some were blank. A wide bank of windows on the far wall lit up the dreary space but not enough that the humming fluorescent lights were unnecessary.

I didn't hear what she said to the man, but when she rejoined me, he got up from behind his desk and led us two doors down on the right side of the office. The door was open as though whoever was inside was waiting for us. The young man leaned in. "Mr. Dunkin? Your guests are here."

"Send them in." A voice came from around the corner. As we entered the room, a man with a receding hairline and a plump belly rose to meet us.

Isi extended her hand first, and for a moment, I wasn't sure if I was supposed to be Bella or Jessica. She introduced herself as Bella.

It was my turn next, and I extended my hand as Mr. Dunkin grasped it and gave it one pump.

"And you must be Jessica," he said.

I had a flash of Mr. Dunkin sitting on a couch in athletic shorts and a plain white t-shirt. He had a beer in his hand, and I sensed his relaxation as he brought it to his lips.

I dropped his hand and stumbled. Isi reached her hand out to catch me by the arm. Mr. Dunkin's mouth turned into an O. Isi's eyes narrowed, like she thought I was a screwup, but luckily, I didn't get any flashes when she touched me.

"Are you okay?" Mr. Dunkin asked.

I nodded my head, embarrassed. "Yeah, I just didn't eat much. Low blood sugar and all that." I bit my lower lip.

"That, my dear, is a problem I don't have." Mr. Dunkin laughed as he patted his belly. "You kids and your young metabolism." He laughed good-naturedly before heading around to sit down behind his desk. "So, what can I do for you?"

The meeting only took a few minutes. Mr. Dunkin pledged money, and Isi took his information. I wondered if they'd be contacting him and actually taking his money. It didn't concern me. He'd only pledged a small amount.

We said goodbye and made our way to the elevator. Once the doors closed, I sensed Isi looking at me out of the corner of her eye. I pulled in a breath. I wondered if she knew something was up. More importantly, I feared what was wrong with me.

The elevator doors dinged open on the first floor, and I followed Isi out. The young man behind the front counter looked up at our approach.

"Have a nice day!" Isi called in a singsong voice as we made our way to the front door.

We got about halfway to the van before she spoke again. "What's wrong with you?"

I shrugged. Nothing that I really wanted to share with Isi or anyone else.

"You're acting weird," she said impatiently as we got to the van. Isi opened the door and motioned for me to get inside. I climbed into the back and slid across the cold metal bench.

"Did I pass the test?" I asked. That was the only reason for this mission. It was to prove I was really in and wouldn't run.

She slid in beside me and slammed the door shut. The metallic sound was enough to make my head ache. Isi nodded. "Yeah, you did."

"Then why do you care how I'm doing?" I looked straight ahead as we drove back to the Agency. She stole glances at me, but I couldn't care less. I wouldn't let Isi know that there was something wrong with me.

"You're right. I don't care." She said to the driver, "Turn the radio up."

He obliged, and for the rest of the trip, the radio drowned out the silence between us.

Chapter 12

When we arrived back at headquarters, I hopped out of the van and stretched, inhaling the fresh air. I didn't even care how cold it was; I missed the outdoors. My thoughts shifted to the cabin. And Brody. That first day when we had arrived after all the madness with the president, we could barely believe we had the entire place to ourselves. We took a walk in the woods, even though Brody was afraid there'd be sharpshooters everywhere, ready to take me out.

Brody held my hand as we walked, and when we arrived at a clearing, he motioned for me to sit with him in the grass. It was damp, but I didn't care. I sat down, inching closer to him in the cold, and he grasped my hand, our fingers intertwining. I pulled our hands up and studied them. He looked at me over the tops of our fingers.

"Can I ask you something?" His words carried on the breeze.

I turned to him. "Of course, Brody. Anything." I inched even closer.

"Are you okay?" he asked. "I mean, with everything that happened. Are you okay?" He lowered his gaze and looked into my eyes. That wasn't what I expected him to ask. I'd assumed we would talk about us. I didn't want to talk about my mother, because then I would have to remember the moment I'd pulled the trigger. I wanted to forget everything and be with him.

"I did what I had to. You understand that more than anyone."
Patting his hand with my free one, I continued, "I'm fine, Brody. I have
all I need right here." Leaning forward, I pecked him on the cheek.

He half smiled. "I love you, Meda." He pulled my hand to his chest.
"And I don't want you to take this the wrong way, but I'm not all you
need. Eventually, you'll need closure, and you'll need to find yourself.
There's no rush, though. Some people don't find those things until late in
their lives, but I don't want that to be you. I don't want you to drown
under the weight of what you had to do."

The way he said it made me flash back to pulling the trigger on
my mother, how she didn't even have time to react before falling to the
floor. I remembered thinking I was more like my mother than I cared
to admit. I didn't want to think about it, and it soured my mood. I
held up my hand to stop him, but he wouldn't let it go. I couldn't help
myself.

"Just stop. I'm okay. I did what I had to, and now it's done. Let's
move on."

He had nodded then, like he was going to follow orders he didn't
agree with, and I felt guilty for scolding him for caring. He didn't
bring it up again, but after what happened with Mr. Dunkin and the
agent, I was beginning to understand what Brody had been saying.
Maybe I needed more time to heal. Maybe my experience with my
mother was affecting my head.

I was still standing on the sidewalk when Isi cleared her throat,
signaling for me to follow her. She gave me her signature eye roll,
and we walked back through the gate and into the front entrance of
the building.

I stopped at the wing where my room was and watched to see
where Isi was going as her shoes tapped down the hallway. She

stopped and turned to look at me. "Yeah? What do you want?" She crossed her arms.

"What comes next?" I asked.

"Nothing. They'll let us know when we have our next assignment. Until then, we just wait." Isi turned from me and began walking down the hall.

"Wait!" I called out.

Isi turned back around, her brow creased. "What is it?"

"What do you do for fun around here?" I took a few steps toward her. I'd never been free to roam. I'd always been on lockdown.

She snorted as though she assumed I was joking, but then she saw the serious look on my face. "Get a life." She spoke without a hint of sarcasm, walking down the hallway and turning right at the end of the corridor.

Her room must have been in a different wing from mine. I got the feeling that they'd separated us for a reason. Isi probably wouldn't help me anyway. She seemed bored and indifferent, but at least she didn't seem like she would stab me in my sleep.

She was right, though. I needed to get a life of some sort here, even if I faked it until I figured out my next move. I shook my head, feeling stupid. Maybe it was time for me to explore the rest of the place. I looked both ways down the corridors. They all looked the same: blank walls, nothing but bricks and tile. I studied the marble patterns on the tiles when a voice interrupted my thoughts.

"Meda?" I looked up to see Chayton walking toward me. "What are you doing?"

"Um, we just got back." I sputtered, embarrassed that he'd caught me walking around like a clueless, lost kid.

He wore a suit with no tie. The top button of his shirt was open, revealing a glimpse of his tan chest. I looked down at my feet. He looked almost casual. I tried to imagine him on a beach, somewhere tropical with kids running around and playing in the sand. I pushed that idea out. That wasn't Chayton. He wasn't a family guy. He never would be.

Clearing his throat, he continued. "I meant, what are you doing just standing here in the hall? Don't you have something productive to do?"

"Yeah, sure." I glanced toward my room. "I just, I wasn't sure if there was some kind of debrief." I glanced down at my hands, embarrassed.

"Meda..." Chayton's deep voice came out in a whisper. When I looked up, he stared at me. He nodded over his shoulder. "Come." He waited for me to join him. As I stepped up to join him at his side, he started walking.

We entered his office, but we didn't stop there. He led me through a door I hadn't seen before. A door that was hidden in the panels of his room, in the wall by the back corner.

As we walked through the secret doorway, I noticed lamps strategically placed around the room to emit a warm glow, rather than the harsh fluorescent lights found everywhere else in the facility. It was like an apartment, with no windows.

"Do you live here?" I asked.

"Sometimes," Chayton answered. "I have homes in various cities. It's much safer if I don't stay here, but sometimes it's a waste of time for me to leave when I'll just be working again. Plus, I like this location." He walked over to the simple red sofa that sat in a corner next to shelves stacked with old-looking books. My father, the librarian, would be impressed with the collection.

Then I remembered that Chayton was my father. I wondered if he'd liked the location because he could be near me. I surprised myself with this hope, and I wanted to smack myself, but I also wanted to ask him what his life was like. I wanted to ask if he had any family besides me and Elan. I wanted to learn if he *could* have a family, or if he was afraid he'd put them in danger. Instead, I kept my mouth shut and waited to see if he would offer any information to me voluntarily.

"Now's your chance. Ask away." He sat down on the sofa, patted next to him on the seat cushion.

I walked over and perched myself to the right of him. The sofa was long enough that I didn't have to sit too close. I opened my mouth to speak, but hesitated. Then I let the words fall out. "What was Ava like when you met her? I mean, the real Ava."

Chayton crossed his legs. "You don't want to know this. Ava was a different person to you, and it's better if you remember her as your mother."

"Did you forget that I killed my mother?" I stared at him, trying to decide if his tone was condescending. Was this his way of saying that he would not tell me anything?

"No." Chayton shook his head. "You didn't kill your mother. You killed Ava, the assassin spy."

"They're one and the same."

"They aren't. You might not understand it now, but the longer you do this, the more you will. As mimics, we have to compartmentalize things. It's hard to really know yourself when you've become so many people. You have to be able to justify the things you do. It's much easier when you consider the job you're doing and link it with whoever you are. Ava was a queen at that. If she killed someone, it was always for the job. It was almost as though that death lay in the hands of the person she'd shifted into."

"So, tell me who she was when she wasn't on the job. That's what I want to understand. Who was Ava when you first met her? When she first came to the Agency." If I had an insight into that Ava, I might know a little more about who my mother was supposed to be.

Chayton looked away, his eyes traveling across the room. He got up and walked over to the bookshelf, running his hands over the titles. "She was wild. I thought she was going to bite my head off." He turned and looked at me. "She was fearless. Well, I thought she was fearless, but that was all part of the act." He came and sat back down. "You could see it, in small moments. Moments when she was unsure or scared." He folded his hands together. "I asked her about it, and she went crazy on me. I knew I shouldn't have. I just wanted to know her."

Chayton leaned back and looked at me sideways. I could tell he had feelings for her. Not exactly love, but something nurturing and caring. It was like he wanted to protect her.

I held my breath for a moment and then let it all loose. "Did you ever want to know me?"

He tried to reach over and grab my hand, but I pulled back. "Meda, I wasn't aware of Ava's pregnancy. Because she was an asset, the Agency tried to get her back, but we didn't know that you existed. I assure you that if the Agency had realized, you could never have lived a normal life. So even though all of your thoughts about Ava are negative, you should be thankful that she kept you a secret."

"Ha!" I scoffed. "The only reason she kept me a secret is because she feared I'd take her position. There were no motherly feelings of concern."

"You don't know that. No one does. Ava was a complex person with a multitude of issues. She may have told you that, but really, she did it for different reasons. I don't want you to write her off."

"Don't you get that it's easier to write her off? It's the only reason I can justify having killed her."

"What you need to learn, my daughter, is that you need not justify anything. We have been put in the poorest of situations. You can't expect people to behave in moral and justified manners."

I stood up from the couch. "You might think that way, but not me. I expect the best. From everyone."

"Then you'll have a lifetime of disappointment." Chayton leaned back and put both arms on the back of the couch.

I wanted to ask why he didn't protect me once he'd realized he was my father, but I couldn't, because he was a stranger to me. Instead, I said, "Thank you for your time." I nodded at Chayton and didn't wait for his response. I made my way back to the hidden doorway and stepped through the entryway, back into his office. Willing myself not to look back and see his reaction, I left Chayton's wing and made my way back to my room.

I stepped into my room and closed the door behind me, leaning up against it. Worried about the hope that bloomed in my chest, I tried to crush it, knowing I shouldn't be thinking about Chayton as my father. He'd never be. I chalked it up to loneliness.

Closing my eyes, I imagined Brody, head tilted back and laughing, his dimple on his right cheek. Prickles in my eyes threatened tears. Swiping at the corners before the tears could form, I walked over to the desk to grab a tissue. I froze.

A scrap of paper lay on the desk. I stood over it, blinking to see if my eyes were tricking me. I reached down and touched it, making sure it was real. On the piece of paper, in block handwriting, it said: "Things aren't what they seem."

I glanced around the room, studying it to see if anything was out of place, but it all looked untouched. I picked up the paper and slid it under my mattress. I needed to focus on the next mission, whatever that would be.

Chapter 13

It was clear I had passed the test when I received our next assignment. The Agency was holding a wealthy entrepreneur and keeping her drugged with a steady stream of Vicodin, which she gladly accepted. I was taking on her identity and pretending to seek to invest money in a local political campaign. Apparently, the woman could barely remember what she spent money on these days, but her name would be useful when backing the politician chosen by the Agency, or whoever had hired the Agency for this job. In fact, the politician's platform went against what her family supported, which would cause a media stir. Isi was going in as my bodyguard, my backup, and I needed to channel my bubbly socialite persona.

"These assignments are stupid." Isi scanned the road as she drove into the shadow of high-rises and big money buildings. "The more you give a politician, the less they do for the people, but that little bit makes them popular among the people."

"I didn't realize you had such strong feelings about politicians." I studied her face, surprised she'd opened up to me.

"You never asked." She squinted at the road, maneuvering through the streets.

"I guess I didn't."

For the first time, I considered who Isi was when she wasn't hiding who she was. Was it possible that a scared little girl lived inside? Ava mentioned seeing Isi crying alone in her cell, and while exposing Isi's vulnerability was a tactic to get Isi to act in anger, there had to be some truth to it. Was she still reeling from the loss of Ava, the only mother figure she'd ever known? She would never tell.

She pulled up in front of a luxury hotel. "Here we are," she said, turning and looking at me. "Why do you still look like you? What is this, amateur hour?" She slid out and slammed the door shut behind her.

I concentrated, and the familiar pins and needles sensation overwhelmed me. When I opened my eyes, I filled up my seat in the body of a large, blond man who had nothing to do with this job. I joined Isi on the sidewalk in front of the building.

One of Chayton's men greeted us at the entrance, and he escorted us to a private room that overlooked the main lobby.

An agent waited at the door and let us in. Once inside, I was ushered into the woman's bedroom. It was lavish with enormous gold framed paintings covering the walls and soft velvet cushioned chairs scattered about the room.

I stood at the doorway, absorbing it all. A smoky haze clung to the air, though smoking wasn't allowed in the hotel, and ashes and wrappers littered the carpeted floors. Someone had thrown a party, and no one had cleaned up.

Isi stood by my side, watching, but I didn't move. A body lay slumped on the bed. She was my target, but she looked so sad in that vast empty room, wrapped in folds of luxurious blankets.

Isi nudged me forward, and I forced myself to walk over to the bed.

I stood over the woman, but she was completely out of it, so I took her hand and closed my eyes. A fevered image of silky sheets and dance floors flashed in my head. There was spinning and spinning, and I stepped back, trying to steady myself, but I dropped her hand.

I looked back at the woman, who had a smile stretched across her face. She was a little older than me and had curly hair and bright blue eyes. Her ruby red lips parted slightly, and she flashed a row of straight white teeth. "You have exquisite eyes," she said dreamily.

I almost tripped and fell. She wasn't meant to be awake. "Um… thank you," I answered as she frowned at me. She was out of her mind, and I had no clue what to do. Her eyes stared off into the distance and lost focus, fluttering half closed. Her breaths deepened.

I closed my eyes, trying to remember the images I'd seen. Isi moved behind me, and a hand grasped my shoulder. "Are you okay?" Her now low voice rumbled in the dark room.

"I…" I tried to say what I thought, but a blankness entered my mind. An unhappiness. Like I wasn't even in my head anymore, and I realized that the images I saw hadn't been my own.

"Meda," Isi hissed. "Are you okay?"

I shook my head, clearing out the images. "Yeah, I'm good."

She looked at me. I could tell she recognized the lie in my voice, but she nodded toward the sleeping woman.

I reached out and grabbed her hand again, this time feeling the familiar prickle as my skin began shifting into the form of the woman. I wasn't worried about the woman seeing me change. She was too out of it to understand what was going on.

Some dry cleaning bags were hanging on the curtain rod, and I grabbed one, opening it and seeing it was a conservative, light pink romper. It would do. Isi turned so I could change in privacy, and as we made our way to the door, I slipped into a pair of velvety heels that had been discarded by the door.

I glanced at myself in the mirror by the door and smoothed my now blond hair. I smiled, noticing how perfectly white and straight my teeth were — and once again, the images and the unhappiness settled in my brain, like smog. I felt the strange distance from my own body and thoughts, and an uneasiness in my stomach came with the change. I briefly wondered what her life was like, but then Isi cleared her throat, prompting me to get moving.

The mission went off without a hitch. I felt guilty for posing as the woman, but it could have been much worse. After taking photos with the campaign managers and some locals, bodyguard Isi ushered me to the waiting sedan, opening the door for me. I slid inside, tempted to shift back to myself, but I knew I should wait until we were back home. I had to play it safe, even with the tinted windows.

Isi opened the door on the other side and got in. She turned and faced me, not bothering to buckle her seatbelt.

I shifted back to myself, and the back of my head throbbed. "That was weird," I muttered to myself, reaching into the glove compartment, where there would be snacks to replenish my energy. I grabbed out a granola bar and unwrapped it, taking a bite.

Isi arched an eyebrow at me. "I thought you did pretty well for your first time back," she said with a smirk. Then her face grew serious again. "You okay?" she asked. She examined my face. I must have looked pretty shaken up.

I nodded, swallowing hard. "Yeah. I'm fine." I straightened up so Isi wouldn't notice anything wrong with me.

I nodded, and the car moved toward the exit. She was telling me to trust her with an expression that I knew all too well from before we were separated. "What happened back there?"

"I don't know what you're talking about." I stared out the window and crumpled up the wrapper, balling it in my fist.

Isi frowned and focused on the road. "Good. Chayton would be pissed if something happened to his precious Meda."

There was the Isi I knew. She didn't care about me. She only cared about herself.

Isi was quiet for the rest of the trip. We arrived back at headquarters and exited the vehicle. As we approached the entrance, Isi grabbed me by the wrist and pulled me close to her.

"Meda, what happened to you in there? Something happened. What was it?" Isi studied me.

"What are you talking about?" I didn't know how to respond to her accusation. She might have been just guessing, but she had noticed something was up.

Isi looked down at her hand on my wrist and quickly pulled away, as though I'd stung her. She glared at me, maybe imagining me reading her thoughts. She had to know something about these abilities, or she wouldn't have guessed that I'd seen something.

I bit my lip, knowing that Isi would use any information I gave her to her advantage. I thought about how this could play out. Would she want Chayton and the Agency to know about my new ability? Would it make me more of an asset than her? That was her usual motivation. But if my abilities scared her, then there was no telling what she would do.

"I just get these flashes sometimes."

She raised an eyebrow, waiting for me to say more.

"I don't get them from mimics, though."

She looked skeptical, and at that moment, I realized I'd made a mistake. It didn't matter if I could read her mind right now. The chance that I might *eventually* develop the ability to read her mind scared the hell out of her. I studied her face, wondering what secrets she held. More than likely, she was afraid of someone finding out what she cared about, or that she actually cared about something.

Isi turned and walked away from me. I should have followed her, but I stood in the remaining sunlight of the day, the clouds of pink cotton candy fading into the darkness.

Chapter 14

After eating a light dinner, I crawled into bed, thinking about Isi knowing my secret, and I considered how my mom would have reacted if she were in that position. Ava would have killed me if she realized I could read people's minds. The power would have made me more valuable than her. Isi wasn't like that. She already recognized her worth. But it would be to her advantage to give that information to others. To sell me out because of my worth, unless it benefited her.

My thoughts then flitted to Brody. It was only a matter of time before he got to me, and I was worried. He would put himself and Aaron in danger in order to reach out to me. Aaron didn't deserve that, but he'd go along with Brody because they were best friends. Even though I hadn't chosen this situation, no matter what I did, anyone who cared about me was in danger. Guilt was a mold overtaking the damp areas of doubt in my mind.

I closed my eyes. Instead of imagining Brody plotting and scheming, I thought about us at the cabin. Our first day alone, after Aaron had left, we slept until noon because we were both so out of it. I awoke to Brody making scrambled eggs.

"Mmm, that smells good," I murmured as I followed the mouthwatering scent into the small kitchenette.

Brody stood over an electric griddle, making pancakes. Some freshly cut pineapple was piled in a container on the counter, and I walked over and popped a piece in my mouth.

He looked at me, his eyes sparkling. "What do you want to do today?" he asked. I watched him flip the pancakes as he concentrated on the task, but when he realized I didn't answer, he looked back up. "Well?"

I shrugged. "I don't know. What do you do for fun around here?" I asked.

"Anything we want," he answered. I saw a blush creep up his neck. "I mean, it's supposed to be a nice day out today. Not too hot, but the sunshine should keep us warm. It would be nice to get outside. We're miles away from anyone, so we should be safe."

"What do we do outside?" I asked. After being locked up and put on missions, I couldn't even conceive of anything that we could do outside.

"I have an idea." He flipped the pancakes onto two separate plates and handed me the syrup. He led the way to the two-seater dining table, and we both put our plates down. I watched him slide into his chair and start eating. I dropped into my chair, letting the legs scrape across the wooden floor.

I looked at him expectantly. He ignored me, turning down one corner of his mouth to fight off a grin. I leaned forward. "Well?" I finally asked.

"Oh." He looked up, tilting his head at me. "It's my idea. I didn't say I was going to share it." He stabbed another piece of pancake and crammed it into his mouth.

"Well, how do you know I'll go along with it?"

Brody rolled his eyes. "It's not like you have any other ideas."

I picked up my fork and pointed at him, taking a deep breath. "True," I agreed and started cutting up my pancake.

"Don't worry, Meda. You're going to love it."

I shook my head. "You're kind of freaking me out."

"Why?" he asked innocently. "There's clearly nothing else to do."

After eating, I followed his lead and dressed in shorts and a t-shirt. We exited the cabin and found an overgrown trail leading into the forest.

He grabbed my hand and led me down the path. I opened my mouth to ask if it was safe, but then my brain reminded me that Brody would never put me in harm's way, if he could avoid it. The dock was at the end of the path. Brody went first, testing his weight by bouncing a few times. When he was satisfied that it was safe, he pulled me to the end of the dock.

I looked across the water. The air was still, and the sun glistened off the small pond. It was beautiful, like one of those Lifetime movies I used to watch when I was younger and had the television to myself. I looked up at Brody, and he squinted in the distance. His face was void of any emotion.

Finally, I interrupted the silence. "So, we're going to watch the water?"

His face broke out into a grin, and he nudged me with his hip. "No, we're going in the water."

"We are?" I shuffled my feet on the worn dock. "But it looks kinda slimy."

"You're telling me after all you've been through, you're afraid of a little slime?" He shook his head and jumped from a standing position. He was fully clad in a white t-shirt and a pair of athletic shorts. I reached my arm out after him but brought my hands up to my mouth as he splashed down, cannon balling into the surface, a wake of ripples shattering the calm.

Water splashed up, and I jumped back a step. It was seconds before Brody surfaced, but in those few seconds, there came a sense of dread, like some water monster had grabbed him and pulled him underneath, holding him down there until he lost consciousness.

When he surfaced, he popped up headfirst but jumped so high, his entire torso came out of the water. He gasped like he couldn't breathe but called out, "That's cold!" Still taking shallow breaths, he treaded water over to the dock. "Come on, Meda!" His teeth chattered.

"That doesn't really inspire me to join you." I laughed.

He tilted his head and pouted. I looked around the open and exposed clearing, thinking I'd rather be in the water with Brody than alone up here on the dock. I slid off my shoes.

"Yeah! Let's go!" Brody yelled, slapping the surface of the water.

I took two steps and launched myself from the dock, pinching my nose and curling into a ball. The cold hit me like a wall, and my entire body tensed, but instead of sinking to the bottom, without touching, I paddled back up to the surface.

"Whoa!" I yelled out as I came up for breath.

Brody grinned and continued to tread water next to me. I was out of breath from the cold, but it exhilarated me. He swam back, and I followed him to the dock. Climbing out, he perched on the edge, and I joined him, my teeth chattering.

He said, "I remember the last time my dad took me swimming. He dared me to go off the high dive at the public pool, but I wimped out. He laughed at me and called me a loser."

I stared at him, mad for him. "Don't listen to him. Anyone who's going to be rude to you doesn't matter."

"But that's the thing. Family does matter. And when they do something that hurts you, it's okay to feel bad about it." Brody was talking about his dad, who used to treat him horribly. It was why Brody was so close to Aaron's family, or he had been until they were murdered.

When I didn't reply, he turned and looked at me. He tilted his head to the side. "Are you okay?"

"Yeah, but I killed my mom." I knew it was my imagination, but it seemed like the entire world halted with my words.

Brody grabbed my hand and squeezed it. He studied my eyes. "You had to, Meda. It was you or her. But it's still okay to mourn the mother that you remember, the one that you keep with you here." He reached his hand up and brushed a stray strand of wet, black hair aside. "It's okay that you're not over it. It just happened. You're not that cold. Your mother pretended to be different people, and even though you don't think you know yourself, you do. No matter who you shift into, when you turn back, deep down you're the same Meda you always were, with a love of books and the ability to be hopeful and see beauty in the world."

He leaned in, his hand gliding down the back of my neck, and planted his soft lips on mine. A fire burned in my stomach, and I settled my arms around his waist.

I opened my eyes, and I was back in my tiny room with my tiny bed, and Brody was just a memory. A whisper across my brain.

He was right. I was still here because I had hope. I would get through this and the next thing because that was who I was.

Chapter 15

The clock read four in the morning, and I sat up in bed, unable to lie there any longer. I slipped on some leggings and a long sleeve t-shirt. No one had told me about any upcoming missions, and I wasn't sure if I was just supposed to sit in my room and wait, so I thought I'd venture down to the cafeteria and see what they had for breakfast foods.

I held my breath as I pressed on the door, wondering if I would find that they'd locked me in at night, but it swung open with little resistance. I tiptoed down the hallway, waiting for someone to stop me or tell me to go back to my room, but when I passed an agent stationed in the hallway, he barely looked at me.

When I made it to the common area, a hotel-style, self-serve, complimentary breakfast surprised me. There was even a waffle maker. It seemed a strange indulgence, seeing as last time I'd lived in this place, they'd hand-delivered me bland food, while I had no say in what I ate.

I snatched up a banana from the fruit bowl before making my way over to the waffle station. The waffle maker was shiny and clean, and I glanced around as I waited for someone to walk in and yell at me or tell me to get back to my room, but I was alone.

Once my waffle was done, I added syrup and topped it with

some cool whip. A tray of utensils sat nearby, and I reached down, swiping a fork and butter knife, once again glancing around to see if anyone would stop me from grabbing this potential weapon. When no one did, I was bold. I placed my tray on a nearby table to eat. No one told me I couldn't be seen — and come to think about it, it was probably better that if anyone was in the building, they witnessed me moving freely around the facility. Maybe it would convince them of my loyalty.

Picking up the knife, I began cutting my waffle into smaller, bite-size pieces when I heard someone enter the room. I looked up, stunned to see Isi. I'd never thought of her as a morning person. She seemed the type to like the shadows. Moving over to the Greek yogurt, she grabbed one from the ice bin before glancing over at me. She sighed and selected a spoon from the utensil tray, then walked over to an empty table.

"Isi!" I called, as though we were in a crowded cafeteria. "Come sit by me."

At first, she looked horrified. I kept my face passive and held her gaze. She drifted toward me and stood by my table. I felt uncomfortable with her glare.

"What?" I whispered.

She glanced around the empty room again and leaned in. "You have no clue what you're doing, do you?"

"Of course, I do," I whispered back. "I'm just eating my waffle."

She raised an eyebrow and glanced at her yogurt before looking back at me. "You're sure?"

My knife clattered to my tray. "No, I'm not," I answered honestly. "I'm not sure of anything," I admitted. "I don't know what I'm supposed to do or what I'm *allowed* to do. Can I eat here? Are waffles okay? Should I have made another decision?" My voice rose with panic, so I chewed a bite of waffle and put on a friendly face.

"Wow," Isi said. "You are a hot mess."

I didn't answer. She placed her yogurt down and walked a few steps away from where I sat before turning around. "Come on," she said. "I'll show you something." I looked at her discarded food, wondering what she was up to.

"What about..." I motioned to the plate of food.

"Don't worry about it. Someone will clean it up." She walked to the entrance of the room and crossed her arms, waiting for me. I glanced around one more time, wondering who was going to clean up. I didn't see anyone working here, but they probably trained the staff to be just as invisible as the rest of the agents.

I pushed back from the table and followed Isi as she led me away from my breakfast and weaved her way through the maze-like hallways to a set of double doors I hadn't seen before.

Isi reached out and pushed the door open. I took a step back, eyeing the space in front of me. It looked like an indoor target range. It was a large room with many lanes marked by yellow tape. Along the walls were various types of targets. Some were realistic depictions of humans and others were more abstract.

"Whoa." I stepped into the room, my eyes widening with wonder.

"This is where we train."

Isi led us closer to one lane with equipment piled up next to it. She lifted a small tube that rested on the top of a box and pointed it at the target to her right, which was a heavy bag suspended from the ceiling by chains. She pressed a button on the device and pulled the trigger. A loud, corrugated pop was followed by the bag swinging with the weight of the ammo.

"What was that?" I noticed the tiny hole in the bag's surface.

Isi pulled another device off the nearest wall. This one looked more like a gun. I heard a tiny click. She aimed it at the bag, and a bright blue light surrounded us.

"What the?" I asked, but she interrupted me.

"Shh." She waited until I fell silent before pulling the trigger. We watched as the bullet pushed on the bag and slowly sank into the surface.

"What is this?" I asked Isi as she put it back on its hook on the wall.

"This," she said, "is a gun that uses light to dispense layers of solid matter. In short, it's an awesome weapon."

I stood up straight. "Is it like a laser beam?"

Isi nodded. "Yes, it's made to cut through the surface of anything solid. It's called a photonic laser. It can cut through metal and, with enough energy, could even cut through a tank."

I looked at the weapons, hoping I wouldn't be assigned to use them. I couldn't fake shooting someone.

"Your face," Isi said. "Don't worry. I didn't bring you here for weapons training. I brought you here for hand-to-hand combat training." She waved me over to a doorway that led to a smaller room lined with wall-to-wall mats. "This is where we fight. Instead of wandering around this place and getting yourself in trouble, or annoying the heck out of me, you can train your boredom away."

The room smelled of plastic and sweat. There were mounds of exercise equipment on the far wall, so I walked over to them. I tapped the speed bag hanging from a movable metal structure. A heavy bag hung from another metal contraption. I couldn't see myself spending time in here pummeling these things. Violence just didn't appeal to me.

"This is where you get your hands dirty," Isi said from behind me. I turned around as she pulled out a set of black bands from a bin nearby.

"What are those for?"

"You can use your hands in this type of fight, so you'll need to wrap them to protect your knuckles. Like before a boxing match."

"I'm not going to—" I began, but she cut me off sharply.

"Just do it."

So, this was her plan — get me here so she could beat me. I didn't even know how to wrap my hands. I'd had only basic fight training for self-defense.

"Isi, I'm not fighting you. I don't stand a chance." I stood with my arms dangling at my sides as Isi finished wrapping her hands and bounced from foot to foot.

"You never stood a chance." She smirked. "It's better than nothing, right?" I sighed and wrapped my hands. She continued, "I didn't think you'd actually want to come back here." She walked out into the main room, where there was an open space.

"Really? Why?" I asked, following her.

She furrowed her brow. "You know why," she said with a scoff. I had no clue what she was talking about. "Don't worry." She backed away from me. "I'm not going to hurt you. You know I'd be dead if I did."

I stood in the center of the room, thinking about what she'd said. She made it sound like I had some standing or power here at the Agency. If I did, I didn't feel it. "I don't want to fight." I felt the heat rise in my face.

"Why not? Afraid you'll hurt me?" Isi laughed and slowly approached me. "Don't worry," she said. "This is just hand-to-hand, and I won't use my full strength."

She lunged at me, and I backed away, nearly stumbling. "Hey," I said, holding up my hands. "Calm down."

She threw another punch, and it grazed my jaw, knocking my head to the side.

I reached up and rubbed the spot where she hit me. "Isi, stop it!" I shouted.

Isi grinned and lunged for me again. She punched at me again, but this time I moved out of the way, causing her to stumble, but she righted herself.

"Stop it," I said, shaking my head. The heat was leaving my face and was replaced by cold chills.

Isi stood up and shook herself off, brushing imaginary dust from her clothes. "Oh, come on," she said. "You're not even fighting back."

I backed away from her slowly, shaking my head. What did she expect? For me to fight her? She clearly knew how to handle herself.

She lunged again, and I dodged her. "That's it!" she yelled, swinging at me again. I ducked and punched her in the stomach. She exhaled sharply and doubled over. "What was that for?" she gasped, raising her head up to look at me.

"You deserved it." I stood up straight and crossed my arms, showing her I was finished with this game.

Isi raised an eyebrow and stood up straight. "You're going to have a tough time in the field." She shook her head. "You have no natural fighting instincts. You could have just shifted into someone else."

It was clear now that she had brought me here to embarrass me, and I was already feeling all mixed up. "I'm going to have a tough time in the field?" My voice was near a shout when I asked. "I don't even want to be here!" I clenched my fists.

She stared at me with disbelief etched on her face. "What?"

"I didn't want to come here. I was forced here. So don't act like you're trying to help me or that I have a say in anything. I never have."

"Let's get one thing straight, okay?" Isi ripped her wraps from her hands as she got close to me. "You need to pull it together for this to work. There are many people counting on you." Her voice was a growl, and I glanced to see if anyone had entered the room.

"You know why I'm here?" I asked, my voice quiet.

Isi looked at me for a moment, realizing what she'd just said. "This is going nowhere," she said, tossing the wraps to the mat. "I'm going back to my room." And she was gone.

I leaned against the wall and sank down into a crouch. What did she mean by that? Why was I here? Once again, I felt like I didn't have access to full information. Maybe Isi was in on something with Chayton. Of course, she would be loyal to him, even if it had seemed like we'd worked well together in covering up what had happened with the president and my mom.

When I got up, the sickening sweetness of the waffles left my stomach sour. Why hadn't I shifted into someone else, besides the fact that Isi could do the same? She was right. I had no natural instincts as a mimic. I was finished with my little outing. I returned to the comfort of my room, waiting until someone told me my next move.

Chapter 16

A knock on my door jolted me awake. I must have dozed off for a bit, but it was still too early in the morning for anyone to be knocking on my door. Instead of yelling out, I walked over and opened the door.

Isi stood in front of me, clad in black, topped off with her signature battered leather jacket.

"Morning, sunshine." She stared back at me with her ever-present smirk.

"It's not morning yet. Not really." I rubbed my eyes.

"But you already ate, so you're good," she said. "New job. Follow me." She turned, walking down the hallway. I sighed and jogged to catch up with her. She always walked fast.

"What new job?" I asked as she slowed down, looking both ways, like she didn't want to be spotted.

I looked up at the camera and spotted no light. I wondered if Isi somehow disabled the cameras — and if so, why?

"Where are we going? Whose mission is this?" The tap of our shoes echoed down the hallway.

Isi wore her usual expression, like she was in on some joke that no one else could get. "Just shut up and follow me."

We crept down the dark hallway, even though Isi had clearance through every security stop. It was as though they let her come and go as she pleased, but I knew that couldn't be true, because even Chayton understood that Isi only did what was best for her. She could never be trusted. Unless something had changed.

I remembered the note that was left in my room. *Things aren't what they seem.* I stared at the back of Isi's head, wondering once again who had left the note, and what did they mean by it?

When we arrived at the big metal door that led to the garage, she stood in front of the retinal scanner. I expected a trick so that there wouldn't be a record of her, but instead, she let it scan her, and the light above the panel turned green as the lock on the door clicked. She pulled the door open and looked back at me, motioning for me to follow.

We weaved through the cars until she stopped at a black sedan with tinted windows. She glanced at me, her lips a thin line, as she pointed at the vehicle. The click of her lifting the door handle echoed through the cavernous space, and Isi tensed at the sound. She glanced at me, and when she saw me observing, her face went blank. Then she nodded at me to follow.

I walked around to the other side and opened the door, wondering again why she was concerned about the noise, as she'd already been cleared to enter the garage. I didn't move, my thoughts waging a debate. Could I trust her or now? My mind flashed back to when I'd first met her, and she'd mimicked my mother. This high-ceilinged garage reminded me of that dark, open space in the parking lot at the rest stop. The red lights on the camera were tiny stars in the night sky. She'd lured me out, and I followed willingly, with the hope of speaking to my mother. The Agency had thrown Isi and me together so many times, and she hadn't killed me yet. Deep down, I trusted her, even though I shouldn't. I slid into the passenger seat next to her and let the door fall shut. Without hesitating, she shifted the vehicle into reverse as the garage door rolled up.

"Where are we?" I started, but she put her hand up, stopping my incoming questions. She cleared the still opening garage door, backing out and then pulling forward onto the road that led from the garage to the parking lot, to the front gate.

"Get down," she whispered out of the side of her mouth. I crouched down, realizing that she needed me to be out of sight as we passed the guard.

I stayed hidden as she lifted her hand in a salute and then pulled through the gate. I looked up through my window, and the sun was coming up. As we picked up speed, she nodded again at me, signaling that we were in the clear. I got up from the floor and settled into my seat, pulling the seatbelt around me.

The tree-lined road was wet with fresh rain. I cracked the window open, smelling the aftereffect of a storm that I hadn't even heard from the confines of the facility. "Can you tell me what we're doing now?" I stared at the side of her face.

"We're going to pay a visit to your bro." She reached down and flicked on the radio to some news talk show.

"What do you mean?" I asked, feigning innocence. No one was supposed to know about Elan.

She turned and looked at me, lips pursed. The men on the radio argued back and forth about some environmental protection bill.

She waited me out until I finally asked, "You knew Chayton had another kid?" I sat up straighter in my seat.

Isi kept her eyes on the road, and her face relaxed. "Meda, you still don't understand. I don't just work for the Agency. I'm a collector of information that can be useful to me."

"How long have you known?" I reached up to tug at my ear, but there was no earring there. She turned to watch me, but I let my hand fall to my lap and folded it into its partner.

She shrugged. "I was aware Chayton was up to something."

"Why didn't you say anything?" She took a hard left onto another road. I grabbed the armrest to keep from being thrown from my seat.

"I wasn't about to get involved with whatever Chayton was up to." She took her eyes off the road and looked at me, waiting for a reaction. Her face was like a mini-fortress with every security feature, and I wouldn't break it down.

"Elan said they lived on a reservation."

"Chayton had them moved. He thought it might delay the Agency from getting their hands on them. I don't understand why he's protecting them."

"Um, because they're family?" I said before realizing that Isi wouldn't understand that.

Isi looked away from the road, tilting her head at me and letting out a snort. "You're his family, too." She laughed. "You're his daughter."

I didn't join in. I'd considered the same thing.

When Isi saw I wasn't laughing with her, her smile disappeared. "Sorry, Meda. It's not that bad. You have your dad and your sisters." She shrugged. "At least when you don't have family, you don't have anyone you can let down."

I had people in my life who were like family that I did let down. Both Brody and Aaron would be disappointed in me right now. They'd given so much already to take down the Agency, and yet here I was, back with them. Aaron wouldn't believe that the good I was trying to do was worth it, because even after all we had gone through, he didn't trust mimics.

"So, how do you know where Elan is?" I asked, changing the subject.

"I hacked into the Agency spending account and found a payment made to a realtor nearby. I went and checked it out. Actually, I staked it out. That's when I saw Elan and some of his friends, his girlfriend, and another guy, I think he's his girlfriend's brother, staying at the same place. A crappy apartment complex." She smiled and stepped on the gas pedal. I worried she was going to get pulled over.

"So, why are we visiting?" My palms were sweating as I tightened my grip on the armrest.

"We need to get Elan on our side, but I don't think he's going to take your side just because you're his sister. I don't know why... probably because you worked for the Agency. Or that you're related to Chayton. Either way, it's always helpful to have allies, or at least to learn about potential enemies." She was good at this in a way I never was. Isi was always thinking about angles. I had to remind myself to be careful around her.

The thought of facing Elan made me nervous. He had an intensity about him I couldn't trust. I rubbed my free hand on my leggings and looked out the window at the houses sliding by, wondering why we had to do this right now.

The rest of the trip remained quiet as we passed through some smaller towns on our way to visit my brother. The sun was more visible in the sky. As we weaved through the city streets, the GPS on the dash indicated the apartments were nearby.

"You think he's just going to let us in?" I asked. "We show up uninvited... Seems suspicious."

"You realize what Elan is asking you to do? He owes you." She slowed as she approached a sign that said *Shady Acres Apartments*.

I shook my head, staring out the window. "I don't think he sees it that way."

Isi pulled into one of the parking spots at the back of the

apartment complex and turned off the engine. It was a generic-looking building, probably about ten years old, with two rows of identical apartments facing each other.

"What are we going to do?" I asked, eyeing the parking lot. A black car pulled in on the far side of the parking lot.

"What do you mean? I'm going to knock on his door." She got out of the vehicle.

I followed, opening my car door and stepping out onto the damp pavement. I looked down at my clothes, wishing I'd changed. I sighed and followed Isi to the second floor.

We walked up to apartment 214, and Isi knocked on the door, then rang the bell twice before glancing at me over her shoulder. I thought he wasn't going to answer. That he'd seen us approach and they were sitting in there, waiting for us to leave. Then, a young woman opened the door a crack.

"Yes?" she asked, just her head peering around the door. She was smart to be careful.

A man yelled from behind her. "I told you not to answer the door!"

"You must be Briar." Isi stepped forward into the doorway. She was inches away from the young woman's face.

"Who's asking?" She eyed Isi suspiciously. There was the sound of someone walking across the floor behind her.

"I'm Isi, and that's Meda." She glanced at me when Isi said my name, her eyes widening. She let the door open, and I felt a wave of heat pouring out and the flickering glow of candles reaching out onto the balcony.

"Elan! Your sister is here," she said, calling back into the room. I heard whispered voices and then my half-brother, Elan, came out to stand next to Briar. He was wearing a white tank top and a pair of jeans. He crossed his arms, his biceps flexing.

"What are you doing here?" he asked me, as if Isi wasn't the one standing in the doorway in front of me. His eyes flashed with anger.

Isi said, "You know what we're doing here." She pushed past him into the room, and he dropped his arms, staring at her, but stood in front of the girl. I kept my head down and followed Isi, stepping into a cozy living room with a couch and chair pushed against the walls and a small television on a wooden stand. The furniture looked worn but tidy. A candle flickered on the weathered coffee table. It smelled of cinnamon and apples. Another boy was in the room. He had dark features and long, shiny dark hair. He rose from the couch, watching us, and I realized all he had on was a pair of athletic shorts. There were blankets on the couch as though he'd been sleeping there.

Elan reached back and pushed the door closed while Briar slid the dead bolt in place. Elan asked Isi, "Who are you supposed to be?" He folded his arms over his chest again. "And what do you want?"

"Meda, get over here." Isi motioned at me, and I realized I still stood in the entryway and up against the closet, as though waiting to be invited.

I looked at Elan, and he nodded and rolled his eyes, motioning toward Isi. The girl, Briar, put her hand on his shoulder and gave him a questioning look.

I took the three steps over to Isi and straightened up. The boy from the couch tilted his head and eyed us.

"So, what are you doing here?" he asked again, turning his attention to Isi.

"We need your help," she said.

My eyes darted her way — Isi never asked for help. Elan's eyes traveled from Isi to me but stayed on me as though checking for a reaction. I let my face relax as I met Elan's gaze. I didn't know what

Isi was digging for, and maybe it was for the best, because then I couldn't mess it up.

Elan looked back at Isi. "Well?" he asked, waiting.

Chapter 17

"You need my help?" Elan asked, one eyebrow raised. The other boy stepped around the coffee table, joining our standoff.

"That's what I said, isn't it?" Isi cocked one hip and arranged her hand on it. "But first I'm going to tell you something and let the pieces fall where they may." Elan crossed his arms over his chest and waited for her to go on. "I'm sure Chayton told you that you guys are safe, but you're not. You're all on the database."

"What?" Elan raised his voice. "No." He shook his head. "Chayton said we were safe. It's why he moved us, to make sure they didn't find us." His words were confident, but his face told a different story.

I interrupted their exchange, speaking to Isi first. "I thought they were in the database." I turned to Elan. "I thought you were in the database. Isn't that why you wanted me?"

Elan looked at me and then at Briar, who raised an eyebrow. "What's she talking about?" she asked.

"I'll explain everything later," Elan said.

Briar crossed her arms, and her friendly face now turned dangerous. "No, you'll explain now. But first, introductions, please." I was glad she wasn't looking at me the way she looked at him.

Elan took a deep breath. "Meda, this is my girlfriend, Briar." He waved his hand between us.

The young woman reached out to me. "Briar Barber." I looked at Elan, and he glanced away as I placed my hand in her firm grip. I waited for any kind of strange sensation, but nothing came to me. As I let go of her hand, I felt Isi's eyes on me.

"I'm Bly." The other boy came forward. He had a chiseled chin and long, shiny dark hair. His skin had a healthy glow, and I tried not to stare at his smooth chest and six-pack of abs. "I'm Briar's brother and, unfortunately, I'm Elan's best friend. Oh, and we were friends first, before he started messing around with my sister." Briar reached over and gave Bly a playful shove.

"Are you twins?" The words rushed out of my mouth before I had time to think.

Briar looked me up and down. "How did you know? Most people think I'm older than my brother."

"Ha!" Bly blurted out. "You wish."

I continued. "I have twin sisters, Ginger and Georgia. They look at each other the same way you do."

Both Bly and Briar fixed me with stares before turning on each other. "Stop looking at me weird!" they both yelled at each other before breaking out into laughter. Then, they looked at each other and said, "Twin moment," at the same time. They doubled up again in laughter.

A smile broke out on my face, and I could see Elan fighting a smile, too.

Isi stared daggers at them before saying, "Okay, sorry to interrupt the love fest going on here, but we need to get some things straight. Do you understand what it means that all your names are on the database that tracks where all the mimics live?"

Elan's face turned to stone. Isi didn't mince her words. She understood how to get through to people with this kind of information. He cleared his throat. "You mean *all* of our names?" He gestured at the group.

"Wait, so you're a mimic?" Bly asked, looking me up and down, making me feel self-conscious. "And your friend?" He glanced at Isi, and a devilish grin played across his lips.

"Cool it, hot stuff." Isi crossed her arms, not liking the way he looked at her.

"That's not what I meant," Bly started, but Isi put her hand up, stopping him. He looked at me and raised his eyebrows. "I like her."

Briar spun around and stared at Elan. "What is all this? Why didn't you tell me this? You said he kept our names off the list. We're supposed to tell each other everything."

Elan, shaking his head, reached out to touch Briar. "Baby, I didn't know. He didn't tell me. I thought we were safe."

She moved away from him. "And you believed your crazy father?"

It was strange hearing someone talk about Chayton that way. He seemed all-powerful. All knowing. That there was someone in the world who didn't care for him gave me a strange feeling. Not good, or bad. Just strange.

I suddenly felt sick to my stomach. Maybe it was the warm room or the overpowering cinnamon scented candle. I stiffened my back, not wanting anyone to notice my lack of composure.

Elan reached out and took both of Briar's hands. She didn't resist. "He's not crazy, Briar. He put us here to help us."

Invisible words passed between them before Briar pulled him closer. "I'm sorry. I know he's the only parent you have." Elan wrapped his arm around her neck and kissed the top of her head. Another wave of nausea hit me.

"Anyway, Chayton doesn't have the power to keep anyone off the list." Isi interrupted. "He lied to you. He doesn't know who's on the list. You two," she pointed at Elan and Briar, "are in big trouble. Two mimics together have the potential to," she cleared her throat, "procreate."

The room went quiet, our shadows flickering in the candle. "And?" I asked, breaking the silence. Bly shifted from foot to foot.

Elan let out a sigh. "And a mimic born of two mimics is special. They've been known to do more than shift." He avoided eye contact with me when he spoke.

I opened my mouth to defend myself when Isi stepped closer and nudged me. "You know how she feels about being called special, don't you?" She eyed me, and I realized she was onto the fact that something was different with me.

"I'm sorry…" I said, trailing off.

Isi cleared her throat and turned back to Elan. "Anyway, we need to get everything on the table here." She glanced at me and Elan. "Chayton can't be trusted."

Elan was the first to answer. "If we're really getting everything on the table, I can't be trusted, either. Meda knows that." I thought back to his elbow connecting to my face and the flash of Brody's car being run off the road. At least he was being honest. Elan continued, "All I know right now is that if it weren't for my dad, you and I wouldn't have these abilities."

"Wait, are you saying it like you're grateful for him?" I asked. I hated being a mimic. I hated the way it felt, shifting into someone else and the sensation of my memories mixing with theirs. Being born a mimic was why I could never live in peace. It was why I'd had to kill my mother and stay away from the father I had known and my twin sisters. It was why even now, I was changing, and I didn't know if those changes would affect different parts of my life, including my relationship with Brody.

"He's helping me." Elan wrapped his arm tighter around Briar and spoke to her. "He has a plan. He wouldn't just throw us into this situation without a plan."

Briar pulled her hand back, breaking eye contact with him. "So, what is his plan?"

He looked up at the ceiling, took a deep breath, and shook his head. "I guess we just have to play along and wait until he tells us what we need to do next."

Isi put her arms up. "Your blind trust in him is makes me want to vomit."

Elan turned to Isi. "You should talk. You work for him." He jutted his chin out at her.

Isi stepped closer to Elan. "Okay! Okay! I can't be trusted either, but we're all in the same boat, so it would benefit us all to play along but pay attention."

"Wait," Elan said. "So, why did you come here?"

"Meda needs people on her side right now. And you're family, so tag, you're it." She reached out a finger and poked him in the shoulder, but he knocked her hand away.

I opened my mouth to speak but then closed it. Elan stared at me and made me shiver in discomfort. "What?" I asked, knowing he waited for an answer.

He shook his head. "Nothing," he answered. He looked at Briar, pleading for her forgiveness. She took his hand.

I tried not to get invested. I was aware that Elan, my brother through blood, didn't care about me, but he cared about Briar. And from what I saw of Briar and Bly, they seemed to be two people worth saving. The warmth of their kindness made an impact in just one meeting. And though I had now learned that my new "gifts" didn't work on mimics, I also recognized that I had to save these two from the Agency or any other organization that wanted to use them.

"We gotta get going," Isi said, moving past them to the door and beckoning me to follow. "It's been real."

"It was nice meeting you." Bly grinned at the two of us, while Elan shot him a dirty glance.

"I'll be in touch," Isi said as she led me out the door.

I had no words, so I gave Briar a small wave and turned to follow Isi back to the car. The skin on the back of my neck prickled. There was more going on with that meeting, but I wasn't sure what game Isi was playing yet.

Chapter 18

I turned the station from talk radio to a classic rock station and hummed along, pretending to be enjoying the music when, really, I was lost in thoughts about Isi and her intentions. The temperature had dropped, and the interior of the car felt frigid compared to the warmth of Elan's apartment, but the smell of cinnamon hung in the air, probably stuck to our clothes.

"Well?" Isi asked as she navigated the roads back to the facility. She drove faster than I cared for. Maybe she had a window of time carved out for herself with the cameras. She glanced my way, her eyes a shade of dark green in the artificial light of the car.

"What?" I asked. "Weren't you the one trying to get intel?"

Isi turned her attention back to the road, but she looked annoyed. I wished I could figure out what she was thinking, but she wouldn't tell me. I looked in the rearview mirror just in time to catch a black Toyota Camry in the passing lane a couple of cars back. It looked like the car I'd seen earlier. I glanced at Isi. She didn't seem to be paying attention.

I pretended to rest my head on the window and looked out the side mirror. The sky lightened and midday approached. I wondered what would happen if we just kept driving, never going back to the Agency. The black car moved like it was going to pass the next car, but it retreated to its lane.

I lifted my head off the window and shot a sideways glance at Isi, who was now checking her mirrors. "What did you think about Bly?" I asked, trying to distract her.

She looked at me, her eyebrows creased. "Bly?" she asked.

"Yes, Bly. The guy who was clearly flirting with you." I glanced at my mirror but still couldn't see the Camry.

Isi let out a dry laugh and began changing lanes. Instead of asking why she'd laughed, I looked back at my mirror. My breath caught in my throat. I'd recognize that tousle of brown hair anywhere. I could see Aaron in the passenger seat, but I didn't want to take my eyes off Brody.

Isi merged into the other lane and looked up to check her mirror, but I couldn't let her see Brody and Aaron behind us. I didn't know what she'd do if she noticed they were following us.

"Hey, why did you laugh when I said Bly was interested in you?" I leaned closer to her.

She glanced at me, her mouth twisting at my proximity. "He's not my type," she said, her voice flat.

"You're like, what, sixteen? Fifteen? Wait, do you have your driver's license?" Isi smirked at me. "Never mind. Anyway, you're young. How do you know your type?" I studied the side of her face.

She shook her head. "Once again, for being the observant one, you really don't notice shit, do you?"

I watched her, trying to understand what she was getting at. Then it washed over me like a bucket of cold water. "Oh," I said, leaning back. "I'm sorry. I shouldn't have assumed."

"Assumed what?" she asked. Her eyes turned back to the road. "I don't know what you're talking about." She gripped the steering wheel tighter.

Staring at the road ahead, I closed my mouth. Brody needed to see that I was okay, but I didn't know how to communicate that to him.

"I need you to stop at that gas station up ahead." I pointed at the exit sign that advertised the next Quick Stop.

"Oh, my gosh. Just cross your legs." She flipped the visor down as the sun rose higher in the sky.

"I have to pee. And I need a coffee." She didn't signal to get in the left lane. "Just do it, Isi. Please." To my surprise, she turned on her blinker and weaved from the left lane to the right and right onto the exit. I held onto the armrest.

The gas station was packed with people getting their lunches. They were probably heading somewhere important but making a pitstop to fuel their brains and cars. A truck backed out of the spot closest to the door, and Isi pulled in and threw the car in park. "Five minutes," she said. "We have to be back." Her fingers tapped on the steering wheel.

I jogged to the gas station and slid through the door behind someone. There was no other entrance, so I didn't understand how Brody or Aaron would get in undetected. It would be easier for Aaron to sneak past Isi. She wouldn't be as focused on him, though his six-and-a-half-foot frame made him stand out in a crowd. I realized how badly I wanted to see Brody at that moment.

I didn't go to the bathroom. Instead, I continued right to the coffee station and grabbed an empty cup. I moved over to the cappuccino machine so I could watch the entrance. I eyed the door as I placed the cup under the French vanilla spout and pushed the button, listening to it sputter and hum.

The doorbell rang, and when I looked up, a hooded figure pushed through the door. The man's head was down, so I couldn't make out his face, but he was the right size. I held my breath, and my brain flashed back to the cabin. With Brody.

After our swim, we'd retired back to the cabin and changed into warm, fuzzy clothes. Brody lit a fire and made some hot chocolate. Rather than sit on the nubby sofa, we threw a pile of blankets and pillows in front of the couch and nestled in.

"Brody? Can I ask what you thought when you first met me?" I blew on my cocoa before testing it with my lip to see if it was too hot. I slurped a small sip.

Brody watched the steam rise from his mug. "I was thinking that I didn't want to get shot by those guys in the van." He looked up at me, his mouth hitched in a half smile.

I shook my head and closed my eyes before speaking. "It's so crazy how we met. And now we're here together." I opened my eyes and looked at him. "Why do you think we're here, together? I still don't get it. We were on opposite sides. We weren't honest with each other. If we were normal people, would you have even given me a second glance?"

Brody laughed. "I love how you talk like it's all in my control, but I can tell you, I would have given you many glances." He reached his hand up and traced the edges of my face, rounding out my chin. "I'm going to be honest here with you, Meda. I understood what I was getting into with you." He studied my gaze.

"What does that mean?" I asked.

"Well, we knew about you. Aaron had notes from his dad, notes about the mimics. When we started down that paper trail, and we found several of your victims…" He paused. My face dropped. "That's not what I meant. I'm sorry, Meda." He put his cup down and took my hand. "What I meant was that I found out that they'd forced you to join the Agency. When I met you, I already knew that what you were doing was against your will." His revelation surprised me.

I'd assumed that he'd come to that conclusion along the way. "Honestly, I bought your sincerity. You're the only one who thought about my side. But if you knew that already, were you using it against me?"

"Does it matter if I was?" Brody asked.

I thought about that for a moment. Did it matter? At that point, we had all been playing a game.

We still were.

I walked to the back of the gas station, where the bathrooms were located. A woman walked into the women's restroom, so I turned left and entered the men's. I put my coffee down by the sink and scanned the room. There was no one at the urinals and I bent over, looking for feet in the stalls. All clear. I turned back just in time to catch the hooded figure walk through the door. He turned back and locked it behind him, then turned to face me, dropping his hood.

Meda? His lips moved, but no sound came out. He studied me, maybe trying to determine if I was actually myself. I didn't give him the chance. I rushed to him and wrapped my arms around his neck.

He lifted me off the ground and squeezed me. I pulled back and brought my lips to his and then pulled away, words spilling out. "Brody, I thought… When they ran you off the road…" I couldn't finish and kissed him.

"I'm sorry I couldn't protect you." There was too much to say and not enough time to say it. "Come on. We're getting out of here." He grabbed my hand and pulled me to the door.

I resisted his pull, standing firmly in my spot. He turned back to look at me.

"I can't, Brody. I have to go back." The hum of the fluorescent light filled the silence, and the toilet began running.

His hand dropped from mine. "What are you talking about?"

I was babbling. "We have a plan to wipe out all traces of mimics, to free them." I felt my voice rising in excitement.

"Who's *we?* The Agency uses mimics — like what they did to you." He put his hand on my shoulder and ran it down my arm, gripping my hand again like he was trying to get me to stay with him. I wanted to. Badly.

It's different this time," I said, trying to get him to understand but not finding the right words to convince him. "Chayton is in on it."

"Meda, don't be a fool." His words were a slap.

I stared at him. "A fool?" I asked, shaking his hand away. I felt my cheeks flush. Brody had never talked to me that way.

"I didn't mean it that way. I only meant that they tricked you before. They used your trust against you." He reached out to me, but I backed away.

"Didn't you do that same thing when we met?" It was Brody's turn to look hurt. "That's not what I meant, Brody. I'm sorry. This is coming out all wrong." I covered my face with my hands. Nothing had changed. Maybe Brody was right. I was too trusting and fell for everything. Maybe I should just go with him.

He looked at his watch. "We've been in here too long. What'll it be, Meda?"

"I have to go back. I have to save young mimics from being ripped away from their families and forced to be agents. Besides, we'd never get out of here without Isi seeing us. Follow us to the Agency. I'll signal you if I need you." I was asking a lot of him, but I also knew he'd do it.

"If I sense you are in any danger or that they're hurting you or using you to hurt someone, I'm pulling the plug." He grabbed both of my hands and squeezed. "I hope you know what you're doing."

"Trust me, Brody. Don't do anything stupid. I couldn't stand it if anything happened to you." I moved closer to him, standing on my tiptoes. On the corner of his mouth, I kissed him softly. A whisper of words flitted across my brain. *I should just make her come with me. Just grab her and force her to come with me. This is stupid.*

He stared down at me for a moment before speaking. "I feel the same way. That's why I'm here. But if you're sure, I'll go along with it. For now." He pulled me in for another hug, and the smell of his freshly shampooed hair drew me in. I didn't want to let go, but I had to.

I pulled away from him and studied his face one more time. "I better go." We traded spots, and he backed away from the door, pulling his hood up again. I unlocked the latch and slid through the opening, leaving Brody behind.

I spun around, and Isi stood in front of me. I nearly bumped into her. "Hey, sorry." I didn't know what she was thinking as she stared at me.

"What took you so long?" Her eyes traveled to the sign on the door and back to me. "And what were you doing in the men's bathroom?"

"There was no one in there, and the stalls were full in the women's restroom." Isi looked over her shoulder at the women's restroom. I hoped she wouldn't go in there. I had no clue if it was busy in there or not, but the interior of the gas station had cleared out.

She turned to face me. "I thought you needed coffee?"

I thought of the cup I'd left by the sink. We would run into Brody if I went back for it. "I'm good. Let's just get out of here."

I pushed past her and weaved through the aisles. She followed closely behind. When we got to the door, I looked back at her. She was looking back at the bathroom, as though waiting to see if someone was going to follow us out. I turned and closed my eyes, hoping Brody knew to wait long enough for us to exit.

We got to the car, and I climbed inside. I watched the door to the gas station, but Brody didn't emerge. Isi slid into the driver's seat and turned to stare at me. "Why are you being so weird?" She reached over her shoulder and pulled her seatbelt down, latching it in place.

"Nothing. It's just been a long day." I slouched down in my seat, staring out the window.

"Maybe you should have gotten a coffee." Isi started up the car and put it in drive. Brody still didn't exit the gas station, and there was no sign of Aaron and the Camry.

"I'll be fine. Let's just get back."

While I wanted them to follow us, I was also afraid that if they found out where the Agency was located, they would try to break in and get caught. There were too many security precautions. They would get caught. My thoughts were jumbled and the entire trip back, I checked the mirrors for the Camry. If they were following us, they were doing a good job, because I didn't see them.

Chapter 19

The sun was seated high in the afternoon sky. It would have been a pleasant drive if I wasn't so worried about Brody and Aaron following us. I hoped I'd done the right thing. If either of them got hurt, I wouldn't forgive myself.

A thought occurred to me. Now that Isi seemed to cooperate with me, maybe I could get some information from her. I turned the radio down before shifting toward Isi. "Did you and Ava do a lot of assignments together?" I asked, trying to keep Isi's attention.

"Sure." Isi stared ahead at the road. I folded my arms in my lap. "What was the craziest assignment you guys had?"

Isi sighed. "You want to learn more about your mom, but you're not going to be happy with anything I tell you. You either want confirmation that she was bad or that she was good, but I can't give that to you. Ava was Ava. When she was being nice, she was really freaking nice, but when she was being bad, well, you didn't want to be around her."

"That sounds about right," I said. "Can you tell me anything?"

Isi drummed her fingers on the steering wheel as she drove. "There was once an agent who caught the attention of those who make the decisions." She twirled her finger above her, and I wondered who she was talking about. I thought Chayton made most of the decisions.

Isi continued, "An American agent living in England who couldn't be identified by any of our sources."

I sat up straighter. "What was his, or I guess her, name?"

"We called her Nancy," Isi said. "Anyway, Ava got herself assigned to Nancy's case, and she worked on it for months, letting me do some of the grunt work. Nancy had contacted five different agencies in five European countries, but no one could identify Nancy. They identified her as American because of certain technicalities in her work, and that was how we found out about her. Ava was obsessed, and she finally exposed Nancy here, in the United States."

"What happened?" I asked.

Isi shrugged. "Everyone knows this story, Meda. It's why we call agents like her 'ghosts,' because they leave no trace of themselves behind."

"She killed Nancy?"

Isi shot me an annoyed look. "Yes, but not before getting some information out of her. The agencies worked together, and they eliminated all evidence that Nancy was ever involved in any agency, so no one would learn what happened to her. She just disappeared."

"And Ava got credit for her disappearance," I finished.

"She did," Isi said. "It was one of her biggest accomplishments." She glanced at me quickly before turning her attention back to the road. "I'm sorry you didn't think so, but Ava did what she had to do. It's not our job to have feelings."

"But it's our job to be human," I said. "What if Nancy was someone's daughter?"

Isi snorted. "If you want to believe that the work is about protecting people, go ahead. But it's not. The Agency sells out to the highest bidder. Someone with money needs someone with a massive security team taken out? It's easy for me to slip into place, do the job, and get out. It's always been about money. And power." Isi turned down the road that would lead to Agency headquarters. I studied it, looking for familiar land markings in case I ever needed to find it later. "It might be our job to deceive people," she said, turning the steering wheel, "but it's not our job to deceive ourselves."

When our car pulled up at headquarters, sunshine bore down on us. We drove through the security checkpoint, and I saw a man in a white suit standing on the sidewalk outside the building. Chayton. He folded his arms across his chest, and as we pulled up the driveway, even though his sunglasses reflected the sunlight, a scowl was visible.

"Are we in trouble?" I asked Isi. I reached up and wiped my brow, feeling claustrophobic without the breeze coming in through the window.

Isi remained silent as she parked the car in front of him.

Chayton's arms dropped as he leaned forward and pulled the door open. He reached his hand out, but I still had my seatbelt on. I again looked to Isi for a sign of what was happening, but she wouldn't make eye contact with me. They looked at each other for a second, an unspoken communication passing between them.

I unbuckled my seatbelt and grabbed my father's hand, letting him guide me out of the car. As I pushed the door shut behind me, I heard the engine shut down and Isi's car door close. I let go of Chayton's hand as I stood before him, and Isi strode around the front of the car, joining us on the sidewalk.

"What's going on?" I looked between them. Did Chayton find out we had just visited Elan? Did they know about Brody?

Chayton spoke first, "So, Isi says there's something going on with you." My breath caught, and I wondered if he was talking about the quick gas station visit. His eyes bore a hole through me, and goosebumps broke out on my flesh.

"It's true," Isi said to Chayton. "There's something. She's different."

I stared at her. Her stare didn't waver as she spoke only to Chayton. This wasn't about our road trip. It was about me and my new abilities.

"What are you talking about?" I asked Isi. I still couldn't believe she'd just turned me in to my father. I stepped closer to her, clenching my fists to avoid my urge to shove her. Rage boiled beneath the surface.

She finally looked at me. "Come on, Meda." She crossed her arms. "They knew all along that you were better than the rest of us. You proved it." A tinge of jealousy painted her voice, but she wouldn't say exactly what I had proven, and I wasn't sure how much she had learned or understood.

"I proved what?" I asked, playing along.

Isi stared at me, and a muscle in my jaw twitched as I fought against the string of words that threatened to rush out at her.

Chayton stepped between us, breaking our eye contact. He turned his back on me, speaking to Isi. "You go ahead. I'm going to have a little chat with Meda." He stepped back and turned to face me.

Isi nodded and glanced at me one more time. She was playing a game, and I cursed myself for going along with her. I needed to be smarter than that, better than that. I kept my face straight as she turned away from me, walking through the doors to the complex.

It was just me and my father. His green eyes were watery, and he had dark circles beneath them. I attempted to imagine what could bother Chayton so much that he wouldn't be able to sleep. After all he'd done?

Chayton sighed and motioned for me to follow him. "C'mon, let's go for a stroll."

I hesitated, glancing around. My body tensed with the urge to run, but there was nowhere to go. The fence around the facility would prevent me from getting away, and the armed guard at the gate would surely stop me.

His hand cupped my elbow as he guided me around the paved walkway that led to the driveway and the guard's booth. "So, it's true?"

I looked down at the ground, thinking about how much he knew and how much I should say. I cleared my throat. "Why don't you tell me what you know first, and maybe I can help." I gave him a thin-lipped smile. The air was still, and a cool breeze sent goosebumps up my arms.

"There's been theories, but no actual proof." He led me down the sidewalk. It was odd that we were out in the open. I looked around, wondering what kind of game Chayton was playing. "I'd like to see it in action."

"I don't understand what you're talking about. Can you elaborate?"

Chayton ignored my questions as we walked over to the guard at the gate. He nodded at the man in the booth, who eyed me and then turned to open the door behind him. He walked around the building; his hand was close to the gun holstered on his hip.

Chayton addressed the man. "Kramer, I'd like you to meet Mary, one of our newest agents." Kramer's eyebrows creased in confusion, but he extended his hand as he approached me.

I didn't want to touch him. Though, it might come in handy if I could shift into the guard. Chayton nodded at me, watching, and I forced a smile on my face as I reached out to grasp the man's hand.

Everything shifted, and I was looking down at our hands, but from a different perspective. The sensation was disorienting. I saw his apartment. It was messy, like he lived alone. I felt a warmth. He was happy. I let go of his hand and heard his voice in my head. *What just happened? What is this about? They never introduce me to new agents. What in the world is going on?* I realized he sensed something, and it scared him. He wasn't alone.

The man stood there, slack-jawed, until Chayton's words broke him out of his trance. "Thank you, Kramer. That's all we'll need."

His eyes focused again, and Chayton gave him a nod. He glanced my way once before turning his back on us. He stumbled and caught himself, glancing over his shoulder and giving us a wave and a smile. "Low blood sugar. I should probably eat something," he said, but his smile was forced. He returned to the booth and collapsed in the chair.

Chayton steered me away from the building. "Well, what happened?" he asked. I wasn't sure how much I wanted to tell him, only because I wasn't sure how much he already knew or how he could even learn about these things.

I opened my mouth and then closed it.

"You'll have to tell me. I'm the only one who can help you with this. I'm sure this has been confusing for you." He walked beside me, his elbow brushing my side as we walked.

I weighed my options in my head. I could pretend nothing happened, but my touch had had an effect on Kramer. Before I spoke, I let out a huff of air between my teeth. "I see images — flashes. He lives alone in a small, messy apartment, but he's content." I twisted my hands together, hoping I was doing the right thing.

"You perceive how he feels? Can you hear his thoughts?" Chayton's eyes were afire with this new knowledge. His excitement worried me.

"That's not clear," I lied. He looked too eager. I needed to keep something in my back pocket.

Chayton studied my face, trying to determine if I was being truthful. "Give it time." He nodded. He looked back over his shoulder at Kramer, and I followed his gaze, wondering again why he was acting so strangely. Kramer was opening his lunchbox, probably trying to quell the dizziness in his head.

I stopped walking, and he turned to face me. "How did you know?" I asked. "Is this why you brought me back? Was this all a ruse so that you could test me?" Once again, my anger bubbled inside me.

"Would it have changed anything if that were the case?" The silver in his eyebrows reflected in the sunlight, and for the first time, I wondered how old my father was. How old was he when he'd met Ava? Had he had plans for her?

I didn't answer him. Instead, I asked, "What happens now? What do you want me to do?"

"We'll see." Chayton took a deep breath and sighed heavily. He glanced over his shoulder at the guard at the gate again, but Kramer was facing the other direction.

I was dizzy with lies, trying to determine what was for the good of the mimics and what was for the good of Chayton. I wanted to believe he had good intentions, but everything that had happened was cluttered in my brain. And that note — the warning. Something else was going on here.

He turned to face me. "Can I see your hands?" His face was blank, and I wondered what would happen if I refused him. It didn't matter. He had me, no matter what I did.

I held out my hands, palms up. Even though he looked down, his eyes were not seeing what was in front of him. I wondered what he was searching for, but as he reached behind his back, I saw the glint of silver in the sunlight. Before I could withdraw my hands, a pair of silver handcuffs clicked in place around my wrists.

"What are you doing?" I asked, tugging at the cuffs and backing away from my father. This stranger. I fought the tremble in my lip.

I didn't want him to see the disappointment and hurt in my eyes. "Why?" I asked.

He took a step back and looked at me from under his eyebrows. "I'm sorry, Meda."

I shook my head, trying to convince myself that nothing was happening, but as the world spun around me, the green grass rushed toward me. I felt Chayton's arms grab me, but my thoughts faded to black.

Chapter 20

I blinked, the bright lights searing my eyes like some far-off sun. A shadow loomed over me, and I struggled to sit up, my hands still locked in place by the cuffs.

"Feeling better?" Isi stood over me, her face blank.

"What is going on? For real. What is happening?" I wrestled with the cuffs on my wrists. My mind raced, but all I could think was that my dad had betrayed me. I swallowed the emotion back down and looked at Isi to calm myself. My head was still foggy from my reaction to the silver cuffs.

"It's not what you think. Nothing is what you think."

I looked down at my raw wrists, trying to slide out of the cuffs. I let out a cry of frustration, slamming my fists into my lap. Then I considered the note I'd gotten earlier. The note hidden under my mattress. "It was you," I said to Isi.

"Chayton didn't tell you the entire plan. He couldn't." Her voice was soft. I waited for her to continue, stunned by the new revelation. She sat down next to me on my bed.

"What do you mean?" I stared at her, leaning away.

Isi sighed. "He knew that if you were aware of his plan, you would try to change things." She paused, considering how to continue before letting out a sigh. "He needed Brody to conclude that the Agency had taken you again. He needed Brody and Aaron to break in, rescue you, and take you back to Opposition headquarters. He needed to confirm that you had some kind of special abilities… That you could read minds. And finally, he — I mean *we* — need you to find the database at Opposition Headquarters and destroy it once and for all."

She struck me speechless. There was a lot to unpack in what she said, but also, how could I trust her? "Wait, what? You guys wanted Brody and Aaron to find me?" Then it dawned on me. If they rescued me again from the hands of the Agency, it would give us a good reason to head back to Smith and the Opposition. "Why are *you* a part of this?"

"Again, if no one knows who the mimics are, my stock increases. They need me to do the job." Isi shrugged.

I pulled at my wrist cuffs again. "So, you're asking me to deceive Brody and Aaron. Didn't we try that once before? That didn't work out so well for me." I remembered how painful it was when Brody couldn't even look at me and Aaron realized all his hatred toward me was justified. I couldn't return to those days.

"I think it did. Look, Brody will always forgive you. That boy is crazy about you." She reached into her pocket and pulled out keys to the handcuffs. She leaned over me and unlocked the cuffs. They slid off and onto the bed.

I rubbed my already raw wrists. "So, what was that?" I gestured to the discarded cuffs.

"We had to be sure they felt you were in danger." They knew about Brody and Aaron. Isi must have known they were following us after the gas station, and that was why Chayton took me on my little walk and then cuffed me. It was all a setup.

"So, our brief trip to see my brother wasn't a spur-of-the-moment girls' trip? It wasn't one friend trying to help another friend out."

Isi let out a sharp laugh. "No. That was Chayton's idea. He wanted us to bond." She emphasized the word *bond*, so it sounded sarcastic. "He didn't give me any specific orders, so I went with my gut. I understand how important family is to you." She rolled her eyes, but I saw that beneath her act, a small river of jealousy flowed. Isi didn't have a family. She had a boss and her job. And no matter how tough she acted, she was just a teenager.

"So all that sneaking around was just an act?"

Isi shrugged.

A thought occurred to me. "Why would Chayton want members of the Opposition to learn where his son is?"

"He didn't. That was all me." She leaned back onto her hands.

"But why?" It seemed like a dangerous game to play, even for Isi.

"You know what? Screw Chayton. He wants to protect one kid and offer up another? What kind of father does that?" Her eyebrows scrunched across her forehead, and her hands balled into fists, gripping the top layer of blanket on the bed.

I studied her face. She seemed sincere, but I couldn't identify where her anger was coming from.

She bolted off the bed, turning from me. "Meda, you were supposed to be the most observant of us all."

I froze, my mind calculating every one of those words. She knew something, but I wasn't sure what it was she was referring to.

I rolled my eyes, putting on a show for her. "What are you going on about now?" I asked. She was uncertain in her current position with Chayton as director and me as her partner.

Isi said under her breath, "I thought you would know me by now. I thought you would know that I'm an opportunist."

I said nothing, worrying about what was going on in her mind.

She turned back. "After all we've been through, I would hope you would remember what I told you. I do what's best for me. I don't do loyalty. I look for the best deal."

I held my tongue, afraid that just a few small words might cloud her judgement.

"Think about it," she continued. "If we can eliminate contacts with other mimics, it increases my value. Why wouldn't I want you to destroy the database? Why wouldn't I help you?" I watched her eyes. Her pupils were dilated. I tried to perceive what she was thinking, but again, it didn't seem to work on other mimics.

This was a lot for Isi. There was something under her words, but I couldn't quite grasp what it was. I looked at the white walls around us, wondering if anyone was recording the moment. I'd been looking for cameras in my room, but I hadn't found one.

"We're clear," Isi said, reading my mind. "There's no camera in here or in this hallway. The end of your hallway just leads to a storage closet. Not really top priority. Now, the storage closet has a camera." She was rambling, and again I was concerned with this erratic new Isi.

"What about the mind reading thing?" I asked.

She pressed the palms of her hands against her forehead. "Come on. There's someone Chayton wants you to meet. Don't talk though."

I stood and moved to face her. "Are you okay?" I asked.

She waved me off. "I'm fine. Don't ask me that." She looked away, staring at the wall for a few minutes before unclenching her fists and opening the door.

I said nothing else, but I felt that for the first time, I might have gotten a glimpse of the real Isi, and no matter what she said, something was bothering her. It had something to do with Chayton.

Chapter 21

The world was spinning out of control as Isi led me down the hallway to Chayton's office. I thought I had been working with the Agency, but I was being played the entire time. I scanned my memory, trying to recall in the last day or two if there was a moment when I could have run away, gone back to Brody, but I was searching for my innocence, an excuse for what I'd done.

Isi knocked on the door. "Come in," someone called from inside the office. Isi opened the door and waved at me to follow.

I walked behind Isi, looking up from under my eyelashes. A stranger stood by Chayton's desk. She was tall and lean with white-blond hair pulled into a bun. She didn't acknowledge Isi or me, but she turned and sat down behind Chayton's desk.

She looked vaguely familiar, but it was difficult to decipher one woman in a pantsuit from all the other pseudo-political assignments I'd had. I closed my eyes, trying to reach into her thoughts. I'd never shifted into her, and I wasn't sure if she was a mimic.

"Ms. Abbott." Isi nodded, no longer turned to me but facing the woman who continued to ignore us. The door opened to Chayton's private room in the back of his office, and Chayton walked through.

I opened my mouth to say something, but with a slight jerk of his head, he signaled that he didn't want me to speak. Isi leaned over and knocked me with her elbow. I scowled at her, still enraged they'd set me up and that Chayton had been lying to me the entire time.

I watched Abbott log in on Chayton's desktop. So, she had clearance — probably more than he did, seeing as how she walked into a room.

The woman finally looked up when Chayton approached and stood at her side. She motioned to the desk; her mouth was tight. "I hope you don't mind."

"By all means, Chelsea. Make yourself comfortable."

She leaned back in her seat, narrowing her eyes at him. "It looks like you have," Abbott said without skipping a beat. She surveyed Isi and me.

"I don't know what you mean by that," Chayton stuttered, but Abbott put up her hand.

"Making this a family affair. You never could control your urges." He glared at her. I'd never seen Chayton submit to anyone. This woman had power, and I didn't know what that meant. "You swear on your life you can trust *that* one after everything that happened?" She spoke like I wasn't in the room.

Chayton was quiet, and the muscles in his jaw twitched.

Abbott stared at him for a moment before answering. "I would have thought that you'd learn your lesson."

Chayton's face turned red, but he said nothing.

She turned and faced us. Her eyes were a deep chocolate brown, and I felt like she could read my mind. "You," she spoke to Isi. "Any funny business since she's been back?"

"No," Isi said. She offered no other details or explanations.

Abbott acknowledged me. "You could be in a prison, but you're not. Remember that."

My cheeks burned. I wanted to say something, but remembering

Isi's words, I bit down hard on my teeth, making it impossible for me to speak. I didn't even know this woman, and I hated her.

Turning back to Chayton, she said, "Ladies, out," with a flick of her wrist. Isi grabbed me by the arm and steered me to the door. I looked back over my shoulder and watched the woman turn the laptop so Chayton saw what she was looking at.

As soon as the door clicked behind us, I heard low voices rumbling from the other side of the door. "What was —" I started, but Isi motioned for me to be quiet and follow her.

We weaved through the maze of hallways, and when I noticed what door we were approaching, my eyebrows shot up in surprise. I'd never been to Isi's room. I'd imagined it as a room with nothing but a mat on the floor.

But when she opened the door, the room was almost identical to mine. She pushed me through the doorway and closed the door behind her.

In three quick strides, she made her way across the glossy tiled floor. Wiggling the mouse, she woke the computer and clicked on a video camera icon. I watched as a split screen view of the parking lot and the entrance and exit of the compound appeared.

I turned and looked at her. "What are we doing?"

"We're waiting," Isi said, pointing for me to sit on the bed. I obeyed. She met me there and lowered herself next to me. The bed barely gave at all. We sat so close together that I felt the heat radiating off her arm that pressed on mine. She made me uncomfortable, and it wasn't just because she was a trained assassin. I looked at her wiry hairless arm. Scars flecked her golden-brown skin.

She looked down at her lap as she spoke, "Abbott's pissed, and you should do your best to stay away from her. She knows something went down with the whole White House mission, but Chayton wasn't very forthcoming with her. Though Chayton runs this place, Abbott runs him. She's pissed about Ava, and she suspects you. That's why Chayton wanted you there. He wanted Abbott to see you before you leave. Or maybe Abbott wanted to see you. I'm not sure."

I said nothing. My thoughts were jumbled. Once again, I didn't know who I could trust. Then Isi broke into my thoughts. "Meda, you have no reason to believe me, but Chayton brought you here for more than one reason. It wasn't just the database." She paused, waiting for me to respond. When I didn't, she continued. "Ava had this theory. She considered that maybe, because you were the offspring of her and Chayton, two decedents from the direct line of mimics, that you might have special powers. But of course, because she was an egomaniac, she theorized that you'd be more powerful than any other mimic."

"Why would Ava assume that? She was no scientist."

"No, she said it was something about you when you were a child. You were different. You were always calm and set other children at ease."

I shook my head. "No, that's wrong. I was paranoid. I was awkward. When my mom…When Ava left and my dad told me I was a mimic, I had to hide everything."

"But I don't think it was always like that," Isi said. "Ava just recognized something special about you. I think that was why she wanted to get rid of you. Anyway, Chayton wanted to know, too."

"Is that why he came to me when I was locked up?" I asked, wondering if what Isi said was true. What if Chayton had come to visit me only because he'd wanted to test Ava's theories? If that was true, what was his actual plan for me? It had to be more than just hiding the other mimics.

"Okay, enough of all that. Chayton and Abbott are busy, so this is it."

"This is what?" I asked, confused.

"We're getting out." She glanced at the computer before turning to face me.

"What do you mean *we?*"

"Oh, I didn't tell you that part of the plan. I'm coming with you." She grinned.

I shook my head. "There's no way Brody and Aaron will take you with."

"They won't have a choice." She looked at the screen and clicked a button, rewinding it back. A black sedan entered the parking lot. She pointed at the vehicle. "Look, they're already here."

She grabbed something off the desk and placed it in my hand. I picked up the small stick and turned it over in my hand. It looked like an old flash drive. "What is this?"

"It will destroy the database. You only need to get it close. Hold onto it. If you lose it, things will be a lot more difficult." Standing in front of me, she nodded at the door. "Go. They'll be waiting for you."

"How do you know they'll be able to get in?" I asked.

She tilted her head sideways at me before shaking her head. She opened the door and sent me out into the hallway.

Chapter 22

I walked into my room, clutching the plastic device in my hand, terrified of losing it or dropping it and breaking it. It would be easy to conceal it though. I turned to shut the door behind me, not bothering with the light.

I still was facing the door when I heard someone sigh. My reflexes reacted to the training I'd been doing with Isi, and I ducked and rolled towards the noise, popping up where a man stood. I jabbed my elbow in his face, not knowing who it was or what he was doing in my room, but as Isi had taught me, I needed to show dominance.

"Shit!" came a voice from behind the hand that was now gripping a bleeding nose. My eyes were growing accustomed to the dark, and I made out blond hair.

"Aaron?" I asked as a growl came from behind that hand.

"Meda?" Another familiar voice searched for me in the darkness and found me within seconds.

"Brody." I reached for him, and he ran into my outstretched arms.

His hands grabbed my face as he pulled me to him. He brought his face down to study me. I watched his eyes travel over my face and then, before I knew it, his lips were on mine.

"Uh, guys," a voice interrupted us. "Don't worry about me. I'm just over here bleeding."

I released Brody and turned to Aaron. "I'm so sorry, Aaron!" I crossed the distance between us in two steps and wrapped my arms around him, just happy to see his face. He held his hands up awkwardly, as if unsure how to accept me clinging to him. Brody chuckled, and I finally released Aaron from my grasp.

"What are you guys doing here?" Tears threatened to spill from my eyes.

"Well, remember that watch that Brody gave you?" Aaron asked, smiling.

I glared at Brody. "You've got to be kidding me." I shook my head.

"You have to admit, it came in handy," Aaron interrupted, the grin still on his face.

I couldn't be mad. I was so happy to see them that they could have inserted another tracker in my thigh, and I would still be right here, hugging them.

"I'm so glad you're safe," Brody grasped my face between his hands and landed light kisses from my forehead to my cheeks. He pulled back to look at me, searching my face for signs of trauma.

"I'm fine, Brody."

My breath caught. I remembered that moment when I'd thought Brody might be dead. The familiar blanket of guilt settled over me like freshly fallen snow. This was all part of Chayton's plan. I should have stopped them from coming. I didn't feel like I could stop anything now. As I stared into his eyes, I saw his mind flash to the first night we met — when he, Aaron, and Dan had taken me and shoved me into the trunk of their car. I flashed to him in the trunk with me, holding me so I wouldn't be jostled too much. I flashed to me, shifting to him and him realizing what I was doing. Even stranger, I heard his voice in my head. *She's going to get herself killed, and she doesn't even know it.*

"Meda?" Brody asked.

It brought me back to the present. Brody stood in front of me. I shook my head, trying to figure out what had just happened. Then I heard Brody's voice, even though his mouth didn't move. *There's something wrong with her. Something's different.* I stared back into his eyes as he studied my face.

I hadn't considered how he would feel if he knew he could never have one more private thought with me… I knew what Brody would say. He'd say, "That's okay, I have nothing to hide." Brody was like that. Too good to be true.

"Come on. We're going to get you out of here." He grabbed my hand, and I felt a jolt of guilt.

"Wait, how did you get in?" I asked, pulling him to a stop.

"The Opposition has a guy inside who works behind the scenes. He gave us some swipe cards."

"But they have retinal scanners there," I said. The retinal scanners picked up the difference between most humans and mimics. I wondered if the guy inside was really working for the Opposition or if he was a double agent. Everything was so turned around.

"Yeah, they put us in the system." Aaron answered. "We're registered Agency operatives for now."

"Which is all we need to walk out these doors and never come back," Brody said, squeezing my hand.

"We figured you could shift into someone you know here. Isi? Maybe even Chayton?"

"Guys, if I shift into them, we risk running smack into someone I'm mimicking or someone who just talked to them. It's one thing that I'm in here, but I can't have you guys caught."

"Meda, I'm not leaving you here." Brody straightened up as Aaron looked away.

"You don't have to. Once I'm done, I'm free." I was still pretending that I could get them to leave, and then I'd have to deal with the repercussions. I understood the plan was for me to go with them, but I was stalling because I wasn't sure if I should go through with it.

Aaron shook his head. "You gotta stop trusting what people tell you. Why would they let you go?"

"Because it wasn't the Agency who brought me in. It was Chayton."

Aaron put his hand up to stop me. "Wait, wait. I'm struggling to see how that is any different. Aren't they the same thing?"

"No," I answered firmly. "Chayton is a figurehead but doesn't have the actual power. They would never give that kind of power to a mimic."

"And who told you this?"

My mouth formed a tight smile. "My brother."

"Your brother?" They asked at the same time.

"Yes, I have a half-brother. He came to me at the cabin. He was pretending to be you." I nodded at Aaron.

"Wait. Why didn't you tell me? You went with him willingly?" Brody asked.

"He didn't really give me a choice." I didn't want to tell him how it had really happened. They'd pull me out of here without my permission. They'd seek vengeance on Elan, and for some reason, I didn't want him to hate Elan before he even met him. Maybe it was because I saw how Briar had looked at him, the love I sensed between them.

"And what did he want?" Aaron asked. "What's the plan?"

"Let's get out of here, and I'll tell you on the road." Both boys looked at me with confusion.

I was sure Aaron was flashing back to the time I'd betrayed them with my mom. I told myself I would tell them the truth when we were on our way to the Agency. I just wouldn't let them know right away, otherwise Aaron might not go along with it. His ties to the Opposition ran deep, but not deeper than his friendship with Brody.

Aaron moved first into the hallway and motioned for us to follow. We crept down the empty halls, and I found it peculiar that the hallways were always empty when we needed them to be.

Someone cleared their throat behind us, and as Aaron turned, he pulled his gun out, stepping in front of me. Isi stood at the end of the hallway, wearing all black and a smirk on her face.

"Stop or I'll shoot." Aaron kept the gun trained on her.

"And alert everyone to our departure? That would be unfortunate and stupid." She took a gliding step in our direction.

"*Our* departure?" Aaron asked.

"Yeah. You guys are taking me with you." She tilted her head and gave Aaron the widest, fakest smile.

"Why would we do that?" He kept the gun pointed at her.

"Because I'm Meda's sister." She spun on her heel and waved for us to follow.

Brody and Aaron turned to glance at me, but I stared at Isi with my jaw hanging open. "Isi," I hissed. "Isi, wait!" I called, following her along the length of the hallway. I wondered how this fit with the plan.

Chapter 23

Aaron and Brody took us to a spot on the fence that had been cut open, and I saw how they'd made it through. We ran down the street to the parked Camry, making it out without incident, but my mind was racing. Was Isi telling the truth? It would explain her animosity toward Chayton. How long had she known? I was torn between talking to her and ignoring her. Questioning her was useless, since she was a master at masking her emotions. I'd never know if she was telling the truth or not.

Aaron drove, and I looked at Brody in the front seat. Isi sat next to me in the back. I leaned against my seat and watched the Agency headquarters roll past. I closed my eyes for a moment but opened them when Aaron spoke.

At first, I thought he was talking to me. "I don't know why you'd trust her," he said. Isi stared at him; her face was emotionless, her eyes as hard as flint. "Are you really her sister?" Aaron asked. "Or is this one of your tricks to get Meda to work with you?"

"I don't need to explain anything to you." She clenched her fists and narrowed her eyes as she spoke between her teeth, but she spoke loudly enough that we could all hear her words through the car's quiet hum.

I interrupted, "But you will need to explain it to me."

She crossed her arms and slumped in her seat, looking out the window. For once, she looked like a kid. I had to remind myself that she was only a couple of years younger than I was, but she still looked thirteen.

"Isi. Please," I said.

"You don't have to beg," Aaron said. "She's in no position to keep information from us."

She turned back toward me and stared at the floor of the car for a moment before she spoke again. "I don't want to talk about this in front of them," she whispered, her voice shaking. "I swear. We'll talk later."

Again, the emotion in her voice surprised me. Isi was stone cold, so something had to have shaken her in order for her to show this kind of weakness. It nagged at me that maybe she was acting. That was our job as mimics. She could mimic emotion right now.

"Okay," I said.

Isi sat up and stared ahead.

"Where are we going?" Aaron's voice cut through the tension. I shifted to see Brody's face, but he wouldn't turn and look at me. He remained quiet.

"We need to go to Opposition headquarters," I said, shifting in my seat.

"You don't just go to headquarters. You get invited." Aaron glanced over his shoulder.

"Well, make the call." Isi's voice had returned to its normal cockiness.

Aaron pulled the steering wheel to the side and slammed on the brakes.

"What are you doing?" Isi asked as we pulled to a stop at the side of the road. She gripped the door handle to keep herself from flying into the seat in front of her. Cars whizzed by as Aaron opened his door and walked around the front of the car. Isi looked at me, and I motioned for her to exit the vehicle. Brody opened his door and got out, too.

"We should keep moving," I said as I slid out of the vehicle. I stood up straight as Aaron spoke.

"Why?" He looked down the road. "No one is following us. No one is looking for you two. It's highly suspicious that they left two trained mimics to be taken by two unknown agents. And if you're both Chayton's children, I'm sure he wouldn't let that happen. So, what gives?"

Isi looked at me, crossing her arms.

I stepped toward Aaron. "Here's the truth." I glanced between Aaron and Brody.

Isi shook her head in objection. Obviously, she would prefer if I kept them in the dark about our plan until we were safely in Smith's office, but I couldn't do that to these boys. I had to trust that they'd understand how important this was.

"There's a database that holds information on all known mimics in the US." Brody was finally looking at me. "Including my sisters." He closed his eyes and sighed. "I'm going to destroy it." I pulled the device out of my pocket. "Using this."

"Wait a minute." Aaron threw his hands in the air. "The Agency gave this to you? They want you to break into Opposition and destroy their database? The Agency are the ones that are using mimics. It makes no sense." He paced back and forth.

"Not everyone at the Opposition works for Smith. There are double agents who are working to get access. I have to destroy it before they get their hands on it and destroy the lives of all mimics." I slipped the device back in my pocket and patted it to make sure it was there.

Isi motioned at Aaron with her eyes, and I understood what she wanted from me. She wanted me to touch him and read his thoughts. She wanted to know if he'd go along with us or double-cross us. I shook my head no. I had more reason to trust Aaron than he had to trust me. There was no way I was going to invade his thoughts.

"I've worked with Isi." I hoped they could hear the sincerity in my voice. "And if she's going to risk her life for this mission, then we have to help her, too."

"How will breaking into headquarters help?" Aaron asked.

I looked at Isi again, and she was shaking her head vehemently, but I didn't back down. "The database is somewhere inside. Probably in Smith's office," I said.

Brody laughed. "You think we can just stroll through the front door?"

I turned to Brody, surprised to hear his laugh.

Isi raised an eyebrow. "Why can't we? Doesn't Smith trust you?"

Brody stared at her with a look I didn't recognize. He turned to me. "Are there other agents who have this information?"

"Nope," Isi answered again. "This information is too valuable. Only Chayton and Abbott know it's on the mainframes at the Opposition."

Aaron stopped pacing and stood in front of Isi. "Who's this 'Abbott'? Is she on Chayton's side?"

Isi nodded her head. "No, Abbott is not on Chayton's side. She's the true enemy. Abbott can't know, otherwise she'll be upset that the database is destroyed. She wants it for herself, to continue their political dealings. It's power she seeks. She's got so many people in her pocket already."

"But if only those two knew, wouldn't she suspect Chayton?"

Isi raised a brow. "Not if he's in a meeting with Abbott. Can't be in two places at once."

"Technically, he could," Brody said.

"Oh, Abbott is no fool." Isi folded her arms. "Even though she trusts Chayton, there's a reason she keeps a silver paperweight on her desk. Anyone who enters has to pick it up, so she can see if they are who they're supposed to be."

I nodded my head. "That's pretty clever."

"Abbott's very clever." Isi turned to me. "That's why we're going to need to be very careful, and not let the *Bumble Brothers* muck this up."

Aaron's eyebrows hit a severe slant. "I think we've proven ourselves pretty efficient. You know, capturing a mimic. In fact, I believe we ended up capturing you as well, Isi. We also helped the Opposition foil the Agency's plan."

Cars whizzed by, muffling Isi's next words. "The question is, can you do it without getting anyone killed?" I watched a shadow fall over Aaron's face, and I realized he was thinking about Dan. I was, too. And my mom.

"No more talking," Brody snapped. The anger in his eyes surprised me. He rarely talked to people that way, but Isi had a way of getting under everyone's skin. "Everyone back in the car."

He slid into the passenger seat and slammed the door behind him before the rest of us could react. I shot Isi a death glare, and she shrugged her shoulders at me before walking over to the vehicle and getting inside.

When it was just Aaron and me, he spoke in a low growl. "I hope you know what you're doing." I stared at him, and I realized that Aaron really was my friend, or he wouldn't go along with any of this. He turned and walked back around the front of the car to the driver's side, giving me one last glance before opening his door.

I looked up at the sky, the wind chilling me to the bone. *Please let this be the right thing*, I chanted to myself as I slipped into the back of the vehicle.

Chapter 24

We rode in silence for the next half hour. I listened to my heartbeat while trying to ignore the sideways glances Isi kept giving me. My eyes were on the back of Brody's head. I wanted to talk to him. He focused on me and every once in a while, when he glanced back at us, I saw his eyes soften. Then he turned to the front again, his face hard as stone. I wondered if I'd pushed him too far this time.

I cleared my throat and turned to Isi. "How long have you known?" I asked, causing Brody to glance at us again.

She blew out an exasperated breath, and she shook her hands out at her sides like she was trying to get rid of a terrible memory or something. "Since Chayton came up with this plan."

I studied her for a moment, weighing my words carefully. "So, you never told me in the first place because you didn't want to hurt my feelings or something like that?"

"I didn't want to tell you unless I had to," she said, her eyes darting over to mine and then back to the road. "I knew how you'd be. This changes nothing."

"What does that mean?" I asked.

Something in her face changed — even though she was looking straight ahead. A heavy pause settled over us. "It means I still need to do what's best for me," she said, before glancing at me. "I'm the only one looking out for me."

Brody's eyes shot to Isi and then back to the road in front of us.

A lump formed in my throat, making it hard to swallow or speak — or do anything other than stare at her. I thought she'd been acting strange, but the more time I had spent with her, the more I saw the real Isi. The girl beneath the bluster. I wanted to reach out to her and let her know it was okay if she was confused or feeling vulnerable, but I knew she'd smack my hand away.

"We'll need to find a place to stay for the night," Brody said, cutting through the awkward silence. "We can't use the safe houses anymore." He looked at me, and I remembered the last time we'd used an Opposition safe house. The leers of the men who had looked at me like I was a monster.

"You don't have to worry about that," Isi interrupted. "I've already got somewhere to take us."

"Really?" Aaron asked, sounding skeptical.

"Yep." She smiled at his doubtful expression. "I've been in this game longer than you. Don't you think I'd set up places to hide out when I need to get away?" She looked out the window. "Sheesh. Amateur hour."

"Okay, Miss Super Spy. Tell me where we're going," Aaron said.

"Just keep driving. I'll tell you when to take the exit." Isi watched out the window, and I rested my head against the cool glass as the hum from the tires lulled me to a half-asleep state.

I jumped when Isi tapped on the window. "Next exit," she said.

Aaron took the next exit and weaved through the downtown section of shops and office buildings to an area of town with large factories and industrial buildings. Everything was hard edges and metal, and all the buildings and warehouses blended together.

Isi directed Aaron to pull into the parking lot of what looked, at first, like an abandoned office building. We could see through windows at the front. The place looked abandoned — no furniture or desks inside. Aaron pulled up to the front door and cut off the engine.

Isi turned to me and said, "I'll be right back." She got out of the car, and the second she closed the door behind her, I glanced at Brody. Finally, he shifted his head just enough to glance at me out of the corner of his eye. I was once again tempted to touch him, to see what he was thinking. But I resisted, horrified by my new instinct. Folding my hands together, I stared at the door, wondering what Isi was up to inside.

We waited for what seemed like an eternity. Finally, Isi came back out and motioned for us to follow. The three of us slid out of the car and walked through the door into the abandoned building. Aaron had his hand on his gun as our eyes adjusted to the light. I gasped and stumbled back when I realized that what I thought was a shadow was actually a man standing in the entrance's corner.

Aaron pulled out his gun and pointed it at the man. "Stay where you are!" he yelled. "What, is this an ambush?" he asked Isi, refusing to take his eyes off the man.

"Why would I bring you all the way here just to ambush you? We could have busted you at the Agency." Isi put her hand up and guided his gun down to his side. What she was saying was true, but this would mean something else if she were trying to hurt us away from Chayton's watchful eye. "This is Zane."

The man smiled, giving us a glimpse of yellowed, crooked teeth. He gave a little wave, and I sensed he had a kind heart. I wanted to touch him to read his mind, but Isi would recognize exactly what I was doing, and I hated being too transparent. Isi nodded at him, her expression softening. Aaron and Brody seemed just as confused as I was, but Isi motioned for us to follow her down the hall.

We passed through several doors until we entered a wide-open space. I imagined it once holding office cubicles, but now it was empty except for the bed set up in the middle of the room. Isi looked back at me and then sat down on the bed. Aaron and Brody looked around, clearly confused. I saw what they were thinking: This was a trap of some sort.

"Okay," she said, turning to Aaron and Brody, her eyes wide open as if that would help them concentrate on what she was saying. "I know this seems strange, but I'm going to need you guys to trust me. I've been planning this for a long time."

"What's going on?" I asked, watching her closely.

Her eyes scanned my face as if she was looking for something. "This is part of the Resistance." She nodded to the man, who followed us into the room. "Zane was living here when I first stumbled onto this place. I'd gotten into a fight with another agent." I opened my mouth to speak, but she shook her head. "No, not Ava. Anyway, I needed a plan in case things went south. Zane was a kind man, down on his luck, and when I asked if he'd look after some stuff for me, he agreed." She patted him on the shoulder.

"So, the Resistance is you, a homeless guy, and an empty warehouse? Neat." Aaron crossed his arms, not taking any of this seriously.

Isi pointed to the back of the room and hopped up from the bed. "Come on." She led us to another door in the back of the room. She was like a kid having her first sleepover and giving the grand tour. When she opened the door, the space was pitch black. She walked over and flicked on a lantern.

It was an office. I didn't recognize the furniture or decorations, but it was pretty clear from the file cabinets, desks, and bookshelves that there had been someone here. Aaron pulled out his gun and held it behind his back as he took three steps inside, then stopped to let me see around him into the room.

"Whoa." That was all I had to say.

I placed my hand on him to calm him, but I shouldn't have touched him. His thoughts invaded my brain. *There's so much we could do with this. All we'd have to do is get rid of Isi.* I shook my head, trying not to focus on Aaron. He had a one-track mind, so I couldn't hold it against him. He wanted to get rid of Isi.

I focused on the contents of the room: cameras, monitors, spy equipment, all Agency issued — stashed for who knew what? I didn't understand what most of it did or how they used it, but I was pretty sure Isi had been hoarding equipment for years.

She moved to the cameras stacked on top of one another and pointed at them. "This is the newest tech. Infrared and digital. They can be planted everywhere, and they upload everything to the cloud, but it's encrypted."

"How long have you been stockpiling Agency equipment?" Aaron's eyes sparkled.

"Long before any of you had anything to do with this." She moved around, picking up supplies and studying them. I tried to imagine Isi even younger, ten or twelve, sneaking gear out of the Agency. Did she have help? Did she do it on her own?

Aaron moved closer to her, finally looking at her like she could be of some value to him. "Tell me about this Resistance," he said.

A grin played across her lips, and in that moment, I realized that Isi and Aaron were more alike than they'd ever realized.

Chapter 25

Isi moved over to a pile of books and picked up a familiar text, *The Art of War* by Sun Tzu. She opened to a page and read, "Supreme excellence consists of breaking the enemy's resistance without fighting."

I remembered another quote she once gave me from that same book. It was something about preparing while waiting for the enemy to be unprepared. She'd also said something about suffering defeat if you didn't know the enemy. I knew the Agency was my enemy, and I knew Chayton, maybe as well as I ever would now. Maybe that was the point of this whole journey.

"Okay," Aaron interrupted. "But who's the enemy?"

"In order to understand your enemy," Isi said, shrugging and placing the book back on the pile, "you must become your enemy."

Aaron eyed her like he didn't trust her. "Again, the question remains. Who is the enemy?"

I stepped forward. "Anyone who wants to use mimics for their dirty deeds? Anyone who wants to track us and label us monsters?"

"So, anyone who isn't a mimic?" Aaron asked.

"Yeah, that's about right," Isi said. "And what's your goal, Aaron?" She drew out his name.

Aaron shot another pointed look at her. My face sunk a little as I waited for the answer. I wanted to believe that Aaron could think of all mimics as people who deserved to be rescued. Aaron obliged in a reluctant voice. "We want to find a way for humans and mimics to live together peacefully."

I could still feel Isi's words bouncing around my head. The Resistance, preparing for the Agency to make a mistake, getting to know all their secrets until she could use those secrets against them. This was her plan or backup plan if anything went wrong at the Agency. She had clearly thought this through more than me if she had been hoarding Agency goods for years. The more I thought about it, the more confused I became.

We exited the equipment room and walked back to the main room with a high ceiling and exposed metal beams. I couldn't imagine staying here. It was too cold and exposed.

"Is there a place for us to sleep in this joint besides this one bed?" Aaron asked.

"My bed is yours," Zane said, patting the mattress of a queen-sized bed.

"Zane, stop." Isi grinned at him. "There are rooms upstairs. Mostly just mattresses on the floor. You'll want to grab some fresh linens from the cabinet over there. Some guests here haven't showered for a while." She used her right hand to shield Zane from the finger she pointed his way.

He continued to smile his crooked grin before turning and opening up a cupboard that was full of ready-to-eat food and canned goods. "If you're hungry, we have plenty of food." He pointed to another cupboard with plates, cups, and silverware. "We also have a bathroom upstairs."

"Oh, Meda!" Isi cried out. She took me by surprise. "I remembered how much you like candy. Check this out." She walked over to the cupboard and flung the door open. The cupboard was filled with candy, a kid's dream. I still didn't know how old Isi was.

She grabbed something and held it out to me: Megatarts. My favorite candy, though my dad hated it when I ate them. He thought they'd rot my teeth. But he still bought me a supersize pack of them for my birthday every year. He'd look the other way as I crunched through them rather than sucking on them until they disintegrated.

"How did you know?" I grabbed the box of candy and turned it over in my hands.

"You're not the only one who's observant." Isi grinned, and I got the impression she was proud of pleasing me.

"Can we talk now?" I motioned for her to walk with me.

Brody watched us as our footsteps echoed through the cavernous room. A musty yet metallic smell hung in the air and again, it amazed me that Isi had pulled all this off — hiding an entire building from the Agency.

Unless she didn't pull it off and Chayton was aware but let her keep it to humor her.

Or if he was laying a trap for them all.

We walked across the room by the tall windows on the outside wall. As we got to the corner, Isi leaned back against the wall and folded her arms across her chest, looking at me with a serious expression. Her lips tightened as she waited for my questions.

"Isi, were you telling the truth back there, about being my sister?" Her expression changed, but I couldn't read it. "Please, be honest with me."

She turned around and gazed out the window. "Does it matter what I say? You can't trust me, anyway."

I stepped over to her side, but she refused to look at me. "Is that why you were so mad at me when Elan brought me back? I thought we were on good terms the last time I saw you."

Isi sighed. "You still take things too personally. I wasn't mad at you when you came back. I was just mad. There's a difference. You'll know when I'm mad at you." Again, I felt like I was getting a glimpse of the girl beneath the agent.

Aaron and Brody were deep in conversation with Zane behind us. We could talk freely. "How did you find out? Did he know?"

"Of course, he knew." She shook her head. I imagined how I'd feel if I were in her position, learning her parents had abandoned her as a kid and the Agency took her in. My mother had taken her under her wing, while the entire time, Chayton, her real father, was there. I wondered if my mother had been aware that she was helping to raise Chayton's daughter.

"She didn't know," Isi said, studying my face. "That's what you're thinking. But she didn't. Otherwise, who knows what would have happened to me? *That* was his reason for not telling anyone. He said he feared they would use me against him." She rubbed the back of her hand across her face, and I saw a damp spot on her knuckle before she wiped it on her shirt.

"What do you mean, 'use you against him'?"

She shook her head and looked out the window. Brody and Aaron had stopped talking and were watching us.

I tried again for an answer from Isi. "So, why did you agree to this?"

She sighed and glanced at me. "You really don't understand the way things work around here. The Agency doesn't like it when anyone knows their dirty little secrets." I could hear the hint of bitterness in her voice. She paused. "Meda," she began, her eyes trained on the floor. "Sometimes they're willing to do anything to get what they want." Isi's gaze flicked to mine before she looked away. "It's not personal. None of this is. It's a means to an end for you and the others, but not for me. And I'm okay with that."

"You could get out," I said without thinking.

She put her hand up and rolled her eyes at me. "Just stop. I don't want to talk about it. Let's get through the night and see what happens next." She kicked her foot against the wall and pushed off, moving away from me. "Come on, I'll show you guys where the rooms are."

I followed her, letting her words settle in my brain. I felt like she was telling me something without telling me anything. She might be younger than me, but her soul was aged. I hoped it was salvageable.

Chapter 26

We got to the room, and Brody carried the blankets over to the bed and started making it. The room echoed with silence, and I couldn't tell if he was mad at me. He continued to make the bed, and I stood there awkwardly.

The problem was that Brody understood me better than anyone else, even my dad and sisters. He recognized that I didn't want to spy on the Agency or play this stupid game any longer, but my actions contradicted what he knew about me. All I wanted to do was run away with him back to the cabin, but there'd be no going back if we double-crossed the Opposition.

"What is all this about?" Brody broke the silence as he continued making the bed. "I mean, what is the endgame?"

"I don't know." I moved closer to him, willing him to look at me.

When he did, a confused stare marred his handsome face, and he let out an exasperated breath. "You don't know what we're doing?"

"No." I sat down on the edge of the bed. It seemed stupid to be arguing about this when we were finally reunited. "I'm so confused." I looked up at him and realized there was another thing that I needed to tell him, but I didn't know how he'd react to the whole *mind reading* thing.

He crouched down by me. "Since when was there a time that I

didn't listen to what you had to say? After all this, you should realize you can trust me." He reached his hand out to me, but I just stared at it.

I swallowed hard. I was afraid to touch him but even more afraid to tell him about my new abilities. Then again, what did I have to lose at this point? I took his hand and let him pull me back up.

"Brody," I started, "I'm sorry for all the things I said, and for not telling you everything that was going on when I saw you at the gas station. Everything was happening so quickly." I took his other hand in mine and looked into his eyes.

He stared back at me, hurt and confused. I saw his aura and received the flash of his thoughts. He had doubts about us. He thought maybe I was playing him. His hands fell to his sides. He had every reason to feel what he was feeling.

"Wait!" I exclaimed, reaching for him again, but I knew it was no use; my touch wouldn't make him understand what I wanted him to.

He pulled away from me again. "No, you listen for once." He paced back and forth in the small room. "I sat there scared that I'd never get to tell you how much I loved you, but you were fine, making friends with your new sister."

I stuttered, unable to find words. There was the sting of jealousy in Brody's voice, but it came from fear. His fear of losing me. And I couldn't be mad at him for that. "Brody, I'm sorry." Tears began building as he continued pacing around the room. I realized just how much of a mess I'd made of things.

"Tell me what we're doing here." His tone was softer now. "I'm tired of being kept in the dark."

I sniffled and stared at my feet before looking back up into his eyes. "I don't know everything that's going on. Dozens of mimics will be free if we destroy the database. I recognize that."

He stood facing me. "You're asking us to double-cross Smith. If we do this, the Opposition can't forgive us."

"I'm tired of running," I spoke with finality.

I needed him to realize this wasn't about me and him. It was bigger than us. It always had been. I never should have run off to our cabin in the woods. I wrapped my arms around his waist, and his arms wrapped loosely around me. The warmth of his body was familiar and comforting.

"What are you saying?" He leaned down, whispering in my ear.

I breathed deeply, taking in his scent, and melted into his arms. My heart was beating wildly in my chest. "I'm saying… I trust you with all my heart. I just want you to trust me." I looked up at him, willing him to understand me.

"I'm sorry, Meda. I didn't mean what I said. I trust you. I just don't want to talk anymore." His right hand traveled to my face and, as his fingertips brushed my cheek, I leaned into his hand. His lips came closer as his eyes stared deeply into mine, searching.

My stomach sizzled with anticipation, and I struggled to close my mind off from his, but I saw the flash of his memory of me being loaded in the back of the van, of him frantically searching for the keys to the car to follow. Then I saw the image of him following the van and the car crashing and pushing him into the ditch and the only thing that passed through his mind was that he'd let me down.

Tears trickled down my face. How could I have put him through that? Even at the gas station, I should have told him I was fine. I should have told him I was back at the Agency and let him be free of me, but I was being selfish, and I still hadn't told him I could read his thoughts.

I pulled him down to join me on the bed, and the warmth of his lips seeped through me. He was the only solid thing in the swirl of dizzying thoughts, and I clung to his muscular frame, allowing him to be my anchor. The world went silent, and his lips sent tremors down my spine.

We fell asleep in each other's arms with unspoken words on our lips.

A commotion downstairs jarred me from sleep. I wiped my hand down my face, still exhausted. We couldn't have slept for long. I turned to look at Brody, and he was also awake, his eyebrows creased with confusion.

"About last night," I said.

"No. Just promise me you'll tell me everything. This can't work if we're going to keep secrets." And I heard his thoughts underneath his voice. *I can't protect you this way.*

I opened my mouth, knowing that this was the perfect time to tell him about the mind reading thing. But then a loud clanking, like someone hitting a metal pipe against a vent, rang throughout the room.

"I think it's time to go," he said as I disentangled myself from him. We both got up and straightened up our clothes before heading back down the stairs, toward Isi, Aaron, and Zane.

Isi and Aaron were already in an argument as we approached the main room. I grabbed Brody by the arm, pulling him back to me. I didn't know when we'd be alone together again. It might be my last time to have a private discussion with him. "Brody, I'm sorry about everything." I looked up into his eyes.

He nodded. "I'm sorry I reacted the way I did. It brought me back to those first days. Aaron's family. I hate feeling helpless, and I never want to let you down." He wrapped his arms around me and pulled me close. His hot breaths warmed the top of my head.

My brain flashed to crime scene photos of Aaron's family.

His sister, who had been murdered because of the Agency. Then I wondered if these thoughts were mine or Brody's.

Brody pulled away. "Come on. Let's see what the plan is." He put his arm around me as we walked through the doors. I kept telling myself that I would explain the whole mind reading thing to him later. If there was a later.

Chapter 27

When we arrived at the main room, Zane was loading some gear into the back of the van parked in the attached warehouse. I hadn't noticed the massive garage door that led into the empty warehouse space. "What's all this for?" I asked.

Isi looked up from the bundle of wires she held in her fist. "I figured we needed to be ready for anything. If we have to run, we're not running empty-handed." She tossed the bundle into the back of the van. "Can you tell Aaron that I don't take orders from kids who know nothing about anything?" She gave an exasperated sigh.

Aaron was leaning against the wall, watching Isi and Zane pack. I realized that I wasn't sure if he'd go along with any of this. Even after all we'd been through. We might walk into Opposition headquarters, and he could turn us in right away. I didn't want to believe that, but I couldn't blame him.

To be safe, I walked over to him and bumped his arm. He glowered at me. I feigned innocence, but I was abusing my power, and I was afraid he would realize it.

I couldn't see in his head but felt his thoughts. *After all we've been through, she's going to trust Isi? How could she?*

"Hey, I don't trust her." I tried to comfort him. Aaron stared at me, and I realized my mistake. My words rushed out. "I know

155

you think that I'm turning my back on you guys, but I'm not. I would never. I owe you my life." I pushed my hair behind my ear and glanced at Brody, who was chatting with Zane. Isi eyed us as she continued gathering items and loading them into the back of the van.

"You know what my dad stood for," he said. "The Opposition helped us. Heck, they saved us. You know I don't think mimics are bad, but you have to admit, having that kind of power is dangerous." He glanced at me, and I wondered what he would think of my new power.

"Having a gun is dangerous," I said. "It's how you use it. And you understand better than anyone what it's like to be forced into situations."

"Meda, I know how you feel about family. I worry that this new connection with Isi will cloud your judgement, like it did with Ava." He crossed his arms and waited for my reply.

I wanted to scream at him or hit him, but I deserved what he'd said. I took a calming breath before speaking. "It's different. I need you to understand that. I knew Ava as my mom. She was a different person. I've only known Isi as what she is. I'm aware she can't be trusted."

Brody approached us. "What's up?" He looked at Aaron and then at me.

"Nothing," Aaron said.

"Come on." Brody gave Aaron a nudge. "I know you guys were talking about something. Let's promise to be upfront with each other. If we can't trust each other, we can't trust anyone." I remembered again that Dan had told me not to trust anyone.

I said, "Aaron is right to doubt me. I've made poor decisions before. But this one feels right. I have to do more than fix my wrongs."

I glanced at Aaron, and he looked down. "This is about more than what the Agency has done to us. If we can destroy the database, then no one can use it. I understand it seems like we're being traitors, biting the hand that feeds us, but the Opposition can't keep that list safe. No one can."

Brody squeezed my shoulder. I smiled at him and looked back at Aaron. "So, are we good?"

Brody held out his hand, and Aaron stared at it for a moment before taking it. They stood there for a second, not sure what else to do.

"Come on," Isi called. "Let's hit the road."

"I'm driving." Aaron dropped Brody's hand and moved toward the van.

"It's my van," Isi replied.

"Do you even have a driver's license? How old are you, anyway?" He crossed his arms.

"None of your business," she said, "but you're right. You should be driving. It would look odd if we pulled up to the Opposition with me behind the wheel." Isi tossed him the keys, and he caught them with one hand.

It surprised me that she'd admitted Aaron was right. Brody joined him up front while Isi and I climbed into the back. Zane waved goodbye as we drove away from the gigantic building, heading away from the industrial area where most buildings still looked empty. A few parked cars dotted the street.

We weaved through town, and I stared out the window at the people occupying shops and small stores along Main Street in Town Square. Two men stood in front of a cafe dressed in pressed suits, sipping drinks while chatting with one another. They didn't look like they had much to worry about. A woman walked out of a shop.

Her hair floated in the breeze as she clutched her purse against her side.

I eyed Isi, who looked lost in thought. "Could you imagine living in a world where you didn't know about mimics, spies, the Agency and Opposition?" I tapped on the glass. "It's like everyone is at peace here."

She glanced out the window, pretending to take in the sights. "They're probably not that happy," she mumbled. "No one is ever truly at peace."

If that was true, what were we doing? Were we just hamsters in a spinning wheel doomed to fall for the same traps over and over again? No. I had more optimism than that, and maybe one day Isi would find her place in a world that didn't require her to lie and kill. Though, I doubted she'd be at peace in that world.

Chapter 28

We'd been on the road for a few hours, nearing our destination, when Isi yelled to the front, "We need to stop! I gotta take a pee."

Aaron glanced in the rearview mirror and then said something to Brody, who spun in his seat and made eye contact with me. "We're not stopping now."

"What is it?" I asked. I looked behind us to see if anyone followed, but that was stupid. The Agency knew where we were heading and had no reason to track us. The Opposition needn't follow us because we were about to show up on their doorstep.

Brody waved me closer. "Aaron doesn't want to stop. He'd rather keep going, just in case Isi has any tricks up her sleeve."

"That's insane, Brody. How can she have any tricks? The Agency knows where we're going. There's no need for her to trick us along the way."

The car in front of us pumped the brakes, and I reached forward, grasping the back of Aaron's seat. My fingertips brushed his shoulder, and my brain flashed to Aaron thinking about me and Isi, riding together before Ava intentionally crashed into the vehicle to retrieve us from the Opposition. He wasn't there when it happened. He only knew what Smith, the head of the Opposition, told him. And that I'd asked to ride with Isi, making me look guilty.

I leaned forward to get Aaron's attention. "Isi has no reason to trick us. It's not like before. Ava was pulling the strings last time, playing both Isi and me."

Aaron stared at me in the rearview mirror. I realized he hadn't spoken a word, and I had read his mind and responded to his thoughts. He flicked his blinker and pulled over to the side of the road.

"No," Isi objected. "I'm not peeing on the side of the road."

He put the van in park and looked back, motioning for me to join him outside the vehicle. He didn't wait to see if I'd follow. He exited the vehicle, slamming the door behind him.

"What's going on?" Brody asked while reaching for the door handle.

I held up my hand. "Let me talk to Aaron alone."

Isi squirmed in her seat. "I still have to pee!"

I pulled the sliding door open just as Aaron walked around to meet me at the side of the vehicle. Brody stared out his window at him, and Aaron saluted him before pulling the side door shut again and guiding me by the elbow to the back of the vehicle.

Once we were out of sight of everyone else, he asked, "What's going on with you?"

"What do you mean?" I asked.

"Let me tell you a brief story I learned from my dad's files. I didn't learn it from him, because he was gone before he could teach me much about the Agency and mimics."

"What's that now?" I asked, confused by his line of thought. Aaron was usually pretty straightforward.

"He not only found out about mimics, but he also had this theory about the potential enhanced abilities of mimics." He stopped talking and stared at me, waiting for me to spill my secrets.

My cheeks flushed. I should have told Brody right away. Now it all looked suspicious. "I was going to tell you guys," I said.

"So, what is it? Be honest, Meda. What can you do?" Cars whirred by us on the busy road. It wasn't safe here, but I knew I wouldn't get Aaron back on the road without telling him the truth.

"It's not… I can't control it," I said. "I just get these flashes of images from people's lives. It's only after I touch them. I sometimes catch fragments of thoughts. Sometimes they're difficult to decipher from spoken words. I still don't understand it."

"You didn't mention any of this to Brody?" he asked.

"How could I? Would you want to be around someone who could read your thoughts? Would you be able to control what you're thinking?' I studied him as his face twisted, and I could sense him trying to stop me from hearing him.

"So, you can hear my thoughts now?" he asked.

There was a knocking sound, and I stepped off to the side to see Brody, tapping his knuckles on the window. He called through it, "What are you guys doing back there? Isi is going to wet herself if you don't get her out of here."

I looked at Aaron, and he nodded, sighing. He wasn't happy, but he didn't make me promise to keep my new power a secret. We walked to the back door and he reached for the handle, but I grabbed his hand.

My fingers tingled where our skin met. "Thank you," I said. Sometimes Aaron was too good at reading my actions to be trusted with secrets.

He nodded curtly and opened the door to let Isi out and to let me in. His thoughts fluttered about in my head, pressing against my skull until it hurt.

Brody turned to look at me, and without saying anything, I could tell what he was thinking, but I read his face instead of his mind. He reached back, and I grabbed his hand, comforted by the warmth of his skin against my palm. His thoughts pushed against my brain, but I closed my eyes and focused on keeping them out.

I watched Isi disappear down the embankment. She must have really had to go.

"What else do you know about her?" Aaron asked. He must have seen me watching her.

"Not much," I said. "We got to spend a little time together, but I can't tell if she's being truthful or not. A lot of it is a show. Sometimes, I think she's just a scared young woman, and sometimes she's a diabolical lunatic. But I guess being raised by the Agency could do that to someone." I considered my mom and wondered what her role had been in raising Isi. I never thought I'd feel pity for the girl.

"Chayton must be a real creep to take in his daughter but not even tell her they're related." Aaron shifted in his seat. Isi's head appeared up the embankment as she made her way back to the car.

"There's always a reason for what they do. I'm sure he believed he was protecting her." As Isi opened the door, I considered Chayton again. I wondered if he really cared about his children or if we were just a science experiment to him.

Isi settled down next to me and clicked her seatbelt into place. "Let's ride!" she called, slapping the back of Aaron's seat. Aaron glanced at her in the rearview mirror before his eyes met mine.

I didn't expect Aaron ever to trust me completely after all this. He'd learned so much about what I could do now, and he was trying to piece it all together. For now, I would just have to focus on the mission at hand.

Chapter 29

We'd been on the road for hours when Isi began squirming in her seat again.

"Don't tell me you have to pee again," I said to her.

"I'm hungry. Aren't you guys hungry?" she asked.

Brody opened the glove compartment and pulled out some protein bars that he'd taken from Isi's food stash. He tossed a few to her in the backseat.

She held one up, staring at it before sighing. "I think I need proper food. Who knows what will happen after all this goes down? Let's find a drive-through."

"This isn't a family road trip," Aaron said.

The corner of my mouth drew up, but I successfully fought a smile. It sure felt like a family road trip. I glanced at Isi to see her reaction.

She leaned forward in her seat. "And you're not my dad or my brother. If I want food, I get food." Isi reached over and unhooked her seatbelt. I watched to see what she was going to do.

Suddenly, she was filling up the seat. She shrugged out of her leather jacket as her arms bulged and her legs stretched, banging into the back of Aaron's seat. Her hair retreated into the scalp and turned blonde as a shadow of a beard sprouted on her thick jawline.

163

She slammed on the back of Aaron's seat, and he ducked, turning to look at the man who was seated behind him.

"What the..." Aaron shouted, swerving before regaining control of the van. "What are you doing?"

"I'm hungry!" Isi yelled in the baritone voice of the man she now mimicked.

"Stop it." I gave her a stern look.

Isi deflated, shifting back into her own form, and fell back into the seat. She shrugged her shoulders and adjusted her seatbelt as if nothing had happened. I was surprised she'd listened to me.

"Isi," I started, but she cut me off.

"What? This is going to be a long night. I'm hungry, and you don't want me eating all the protein bars before we get there. I'm sick of these things. Aren't you?"

"You could've eaten at your warehouse." Aaron spoke with the impatient tone of a tired parent dealing with an impatient child.

"I was in a hurry. I didn't have time to eat." Isi crossed her arms over her chest.

"You're always in a hurry." I looked back at Aaron and Brody.

Brody checked his watch. "Can we find a drive-through so we can keep going?"

"I'm sure there's one coming up soon." I tried to keep myself calm.

We passed by a sign for a fast-food chain, and Isi pointed out the window. "There!"

"Good, there's a drive-through," Aaron said in relief. He pulled into the parking lot a couple of minutes later.

"I'm so hungry." Isi moaned to herself, slumping down in the backseat.

I swiveled in my seat. "Isi, if you do that again, I'm going to kick you out of this car and leave you there to walk home."

"I was just hungry," Isi said as Aaron glared at her in the rearview mirror. "Did you not hear me? What are you, deaf?" Isi squirmed in her seat. "Would you guys just leave me alone? I'm not doing anything."

"And depleting your energy that way will only make you hungrier. Besides, you know how dangerous that was, right? You could've hurt someone or yourself." I realized the irony in my warning. I was speaking to a trained Agency assassin.

"It was just for a few seconds and besides, it won't happen again," Isi said with a pout.

"If it happens again, you can walk home," I said, reaching for my seatbelt to take it off when we arrived at the drive-through.

"Fine," Isi said with a huff. I gave her a stern look. She looked down, defeated.

Aaron pulled up to the speaker, and as we called out what we wanted, he leaned out of the window toward the speaker to place the order.

We pulled up to the window a minute later, paid, and got our food. Isi was eating hers in the backseat before we even started driving again. "Can you please slow down? You're going to choke if you eat so fast." I stared at the half-eaten sandwich in her hand. "Why are you so hungry?" I asked.

She spoke with her mouth full between chews. "I've been shifting so much lately. It makes me really hungry."

I thought about the last few days. "Why have you been shifting that much? We haven't been that busy."

"Speak for yourself." She stopped chewing to look at me. "Crap," she said, trying to swallow the food in her mouth with a gulp of her soda.

"What do you mean? How busy have you been?" I wondered what she was talking about. Was she going on extra assignments?

"I wasn't going to tell you, but I guess it can't hurt. You're terrible at this whole mimic thing, so maybe you could use some tips." She took a French fry from her container and slipped the entire fry into her mouth.

"Tell me what? What are you talking about?" I took a small bite from one of my fries.

"Well, you know how when you shift, you're as strong as the person you shift into? Like your body knows to mimic not only their form, but their muscle mass and strength?"

Aaron merged onto the highway without touching his food, but I could tell he was listening closely to what Isi was saying.

"Well, it's the same with their brains." She took another sip of her drink, and Brody turned down the radio.

"What do you mean?" I lost interest in my food.

"Say I turn into a neuroscientist. If I pick up a neurosciency book, I can understand it. I have to. It's like the vocabulary comes with me. So, say I want to read something above my comprehension level. All I need to do is shift into someone smarter."

"Wait, what?" I asked, dumbfounded.

"It's how I taught myself to read. It's how I taught myself to fight, shoot, basically do anything that makes me a badass agent."

I stared at her, letting her information seep into my brain.

Aaron spoke up from the front, "So, even if you didn't know how to read, you'd be able to pick up a book and read it?"

"I mean, of course I knew how to read when I shifted, but yeah. It was easier to learn when I was learning as someone else. I started reading more complex texts and practicing martial arts at a young age." She grabbed another fry and popped it into her mouth.

"Who taught you to do that?" I asked.

Isi shook her head at me. "Some of us don't have the luxury of being taught things. Some of us have to figure it out on our own." She took another drink of her soda and stared out the window.

I thought about what she'd said. Isi was much more adaptable than I was, and her skill set made sense. It was probably how she had learned to drive. Why hadn't I thought of that? I wondered if Chayton knew this information. I wondered if Ava did… Isi chewed her chicken sandwich as she watched buildings pass by on the side of the road. I wondered how many secrets she kept inside. I wonder if she'd ever told anyone that information.

I glanced at Aaron through the mirror. He looked like he wanted to ask more questions, but instead, he lifted his soda and took a long pull from the straw.

Chapter 30

The rest of the trip was uneventful, and as we arrived in the city, my anxiety grew at the prospect of seeing Smith again. He'd helped me. He'd put Brody and me up at the cabin, which had given me some of the best few days of my life. Who knew what he would do once he realized I had betrayed him? I hoped he could understand that what I was about to do would be for the best. The world would be a better place if neither the Agency nor the Opposition could use mimics to do their dirty work.

We exited off the freeway and took one of the main roads downtown to the heart of Chicago. Opposition headquarters — that familiar high-rise building which doubled as a luxury hotel — waited in the distance, and I remembered the first time I'd come here. I was terrified, but also, I had found a family with Brody, Aaron, and Dan. We were a group of misfits, but I didn't need to protect them like I had to for my dad and my sisters. There was relief in that.

We parked around back at the service entrance and exited the van. We stood outside the building.

"I don't know if I can do this." Aaron looked at each of us.

"We have to do this," Isi said.

"No, I meant to come here. This is not what I wanted." He looked at Brody. "The Opposition has only helped. I can't betray them."

"Who's betraying anyone?" Brody asked. "We just need to figure out if Smith is the one who has the database. We'll confront him, get some answers, and then convince him we need to destroy it. Tell him he has traitors in his house."

Aaron looked at us all. "I don't think that'll work."

"It might," I said. "You just have to talk him into it."

Aaron was quiet for a moment. "I don't know how to convince him to do this."

"We'll figure it out together, I promise," I said.

Aaron looked at the ground and nodded. "Okay."

As we walked into the lobby of the pristine building, all eyes turned our way. The receptionists stared as we entered, and the guards looked confused as we walked freely into an unauthorized area. Four men in suits moved toward us. A silent communication passed between them as they converged on Isi.

Two men grabbed her and yanked her arms behind her back, while the third patted her down. "Leave her!" I called out. "She's with us." I moved toward her, but she shook her head. She let them put cuffs on her without putting up a fight.

"Brody? Aaron?" My gut twisted as my brain helped me understand what she was enduring, even if my new skills didn't work on her.

Aaron said, "You have to let them take her. There was no way they could let her just walk in the door."

How can this be part of her plan? I asked myself. She had to have a way to get out of this. I stood and watched helplessly as they shoved her in the opposite direction down the hallway.

The remaining man in a suit walked us behind the receptionist's desk to a back room, where they patted us down and used a silver plate to test us. It burned against my flesh, but when I didn't change, they confirmed that I was myself.

We approached the private elevator, and I noticed the grim expression on Aaron's face. Brody, noticing it too, leaned over and whispered, "You can do this. It'll be fine."

Aaron nodded as the elevator door opened, and we all climbed inside. The agent pushed the button that led to the penthouse, where Smith's private suite and office were located.

The lurch of the elevator made my stomach jump, and the hum was like a gnat buzzing in my ears. Beads of sweat sprouted on my forehead, and I concentrated on my breathing. Brody reached over and squeezed my hand, and I saw Aaron catch the movement out of the corner of his eye, but he looked away. When the elevator dinged, I held my breath as the doors slid open and the suited man exited first.

We walked back into that familiar room, and I remembered being here with Dan. Goofy Dan. We'd all been through so much. There came a pang of guilt because Smith had helped me last time, even if that hadn't been their intention at first. I convinced myself that if he really never intended to use mimics in the Opposition, then he couldn't be too mad when we erased the database.

The agent spoke to us, "Have a seat. Smith will see you soon. He's on a call."

We all made ourselves comfortable, and for a moment, I wondered where they held Isi. We'd need her with us when we were done. There was no way I'd leave her behind with the Opposition. Not after all she'd been through.

I nudged Brody with my elbow and spoke out of the corner of my mouth. "We need to find Isi." I saw Aaron watching my mouth move and knew that he'd heard what I said. He looked over his shoulder at the agent who now stood in the kitchen area, rummaging in a refrigerator. "How can we get her in the suite with us?" I asked.

"We'll have to tell Smith she has valuable information. We might have to spill that she's your sister."

Brody asked, "Won't that be a problem if Smith knows Isi is also Chayton's child?"

Aaron whispered across Brody, "I think the bigger problem is the number of people she's killed. That's what I'd be worried about."

Aaron leaned against Brody and for a fleeting moment, I wanted to be the one sitting next to him. He looked over at me, searching my face for any sign as to what I was thinking. "You can't trust her. The Agency isn't good for anyone. And besides, it will hurt her."

I knew he was right, but I didn't have to like it.

The agent returned from the refrigerator and handed us all water bottles. Aaron opened his and took a drink, while Brody set his down on the table in front of him. I held mine, uncomfortable in the silence.

After another minute of silence, Aaron looked at me with an arched eyebrow. "What are you thinking about? You keep chewing on your lip."

I looked away, embarrassed that he had caught me. "Isi. I'm thinking about Isi. We can't let her spend the rest of her life in isolation in the Opposition or the Agency. They could kill her for all we know," I whispered out loud.

"Meda, we've been through this. She chose her side, and she knows they can kill her if she doesn't cooperate. They wouldn't really kill her, because they need her for what she knows, but I get it. This sucks," Brody said.

"No matter what she knows, they can't hold her hostage indefinitely. We have to figure out a way to get her out, or it will be like keeping her in jail forever," I said. I stared at him and watched his face for a sign of what he was thinking, but he gave nothing away.

Smith opened the double doors to the suite and walked in, flanked by two men with their guns at their sides. He looked the same as always, his mocha skin contrasting with the light, perfectly pressed suit he donned. For the first time, I wondered how he ended up heading up the Opposition. In his late twenties or early thirties, he looked like a leading man in an action movie, but everyone here had a backstory — some terrible atrocity committed by the Agency that had caused them to seek revenge. The Opposition didn't have access to the funding the Agency did, but they made up for that in their search for revenge.

"I apologize for the delay. I had some business to attend to," he said as he sat in a chair opposite us. "I understand you brought someone else with you." He stared at Aaron.

"Yes." Aaron nodded slowly. He looked at me as if asking permission.

Smith raised his eyebrow and looked at me, waiting for the rest of the story. I spoke slowly, "We just got some intel that Isi isn't just an agent. She's my sister. Chayton is her father. I just found this out."

Smith tilted his head at me. "I understood you were vacationing? How did you get this intel?"

Brody spoke up, "She found us at the cabin."

"There's got to be a leak in the Opposition," I said, finding the perfect time to plant the seed. "She told me there's a traitor in your organization." I shut my mouth, knowing I had taken it too far by making it sound like I trusted Isi.

Smith waved at one of the men, who then came over. He bent down, and Smith whispered something in his ear. As the man stood and left the room, Smith turned to me. "Does he even know she is his child?"

I nodded my head. "I believe so. I assume that's why she was brought into the Agency, but who knows?" I was wringing my hands, but when I saw Smith glance down, I stopped, clasping them together.

Smith leaned back into his chair and stared at Aaron, then me. "How can you trust her?"

Aaron interrupted this time. "Oh, I don't expect we can. But she seems to want some sort of relationship with Meda. She's trying to work with her, and Meda is doing a good job of stringing her along." His words surprised me. I didn't really consider Isi working with me. She was a pain in the ass and always messing with me. But I still wanted nothing bad to happen to her. Maybe I felt bad for her.

Smith's face was blank as he nodded. "I can work with this information. Has she offered to help us with the Opposition? Or has she just offered you a deal?"

Aaron looked at me and then Smith. "Yes, she has offered her service in exchange for her freedom."

"So, you're saying she isn't here because she wants to help us? I need all the facts before we continue. If Meda were in her position, would Meda do anything to save her own life?" He glanced at me and then Aaron. I knew what he was getting at. He thought Isi was lying about being my sister because she had some angle. He leaned forward in the chair and stared at us for a second too long before standing up and walking over to me. "Will you continue to monitor her here? She knows too much about the Agency, and she will probably try something."

"She won't do anything stupid, Smith. I promise," I said.

His mouth was a thin line as he gestured towards Aaron. "So, you brought us Isi. Can you handle finessing information out of her while keeping her contained?"

"I assure you we will keep her contained." Aaron's eyes darted my way before he extended his hand, and Smith shook it.

Smith spoke, "We can get you rooms here equipped with security monitors." He looked at me. "We only sent you to the cabin for your privacy, but it seems that wasn't the best idea if the Agency still has a way to monitor you. We'll house you here until we determine where the Agency's intel is coming from."

"Thank you," Brody said.

"Aaron, follow me to my office." Smith nodded at his security. "Let's have a private conversation." Smith moved away from us without waiting for Aaron.

Aaron stood and looked at Brody before glancing at me. Panic gripped me. Would Aaron tell Smith my plan? Would he turn us in before we even got the chance to see if the database was here?

Aaron's face was stone as he moved away from us, flanked by Smith's security. I picked up my water bottle to do something with my hands, but when I looked down, I saw they were shaking.

Chapter 31

The two men remaining escorted Brody and me to the elevator. Brody gripped my hand as they keyed in the code that operated the elevator, and as the doors whooshed open, I glanced back at the door to Smith's office, wishing I could read Aaron's thoughts from this far away.

They ushered us into the elevator and pushed the button of the floor below the penthouse. Once again, the elevator jolted and hummed to life. I bumped into the agent standing next to me, but all I saw was the interior of the elevator from a different angle. There were no thoughts. It was like I was closed off, walled away from the suite of senses these people shared. It made me feel separated, isolated, and on edge.

I tried to wipe the man out of my brain as we rode to the floor below in silence until the doors opened again. Brody's fingers tightened around mine while they led us down a long corridor that ended with two large, paneled double doors.

They pushed them open, and the sight that met my eyes made me freeze in my tracks. Isi was waiting for us. She sat on the couch, her hands still bound behind her back. An agent sat behind her with a gun to her head. She stared back at us, her face a mask.

The blank agent from the elevator grabbed me by the shoulders. I flinched. A razor's edge of panic sliced through me as I turned to the agent and struggled against him. He pushed me farther into the room.

"She's innocent! You don't have to point a gun at her!" I babbled as tears filled my eyes. "We came here voluntarily, so why are you going to kill her?" I asked desperately. I couldn't help my hysteria as the man's despair clung to my brain.

The agent holding me yanked me forward so hard that I fell to the floor. My knees stung through my pants as they scraped against the tiled floor at the entrance of the suite. Isi never moved or flinched, just stared straight ahead of her, bound to the couch. The agent behind her didn't move either, his gun still trained on my sister.

A tremor of fear ran through me, and a red haze blurred inside my vision. I wondered if they knew why I'd come here.

"Hey!" Brody fought against the stony-faced agent who held him back. "Leave Meda alone. We're guests here. I work for the Agency. This is unacceptable. You can't treat a guest like this."

The agent holding Brody shoved him down on the couch next to my sister, and then he pushed me over too. I landed with a grunt on top of Isi. Her hair was tangled in my mouth, and her shoulder dug painfully into my ribs.

"We found a tracking system on her." The man behind Isi nudged her with the gun. "Why did you bring her here?"

I sputtered, unable to form words. Why would Isi have a tracking system on her when Chayton knew where we were going?

Isi finally spoke, "That's bullshit. No one needs to track me. Everyone knows where you are. It's no secret. Hell, you have traitors in your own building. No one has any reason to track me." She sat up straight, unfazed by the gun at the back of her head.

Brody turned his head toward her, his eyes wide. "Traitors in the Opposition?" he whispered in disbelief.

I shook my head, ignoring him, and tried to focus on what was happening in the room. Even when none of us were talking, a buzz of nervous energy filled the room, like I was sitting on top of an active volcano. Isi's eyes flicked to mine. I looked back at her, trying to make sense of everything that was happening around me.

"We're calling your bluff," Isi said. "There's no tracker, so there's no reason to rough anyone up." She leaned back on the deep couch, ignoring the gun pressed to her skull, and rested her head on the back of the cushion. "Now, I'm tired. Can I get a shower and have a meal? Possibly a bed? Heck," she rubbed her bare feet on the carpet, "this carpet is so nice. I'll sleep right on the floor, no problem." She closed her eyes.

"Hey," Brody asked the nearest agent, "what's going on here?"

The man eyed me suspiciously before turning away. He motioned for the other guys in the room to follow him.

"Hey!" Brody called again, but the other agents ignored him. "What's going on? What's going to happen to us?" They walked back through the door, and I heard the ding of the elevator door.

"What the heck was that?" Brody asked. I looked over at Isi and noticed a key sitting on the glass coffee table in front of her. Leaning forward, I picked it up. Isi opened her eyes. She leaned forward so I could unlock the cuffs.

Isi rubbed her wrists where the silver had dug into her skin. The silver had barely made marks on her wrists, whereas when I was cuffed, my skin was always/usually raw and oozing. "Looks like we passed the test," Isi said as she continued rubbing her wrists.

I settled back on the couch next to Isi, tucking my feet underneath me. "That's what that was?"

"It was a test for me, not for you guys. They were bluffing, and I called it. I bet they didn't expect you to react that way, Meda." She glanced at me sideways. "What was that all about?"

"I don't know." I resisted the urge to huff out a frustrated breath.

"Right now, I really want some food. And a shower would be nice," Isi said as she sat up and swung her legs off the couch. "I wasn't lying about that." She walked over to the kitchen area and opened the refrigerator. "Score!" she yelled, pulling out prepackaged salads and sandwiches. "Anybody hungry?" she asked.

I stood up and followed her into the kitchen area. "Do you think those agents are going to be back?"

She shrugged as she pulled out a handful of disposable plates from a cabinet. "Hey, do you guys have any preference for bedrooms? Will you be sharing a bed?" She called over her shoulder as she started opening the packages of food.

"No preference, but I am going on record that I don't want to share a bed with you," I said, grabbing the plates and opening the twist tie.

She grinned. "I meant with Brody. Did you guys share a bed in that cabin?"

I glared at her. "None of your business."

"And I didn't ask if you and the pretty boy had sex. Just if you shared a bed." She offered me a plate of salad and sandwich, which I took after she started stacking up her plates with food.

Brody moved to my side. "That's none of your business. How can you be talking about this after what just happened?"

"What? You think I've never been cuffed with a gun to my head? That's par for the course, buddy." She winked at him. "You should try it."

If I didn't know what I already knew about Isi, I would think she was flirting, but I saw now that this act meant she was nervous. She was uncomfortable being trapped in this place, and the way she hid it was with her tough-guy act.

"Okay, Isi. Enough. Eat your food. Take a shower. We'll wait and see what happens when Aaron gets back." I looked at Brody and saw my frustration mirrored in his eyes.

"Of course, Miss Perfect. Yes, ma'am," she said as she picked up her plate and started for one of the bedroom doors.

"I wasn't saying that because I want you to do what I say, Isi. You said you were hungry."

She paused and then shrugged. "Whatever." She pushed open her bedroom door and stepped into the darkness of the room.

Brody watched her go into her room before he turned to me. "She's not doing so well, is she?"

"No," I said. "She's scared."

"Can we trust her? Do you think she was telling the truth about not being tracked?" he asked me in a low voice.

I shrugged my shoulders. "I mean, it makes sense. Chayton even said they had someone in place here." I grabbed my food and started for the couch. I planned to wait it out here until Aaron came back.

Brody followed me with his plate. We settled in on the couch but left our food untouched in front of us. Brody pulled off his shoes first, and then mine, as I moved the pillows around to get comfortable. I situated myself between the pillows and rubbed my eyes. "Do you think we'd be able to get out of here if we tried?" That thought made me uneasy.

He didn't answer right away. Instead, he moved closer to me and pressed his body against mine. "It's going to be okay."

I shook my head, letting doubt creep in. "How do you know?"

He placed his hand on my hip. "Because I've known Aaron for a long time. He's family. He would never turn against me, even in a bad place, and I'm not about to believe he ever will." He sounded confident.

"I hope you're right," I admitted as he slid his hand across my hip and touched the bare skin on my stomach.

He whispered before he kissed my neck, "Let's not think about it right now." His lips moved closer to mine, and I felt myself falling for his touch. "Everything will work out," he promised before his lips found mine. I heard his voice in my head, like a mantra. *Everything will work out*, he repeated the silent mantra to himself. I pushed his thoughts out, just glad that his inner voice matched his outer one.

Just as his kiss became more heated, I heard the elevator ding. We both let go and stood to meet Aaron, hoping that everything had gone as planned.

Chapter 32

Aaron pushed through the double doors, and we stood, waiting to receive the verdict. The double doors swung shut behind him, and he walked around the table to face us.

"What did Smith say?" I asked.

He gave a sad smile. "Smith will give us some time, but he has the final say in this." After a moment's pause, he continued, "He asked if we wanted to keep busy while we're staying here."

Brody looked at Aaron and me. I shook my head. "No. I'm out. See? The Opposition is no different from the Agency."

Aaron interrupted my rant. "Except the Opposition didn't kidnap you."

"Didn't it?" I asked, remembering when I first met Brody, Aaron, and Dan and they'd shoved me into the trunk of a car.

"That was us," Aaron said.

"Same thing," I answered.

Brody stood between us. "Okay, okay. We're not doing any missions. What did he say about Isi?"

Aaron took a deep breath and said, "He didn't say much. They want us to get information out of her or they will."

Brody exhaled with relief.

"Are they talking about torture?" I asked.

Just then, Isi pushed through the bedroom door. "I'd like to see them try," she said.

"How long have you been standing there listening?" I asked, considering my make-out session with Brody.

She raised an eyebrow at me. "Long enough."

"Sit down," Aaron said. "We should talk about this."

Isi pulled up a chair and sat. Her hair was messy as always, but she looked wide awake. She had her arms crossed and spoke rapidly through tight lips. "Let's get this straight. I have two choices: expose the truth about the Agency, or be tortured for information about them."

"What?" I spoke. "Wait a minute."

Isi cut me off. "I can handle the torture if Meda can get to the database. Did you recon for it?" she asked, directing her question at Aaron. "It's somewhere in Smith's office. Is there a safe or a wall hanging? Maybe a desk that opens up into a computer? With the technology they have, it doesn't have to be big."

"Slow down," Aaron said, holding his hands up. "Why would I tell you? I still don't know if this whole thing was some type of Trojan horse ploy for you to get into Opposition headquarters."

I interrupted him, "And do what? She's willing to be tortured to destroy the database. Isn't that proof enough?"

Isi glared at me, but I remained focused on Aaron.

"It doesn't make sense," he said. "Why would they want it destroyed? The Opposition is the good guys. They're the only thing preventing anarchy."

I knew Aaron would be a tough sell on this plan, especially after being welcomed back by Smith. I answered his question before Isi could speak up again. "Because there's an even bigger threat that will destroy the Agency, and that's losing the ability to track mimics. It's more powerful than either of them. Both sides assume destroying their enemy is the only way to survive, but we know that taking away their weapons will weaken them."

Aaron and Brody looked at me and then at each other. "No," Aaron said. "I want to believe that, but it doesn't add up."

"Fine," Isi said, raising her hands in defeat. "Meda's the only one who can break into the database, anyway."

Brody looked at me. "Why's that?"

"Because Meda is the only one who can do her crazy mind-reading thing," she said in a huff before looking at me with widening eyes. She paused. "I wasn't supposed to say that, was I?" Only, she didn't appear to regret it.

"What?" Brody asked.

Aaron put his head in his hands and let out a sigh. I closed my eyes and took a deep breath.

"Meda can read minds," Isi said. "Oh, she didn't tell you yet? Sorry." She pushed her bottom lip in a pout.

There was a moment of silence before Brody burst out laughing. "That's not possible."

"It's totally possible," she said, her voice serious.

This seemed to set him off even more, but his laughter faded into chuckles, then grins. He shook his head before looking back at me with confusion in his eyes. "Come on, Meda. Let's hear it."

Aaron lifted his head. But I didn't want to look him in the eye, and I certainly wasn't going to stare at Isi, but I couldn't ignore Brody. "When I touch someone, it's like they're projecting everything in their mind onto me. It's overwhelming because there's so much noise." Blood rushed to my face, and Isi shifted in the spot where she was standing.

"When did you figure this out?" Brody asked quietly.

"I started getting flashes at the cabin," I said, still not looking at him.

"About my thoughts?" His face was a puzzle I couldn't figure out.

I kept talking, wanting to give him all the information he'd need to feel comfortable around me. "At first, it was like I was projected into your head. I could see what you were seeing. It wasn't until I was back at the Agency that I realized I was hearing people's thoughts, and I wasn't trying to. I would never do that," I said, moving closer to Brody.

"You're a terrible liar," Isi said. "I saw you use it to your advantage. Heck, you tried it on me, but it doesn't work on mimics."

"Would you shut up?" Aaron said, glaring at Isi.

"I love how Meda told you, but not her boy," Isi laughed, clapping her hands together. "I mean, look at Aaron." She was now talking to Brody. "He's not even surprised."

My body was so close to Brody that the warmth radiated off of him, and I wanted to curl up in it. If I could touch him, I'd know how angry he was. Instead, I jumped up and stood inches from Isi's face.

"What is your deal? Since we left your hideout, you've been a completely different person. I thought we were in this together. I thought we were doing this to stop humans from using mimics."

Brody got up and placed his hand on my shoulder. I almost flinched, surprised he wanted to touch me. "She's trying to set you off. She's trying to build a rift between us. She's a sad and lonely girl."

Brody looked at Isi with pity.

Isi crossed her arms. "Stop trying to read me, lover-boy. I'm not sad or lonely."

Brody took my hand, showing a solid front. "It's okay. You're safe here with us."

"You guys are so gross," she said, before spinning on her head and heading back toward the bedroom she'd claimed. She disappeared into the dark, slamming the door behind her.

The room was quiet as we stared at the door to see if she'd make another appearance. After a few minutes, Brody turned to face me. "Tell me everything," he said.

Brody listened quietly as I told him the entire story from waking up to Elan grabbing me and shoving me into the van, right up to the point they arrived at Agency headquarters to take me.

He was quiet for a moment, rubbing his chin with his thumb before sighing and saying, "So all of this was part of Chayton's plan? Have we considered every angle? Is there a way that what we're doing will benefit him rather than just help mimics?"

"Of course," Aaron said, but his eyes sparkled with excitement at Brody's line of thinking. He was always good at reasoning from all sides and deciding based on information rather than feelings — unless it came to me. I realized that the only time Brody screwed up was when he was worried about me. Taking a few deep breaths, I closed my eyes. I wanted to be sure I wasn't making a huge mistake.

Aaron continued, "There's got to be something. Why would he lie to Meda? I mean, he's sneaky, but if he was going to tell her anyway, there was no reason to hide it from her." Aaron looked at me, trying to confirm his justifications.

"It wasn't just Chayton though," I said. "I needed to convince the Agency that I was back, and he didn't believe I was a good enough actor."

Brody shifted on the couch, turning toward me. "But who, specifically, did he want you to convince?"

"Chelsea Abbott. I guess she's the actual mastermind of the Agency. Chayton's the face, but Abbott is behind the scenes."

"Who the heck is Chelsea Abbott?" Aaron asked, glancing at Brody. "I've never heard of her. Have you?" Brody shook his head in reply. "Can we even ask Smith, or will that make him realize something is up?"

Brody answered, "If anyone is going to have anything, it's going to be Smith."

"What about Isi?" Aaron asked. "What does she know about this Abbott lady?"

I glanced at Isi's closed door. "I don't know that she'll be very helpful right now." I considered her strange behavior. Isi was always out of control, but her most recent reactions were just odd. I got the nagging notion that there was something else going on with her.

Chapter 33

There was a knock on the door, and a nondescript man entered the suite. He cleared his throat as we all looked up at him.

"Yeah?" Aaron asked, his eyebrows scrunched in annoyance.

"Smith wants to see Meda." He nodded in my direction and as both boys rose from their chairs, the man raised his hand, halting them. "Just Meda."

"No way," Brody said, and I broke out in goosebumps at the thought of him protecting me even after what I'd just told him.

I stood. "It's okay," I said, and both boys looked at me like I was insane.

"No, it's not." Brody ground out. "If you think—"

The agent turned back to me. "Please."

The use of that word surprised me, but I wasn't stupid. The man was armed. I nodded, and both boys let out protests as the man escorted me to the door.

"I'll be back," I promised.

The man took me down a different hallway than before, not saying anything until we exited through another stairwell door. He turned to the side so his shoulder was to me and pressed a button on his earpiece.

"I have her." Something in the man's tone made the hairs rise on the back of my neck.

We stopped at another door and the man opened it, holding it for me, but I didn't move. "Where are we going?"

His face was impenetrable as he gestured again for me to enter. "Smith wants to speak to you."

Something was off, but I had no choice. I swallowed, and my mouth was dry. Then, I took a step through the door. The room was odd. It was small, like a closet, and it smelled like bleach. I glanced around at the paneled walls, and my vision flickered. It was as though I could see another layer beneath those walls.

Someone cleared their throat, and I realized I wasn't alone. An old man sat behind a small metal desk. "Please, take a seat." He gestured to two chairs in front of his desk, but I stayed standing.

My brain was trying to make sense of what was happening, running through different scenarios. "I'd rather stand."

He nodded and gestured again for me to take a seat. "You want answers? You want your life back, correct?"

A chill ran down my spine at how close he was to what I wanted. "Yes."

He paused as if he were weighing his words, but the longer he sat there without speaking, the more my heart raced with anxiety.

"I'm going to level with you," he finally said. "There is no easy way to say this."

Every part of me tensed as I prepared for something bad. "Okay."

"You aren't who you think you are."

I shook my head, squinting as I tried to make sense of what he was saying. "How do you know that? Who are you?"

He gestured to the chair again, and I finally took a seat, still confused. Then, the old man shifted, and as I watched his face morph and sink into a smaller, more feminine form, it was only moments before I realized that a young woman sat in front of me. She had a defined jawline and a serious face. She looked to be in her twenties. "My name is Moira. I'm the head of a division of the Agency known as TAC—Tapestry Analysis and Control."

"Wait." My mind raced, once again trying to make sense of this new information. "The Agency has divisions?"

Her expression never changed as she leaned forward in her chair and clasped her hands on the desk. "Do you know what a tapestry is?"

I swallowed, my throat dry, and thought about castles with old rugs hanging from the walls. "Yes."

"It's a piece of fabric created through the interlacing of two threads, one from each side of the loom," she said. "In most textiles, the warp and weft threads are visible, but in a tapestry, the warp threads hide in the completed work."

My head hurt—all this talk about tapestries and threads was not helping. "I still don't understand what you're getting at."

"Tapestries are fragile and difficult to make." She paused. "Much like a certain group of people."

I stilled, realizing where this was going even as my mind protested the idea that she could be telling the truth. That there was another agency hidden inside the larger one. And if it was hidden, what did TAC actually do? I let out a long breath. "And you're telling me this because?"

"In the late-1960s, when they discovered how to see the warp threads in order to make invisible tapestries, humanity's fate changed forever." She paused for a second and added, "Just like your parents' figured out that two mimics together can make something special."

I stared at her, waiting for something — anything — that would make this all click. "My parents?" I asked.

"Your biological parents," she said. "You are a part of the tapestry, and once you admit that and admit how rare your gifts are, you will have power."

The room spun as I processed what she was saying. "And that would be?"

She leaned back in her chair, her green gaze never wavering. "There are people who would do anything to destroy all traces of tapestries — to rid the world of them. You must be very careful."

I thought of the device tucked neatly in my bra. How much did she know? Did she know why Chayton had sent me here? Did TAC work with Chayton, or did he even know anything about them? And what did Isi know? A red mist settled on my nerves, thinking about Isi and what she knew. I had to ask her before I made my next decisions. I stood slowly, my legs shaking as I realized that what she was saying might actually be true.

"Why are you telling me this?"

"Because I want to help you. And that means teaching you how to survive."

I stared at her, wanting to believe her but not trusting my own instincts.

"You don't want to go with the Opposition," she said. "Trust me on that one. I've been planted in here just long enough to recognize that this isn't the side you want to be on."

Was this the Agency's spy? I nodded and backed away from the desk toward the door. She stood slowly and reached into her pocket, pulling out a small red box, one that looked like it held a ring. She held it out to me.

I took the box, feeling the weight of it in my hand, my breath catching as I realized what was inside. As I held it, a flood of memories rushed back — memories that were not my own: watching someone open this box before they handed it off to someone who looked a lot like Moira.

I spun toward her, and she held up her hands as if to stop me. "That's all I can tell you right now."

"How did you do that? How did you project images into my mind?"

"There's nothing I'd like more than for us to be on the same side, Meda. I think once you realize that, it will be a very good day for all of us." Her smile faded slightly. "There's someone coming for you." Her gaze shifted to the door.

I followed her gaze but heard nothing, and when I turned back, she'd already shifted back to the older man. "How do you know?" I asked, my voice trailing off.

"Meda?" she prompted. "You've got to go. You've got a job to do."

The door opened, and the suited man at the door cleared his throat, signaling for me to come with him. I looked back and held the box up. "What do I do with this?"

"Keep it. When you want to learn more, you'll know what to do with it."

I closed my eyes for a second, trying to decide what my next move would be, but the agent next to me pulled me out of the room and down the hallway.

"There's no time," he said. "We've got to move."

I pulled my arm out of his grip and faced him. "Who are you?"

His eyes were cold, unforgiving, filled with purpose. It didn't matter what the answer was. There were so many moving parts under the surface of what was actually going on. I needed time to process everything, but I felt like the sands in the hourglass were running out.

As we moved down the hallway, I slipped the small box into my pocket.

We were soon back at the suite, and I stood outside the door. Brody and Aaron would ask me what Smith said, and I would tell them everything. But first, I had some questions for Isi.

Chapter 34

I pushed through the doors with one thing on my mind. Aaron stood in the kitchen and Brody looked up from the couch, but I barely noticed as I took four long strides to Isi's door. With a tightened fist, I hammered at the door until there came movement from inside.

"What's going on?" Brody asked, but I focused on the door in front of me.

The door handle clicked and creaked as Isi peeked through the crack she'd opened. Her hair was a mess, and it looked as though she'd actually been sleeping. I pushed the door in, knocking her back. She stumbled, her eyes widening.

"What the hell?" she asked as I stood in front of her.

"What's TAC?" I studied Isi for a reaction. Her eyes narrowed before widening again. It must have taken all her effort to sweep any trace of emotion from her face.

"What's your deal, Meda?" She moved to push by me, but I stepped sideways, blocking her path. I cornered her, and it made her uneasy.

"What's the Tapestry of Analysis and Control? And who is Moira?" I asked. I was aware of Brody and Aaron standing nearby, having moved in closer to listen in on the conversation.

Isi stepped toward me again, trying to push me aside, but I grabbed her by the arm. With her free arm, she tried to swipe my hand away, but I'd learned a thing or two from her. I drew on my memory of people I'd shifted into and selected a former navy seal who I'd had to impersonate on one of my Agency assignments. My grip was firm, and I pulled her with me out into the living room of the suite. Brody and Aaron backed away as I pulled Isi in front of the couch before tossing her down.

She looked up at me, holding her arm in the place I had just clenched. Her mouth was open as though she wanted to yell at me, and her eyebrows sat at a severe slant.

"Answer the question," I growled.

"I don't know what you're talking about," she said, trying to get up, but I pushed her back down. "I don't know what you're talking about," she repeated, her voice firmer this time. Anger flashed in her eyes, and she tried to get up again.

I shifted my weight, so I was sitting on top of her, pinning her down. She tried to push me off, but I refused to let her go. "I saw it in your face. You know something about TAC. Who are they? What do they want with me? "

Isi stopped fighting and looked up at me, recognition dawning on her face.

"I will not let you go until you tell me what I want to know." I held her by the wrists even though she had ceased struggling.

Isi's eyes met mine, and anger flickered in them. She shook her head and tried to push me off of her again, but it was a half-hearted attempt.

"I know nothing about them. I don't know what they do. I don't know how they do it. They don't want me." She looked up at me. "And you don't want any part of them. They are bad people."

I studied her for a moment, trying to determine if she was telling the truth. I couldn't tell. "Who is Moira?"

"I have no clue," Isi said, and it looked like she was telling the truth.

"Okay," I said and stood up. "I believe you."

Isi pushed herself up off the couch so I couldn't pin her down again. She rubbed her arm and continued to stare at me.

"What's this all about?" Aaron asked.

"I didn't see Smith. I saw… someone else. Another mimic."

Brody stepped closer to me. "Do you think it was the spy in the Opposition that Chayton told you about?" he asked.

I glanced at Isi before directing my attention back to Brody. "I don't know. I get the sense that even the Agency doesn't know much about this TAC thing."

"What's TAC?" Aaron asked. It surprised me that Aaron hadn't heard of TAC. He seemed to know all the Opposition secrets, so if *he* didn't know about TAC, no one in the Opposition did either. Unless it was beyond his clearance.

There was a knock on the door, and a man entered. "Smith is ready to see you," he said.

I turned to Isi. "You're coming with." She shook her head, but I grabbed her arm and pulled her along behind me as I followed the man out of the room. I looked back, and Aaron and Brody followed us.

As we got in the elevator, Isi shook her arm out of my grip. The agent stood in front of us, so when Isi looked at me and shook her head, he didn't catch it. "What?" I mouthed to her.

"You're going to get us all killed," she mouthed back.

Aaron was standing on the other side of Isi and looked past her at me as I felt Brody take my hand. Everything was once again happening too quickly, and I didn't have all the information I needed to make a smart decision. I had more doubts in my mind about the Agency and Chayton than ever before. Maybe he'd just used Elan to get to me. And Isi had only reinforced that when she took me to meet Briar and Bly. Isi was working with Chayton, but who was Moira working with? And what was TAC? I started to think that we should just ditch the mission, but as the elevator jolted to a stop, I realized I still wasn't sure what to do.

Brody's voice whispered in my head. *What should we do? What's the right answer here?* I turned to look at him, and as I studied his face, it occurred to me that he was directing his thoughts toward me. He was asking me through his mind. I lifted my shoulders in a semi-shrug and shook my head, showing him that I didn't have the answers. His grip tightened on my hand.

The door to the elevator slid open, and we stepped out into a large, circular room with glass walls. The agent led us through the room to the looming oak door in the back. I remembered Smith's office from last time, and I hoped the database wasn't even in there because then I wouldn't have to worry about betraying the Opposition, but there was only one way to find out. I'd have to touch Smith. He was the only one who knew for sure.

The agent knocked on the door twice before opening it. Smith sat behind his massive cherry finished desk in the center of the room. It hadn't changed much since I'd been here last. He still had a wall of computers and equipment. I remembered filming my shifting in this room so he could have proof of mimics.

He was talking on the phone and didn't look up as we entered.

"Take a seat," the agent said and nodded toward a few chairs in front of Smith's desk.

I motioned for Isi to take a seat and she complied, but I stayed standing, and Brody stood next to me. I could feel his unease. He was waiting for me to make a move. Aaron stood on the other side of Brody, but he continued to eye me as though unsure of what I was going to do next.

"I'll call you back," Smith said into the phone and hung up. He finally looked up at us, and annoyance flared in his eyes.

Chapter 35

Smith sat across from us behind the glossy desk, folding his hands on the smooth surface. He cleared his throat before speaking. "Meda, I didn't expect to see you so soon. Were your accommodations not suitable?" I noticed a sheen of sweat across his forehead.

I thought about our original plans, the ones Chayton and then Isi had gone over. But I had my own plans. Drawing in a deep breath, I spoke. "I'm looking for my brother. They told me you knew something about him." I folded my hands together, mirroring him. I felt Aaron and Brody shifting behind me.

"Your brother?" He looked confused. "I thought you came here to talk about Isi." He glanced in her direction, and I followed his gaze. She remained slumped in the chair with her arms crossed, pouting.

"My half-brother. Chayton's other child." I leaned forward, and it occurred to me I hadn't asked Chayton if there were any other children waiting in the wings. If so, Smith might know about them with his database.

"If we knew you had a brother, we would have told you right away. We would have helped you try to bring him in." He stood, pushing back from his desk. "How did you hear of him? What do you know? Maybe we can help." His eyes lit up, and I imagined the prospect of adding another mimic to his list excited him, so I recognized that what he was saying was true. That meant Isi had lied when she told Elan that he was in the database. More questions bloomed in my brain.

Realizing I had forgotten the most crucial part of this meeting, I stepped over to the desk and reached my hand out. "I'm sorry. Where are my manners?"

His silence said more than he had, and the tension in the room seemed to change the air pressure as Smith glanced behind me at Aaron and then Brody. He didn't want me to have the power to shift into him, but if he didn't shake my hand in this moment, I wouldn't trust him. I was making a power move, and his hesitation made me nervous.

"Smith?" I asked, glancing down at my hand.

He eyed my hand again, his eyebrows creasing with suspicion before reaching out his hand and grasping mine. A pang of guilt shot through me as he made eye contact with me and nodded. I wasn't even sure why he did it.

I dropped his hand and had a seat, and he mirrored my actions. I had no flashes, and I was too nervous to consider how I might force my brain to read his mind. I wasn't in control of this power, so I shouldn't have expected to be able to use it at will against Smith.

"Now, about this brother," Smith started.

"Have you heard of TAC?" I asked, interrupting him. I heard Isi shift in her seat. This wasn't part of the plan. But Smith had been pretty honest with me in the short time that I'd known him. Plus, he shook my hand. That had to count for something.

He leaned back in his chair and rubbed his temples. "This is a mess," he muttered.

"What can you tell me about TAC?" I asked, leaning forward.

Smith sighed and sat up straight. "TAC is a secret agency that was formed right after the war. They dealt with the shifters who refused agreement to keep their own form."

"And what exactly do they do?" Brody asked, moving next to my chair. I noticed that Isi was suspiciously quiet.

"They're a special forces team," Smith replied. "They're trained in all forms of combat and are experts in capturing shifters."

My stomach dropped at his words. So that was why Moira wanted me. TAC wanted me to help them capture mimics? "Do they have a base of operations?"

"Yes, they do," Smith said, but he offered no details.

I could see the resolve in his eyes. He wouldn't give us any more information than that. "Fine," I said, and I pulled my hand away from the desk. "But I'm going to find it."

Isi spoke up, "He doesn't even know where it is. No one does." I looked sideways at her. She seemed to know more about TAC than she'd let on. I felt annoyance nibble at me, but I pushed it way. I'd deal with her later.

I looked back at Smith. "Well, I'm going to need access to the database."

Smith's eyes widened, and as he stood, my stomach lurched and my eyes zeroed in on the painting on the wall behind his desk. I wasn't seeing through my eyes, but rather from Smith's, as I watched a hand reach out and pull at the painting. The hinges squeaked as it opened up to a computer. Smith reached out to punch in the password, but I couldn't determine what it was. A wave of dizziness hit me as I tried to focus, but my vision blurred, and I was seeing out of my own eyes again. Smith looked down at me, with the painting over his shoulder.

I cleared my throat and stood so that he wasn't looming over me. "What will it cost me?" My hands were shaking, and I wasn't sure if I was recovered enough to convince him that my request was a legitimate one. Smith was smart, and I felt like he could see right through me, but he was just a regular man.

Smith looked at me like I'd struck him. "What do you mean?" His eyes traveled to Brody and Aaron and back to me. "What's going on here?"

"I mean, from what I've learned, you're not really into favors."

Smith crossed his arms. "That's not fair, Meda. We have been very fair to you. Even after the little situation in which you colluded with the Agency and got our men killed."

My cheeks flushed. "I colluded with my mother, who tricked me. How was I to identify who I could trust?" I couldn't be angry that he had brought it up, but the tone in his voice caught my frayed nerves.

"I was straightforward with you." There was tension in his jaw, and once again, I imagined this meeting wasn't the only thing that was on his mind. There was something going on beneath the surface, but I couldn't sense it.

"You realize that before I first came to you, we stopped at one of the Opposition safe houses. It was there that I learned how your people in the Opposition feel about my kind." I remembered that day vividly. Aaron had saved me from the man who tried to attack me. Even the man who had cut the Agency tracking device from my leg treated me like a dog. I glanced back at Aaron, and there was sympathy in his eyes.

Smith threw up his hands, losing some of his composure. "That's not fair. You understand that many of those men joined because the Agency destroyed their families. Whether mimic strings were being pulled by the Agency or not, those men had a right to be wary."

"But Brody didn't. He saw right to the core. He recognized I had no power, that I was a tool for the Agency to use to get what they wanted." I looked at Brody, but his face was emotionless.

"And you still betrayed him. What does that say about your kind?"

I flinched as though I'd been slapped. He was right. But Brody wasn't the Opposition. He was my Brody. And Aaron was only with the Opposition because the Agency had forced me to mimic his father. Aaron had wanted me dead until he found out the truth.

If we could get rid of the database of all mimics, maybe this wouldn't happen again.

"Either you'll help me or not. I think I've given enough to the cause." I nodded toward the portrait of the president that hung on the wall of Smith's office. He looked over and turned back to me, scrutinizing me.

He looked over at Brody and Aaron. "Guys, what is this?" His face screamed betrayal.

I continued, "What's behind the picture?"

Smith studied me as though trying to figure out how I'd guessed the database was there. "It's the database that holds all known information about mimics."

It shocked me when he told me the truth. "What do you do with this information? Can you find my brother?" I tested him.

"I was telling the truth when I said I didn't know about him, Meda. There's no way he's in the database. Your father must have hidden him well."

His words stung. It hurt that Chayton had worked so hard to keep Elan out of the Agency's grip but served me up on a platter. Doubts blossomed in my head again. "Can I look at what you have on my family?" I asked. This was the genuine test of trust. The Opposition had broken me out last time because they needed me. I tried to connect with Smith again, maybe read his mind, but there was nothing.

To my surprise, he walked over to the painting and pulled it open, the hinges squealing loudly. He lifted his hand, but the painting of the president blocked the screen, so I couldn't determine what he was typing, but when he was done, he swung the painting open all the way and looked at me.

I stepped closer to see what he had pulled up on the screen. Skimming the monitor, I stopped when I saw my name. "What is this?" I pointed to the red stars by my name.

His face twisted in concentration. "We've been tracking mimics who are born of two mimic parents."

"But what does it mean?" I asked.

"We don't know. We just recognize that there's something special about you."

A minor earthquake erupted in my stomach. Not only did Chayton know, but the Opposition also suspected there was something different about me. Something flared in the back of my brain, a warning that I would never be safe. I continued my search but halted when I noticed my sisters' names, Ginger and Georgia, beneath mine. My breath caught in my throat.

"Why are they on here?" I asked. "They haven't shown signs of shifting, have they?" Dread filled my gut. I hadn't been in contact with them since before the cabin. What if something had changed?

"It's just a precaution." Smith moved toward me as though he was going to comfort me. I flinched instead.

"A precaution? By having my family in there, you leave them vulnerable. Any double agent can sneak in here and get their hands on this information." I stood my ground. "You think you're helping, but you're only making things worse for everyone."

"The database was the only way we were able to find your family and get them out of the Agency's stranglehold. They're safe because of it. And the database is secure. No one can gain access."

I sighed in frustration and rubbed my hand down my face. "Then how does the Agency know about it? How did they get a printout that I saw with my own two eyes?"

Smith's face scrunched in confusion.

"Smith," I said as he looked over my shoulder, "I'm going to need you to delete this database."

It took a few moments for him to react to my words. "Wait, what did you say?" he asked, turning to face me.

"I said I'm going to need you to delete this database." My voice was firm.

Smith looked bewildered. "I can't do that," he said. "Believe me. We're not using them. We need to identify who the Agency might use."

"Having this database endangers all mimics. How do you know the Agency hasn't infiltrated the Opposition? And if they haven't yet, can you guarantee they never will?"

"I can't do it, Meda. It's a matter of national security. We need to be aware of potential weapons."

"*Weapons?* You mean mimics." I couldn't refrain from laughing. "Weapon? That's how you see me?"

He reached out to touch me but pulled his hand back. "That's not what I meant. You know that. You know what we do here."

"I know what you did to *me*, Smith. I have no clue about the rest. How can you assure me that if someone discovers this database, my family won't be hunted? That the Agency won't come after them when they find out Elan has been hiding in plain sight this whole time?"

"I would never let that happen, Meda. I swear to you. But I can't let you destroy the database. Let me help you."

Smith stepped forward and reached for my hand, but I pulled away so he couldn't touch me. Instead, I reached into my pocket and pulled out the device.

Brody reached into the waistband of his jeans and pulled out a gun. I felt my mouth drop open. I didn't know he had it. This wasn't part of the plan. He pointed the gun at Smith. "Do what she says."

"Brody, what are you doing?" Aaron asked, stepping toward Brody. Isi moved to the edge of her seat, her eyes widening.

Smith held up his hands as if surrendering, and then he backed away. Ignoring Brody, he glared at me. "And after you delete it? What happens then?" Smith asked me. "Are you positive the Agency isn't tricking you into stealing the database for their own use?"

"I don't plan on returning to them."

"And you think you can walk out of here?" Smith's back was pushed against the wall.

I shrugged my shoulders, not sure what to say. "I'm doing what needs to be done. You can decide what you need to do."

Smith spoke, "We didn't mean for any of this to happen to you." He was referring to the incident with my mother, being taken from the cabin, all of it. It was almost an apology. His eyes traveled to Brody and Aaron. "Any of you. We've only tried to help."

"Let Meda destroy it." Brody's voice was flat. "She deserves to be the one, after all we've done to her."

"*Done to her?*" Smith asked. "We helped her."

"Yeah, to use her," Aaron added, and I looked at him, biting my lip to prevent any emotion from spilling out. He was taking my side. Against the Opposition.

"With the database gone, the Agency is going to cling to any mimics they have." He sat down in his chair as I walked over to the hidden computer. I held the device close to it and watched the screen flash and turn to black. "What is that thing?" Smith asked. "Are you sure it didn't collect information?"

I showed him the plastic device before throwing it to the ground. I lifted my foot and brought my heel down on it. It shattered into small shards. I stomped on it again and again, focusing my rage on my memories of everything that had happened to me.

Tears welled in my eyes. I didn't want to cry right now, not here. Not around Brody or Aaron. And definitely not in front of Smith. "It's over," I said.

"We're going to take your private exit." Aaron motioned toward the back wall. Smith nodded, crossing his arms. He didn't even seem that angry.

Aaron walked over to the wall and felt along the paneling, pushing on a section. There was a click and a whirring noise as the small door swung open.

"Meda," Smith said. "I don't know what's going on, but I swear we won't hurt your family."

Brody grabbed Isi by the arm and pulled her along with him to the hidden door. Isi stumbled, and there was a crunching noise as she stood and made her way through the remains of the device. I followed both of them as Smith watched. He didn't move to alert anyone. We'd have a head start on them. Aaron disappeared through the doorway, and Brody waited for me.

Before stepping through, I turned back to Smith. "I believe you," I said. "Please don't make me regret it."

I didn't wait for Smith to respond. We left him standing in the room and ran down the dark passage, feeling our way and hoping it would lead us directly outside. I didn't know where we were going, but we had to get out of the building before Smith alerted the agents to our escape. Even though the database was destroyed, it wouldn't be over until we got somewhere safe, away from the Opposition and the Agency.

Chapter 36

We followed the passageway to a door that led outside into the strategically planted trees on the backside of the building. I looked back at the glass high-rise, knowing that if we ever came back here, it would not be as guests. Brody took my hand, and we followed the curb until we reached the back parking structure, searching for a getaway vehicle.

"Here," Isi called. She waved us to a car parked in a reserved spot. Pulling open the door, she checked for the keys, but of course they weren't there.

"What about the van?" I asked.

Isi scanned the lot and found that someone had pulled it around to a different reserved parking spot. "Good idea." She jogged over to it.

I watched the back of the building to see if anyone was exiting. Still clear.

She pulled open the back door, and we all got closer, but she waved us away. "We're not taking this. They would have put a tracking device on it already." She grabbed a small, solid bag out of the back and opened the zipper, waving us back toward the car she'd opened.

"Go, go." She urged us to get into the vehicle while she pulled out a device that resembled a key fob. Aaron slid into the passenger seat as Brody climbed in the back. Isi clicked the button on the fob a few times, and I realized what she was doing. She was programming the fob for the car. I slid into the backseat and moved closer to Brody as Isi got in the driver's seat and pushed the start button.

"How did you do it?" I asked, finally able to ask what I wanted to know. "How'd you get the gun inside?"

Isi was already pulling out of the parking lot. I turned and looked back, but still no one followed.

Brody shrugged his shoulders, looking at me, then back at the road. "I knew they wouldn't search Aaron and me too thoroughly. Isi gave me this plastic gun, undetectable by metal detectors."

Isi called over her shoulder, "I didn't think you'd actually use it."

"When?" I asked, confused.

"When you were talking to Aaron. She guessed Aaron wouldn't want to bring a gun in." He glanced at Aaron, who stared out the window.

My eyes traveled from Brody to Aaron. "The database is gone," I said. I studied his face to see if there was any sense of relief, but his mouth remained set in a hard line. Somehow, that didn't make me feel any better. "But what happens if they're still after us? What's stopping them?"

"Nothing," Brody answered. "Just us."

Isi drove in silence, and I couldn't tell if Aaron was mad or not. I couldn't tell if he knew that I had to do what I'd done. I sighed and looked out the window.

No one spoke for the next few miles. Every few minutes, I stole glances at Brody as he continued turning and looking out the back window to see if we were being followed. Then his eyes turned to narrow slits as though he was tracking something.

"What is it?" I asked.

"We have company," Brody said. He didn't look at me, but Aaron turned and looked out the back window. It was wishful thinking that they would just let us go.

"Is it Agency or Opposition?" I asked.

"I don't know, but they're getting closer," Brody said. Aaron reached down and pulled the handgun from under his seat. This time, he looked in the mirror at me.

I turned to see three black trucks, all bigger than our vehicle, approaching from behind. They aligned themselves across three lanes, gathering in formation. It looked as though they were attempting to corral us, probably to lead us somewhere.

"What do we do?" I asked.

"We have no choice," Isi said. Brody finally made eye contact with me. I wasn't sure what she meant by that, but a moment later, she said, "Hold on," and pulled the steering wheel hard.

We fishtailed, causing my stomach to bobble like a boat on rough waters. I grabbed the door handle just as one truck rammed us from behind. The impact knocked Aaron forward into his seatbelt before it catapulted him back and slammed his head against the seat. Something clattered on the floor. Isi fought to keep control of the vehicle as she veered to the right, careening toward the ditch.

The back tires bounced on the edge, and the car teetered in space for a moment before falling over the embankment into a cloud of dust, branches, and dirt.

My vision tunneled, and everything was in slow motion and eerily quiet, but for the sound of metal crunching and the tumbling thud of the car turning over. Brody's shoulder knocked into mine as we rolled repeatedly until we finally came to a stop, upside down, covered in debris. The smell of burning rubber was heavy and thick.

The seatbelt was squeezing me. I wheezed as my chest tried to expand but found it difficult to breathe.

My head was still ringing from the impact when something fell onto my face and a warm wetness flowed over my cheek. I reached with one hand to wipe it off. Blood.

Brody coughed next to me, and I was relieved to hear him breathe. "Meda, are you okay?" he asked, a groan escaping his lungs.

I nodded and took a deep breath, searching what I could see of his face and body for any sign of injury. He looked okay, so I glanced at Isi, who was looking back at me. Her eyes weren't focused on me, though. She was looking out the window, and she had a gash across her forehead.

"Isi, are you okay?" I didn't think she'd had her seatbelt on during the crash. She had to be hurt. "Isi," I called, but she didn't answer as she shimmied out the front window, leaving us behind.

Brody had already gotten himself unbuckled and was helping me with my seatbelt. Aaron followed out the window, and I crawled on my forearms out of the ditch until we were clear of debris and broken glass.

By the time we got out, Isi was gone. I glanced around the ditch, looking for any sign of her. There were trees lining the patch of dry grass where we currently stood. It was possible she'd made it to the trees with no one in the trucks noticing, or maybe they had let her go because she wasn't the one they wanted.

As we stared up at the three trucks parked on the road above us, two men stepped out from behind two of the trucks. The first man was tall and thin with blond hair and blue eyes. The second man was shorter and bulkier, a brunette with brown eyes.

"Do we run?" Aaron asked, looking over his shoulder for an escape route.

The two men pulled guns out from behind their backs and flashed them at us, answering Aaron's question.

A third man got out of the lead truck and walked toward us, his hand held up to stop us from leaving. There was something familiar about him. He wore black jeans and a long-sleeved black shirt with the sleeves pushed up to his elbows. His hair was long and shaggy and tied back in a ponytail that fell well below his shoulders. He hid his eyes behind sunglasses, but I sensed he was looking at me. A smile spread across his face as if he knew something I didn't.

"Meda," he said my name.

I tried to respond, but I couldn't. My hands were shaking, and I felt light-headed from the crash.

"Come here," he said.

I looked at Brody and Aaron, and they watched me to see what I would do. I walked toward the man.

"No!" Brody shouted at the man as he stood in front of me, blocking my path.

"There's nowhere to go," the man said. "Let's do this the easy way."

"You're not taking Meda anywhere!" Brody yelled.

The man looked over his shoulder and nodded to the short bulky man, who raised his gun and fired at Aaron. There was no warning, and Aaron yelled out, dropping to his knees.

"No!" Brody and I yelled simultaneously. Brody ran to Aaron's side and bent over. I could see the blood spreading across the thigh of Aaron's jeans. They weren't aiming to kill.

"Come here," the man said again.

I didn't hesitate this time. Raising my hands, I began walking up the embankment, crunching through the dry grass and leaving Brody holding Aaron closer to his chest while gripping Aaron's leg, trying to stop the blood flow.

"Meda, don't!" he called. But I didn't have a choice. There was nowhere to go. And I couldn't allow them to hurt Brody or Aaron. I continued walking toward the man with long hair and black sunglasses.

The man looked at me with an unreadable expression on his face before winking and turning around to walk back toward the trucks. A sound came from behind me, and someone grabbed my shoulder. They dragged me over to the back door of the truck.

"Meda!" Brody screamed. "Let her go!"

The man kept a firm grip on my shoulder while he pushed me toward the truck. I stumbled forward, catching myself on the side of the vehicle. A moment later, hands ripped at my clothes. They were searching me for weapons, but I didn't like the careless way they brushed against me.

"No!" I yelled, squirming away.

A hand clamped down over my mouth as something brushed against my skin.

"I would stop fighting if I were you," the man holding me said, his hot breath hitting my ear as he spoke.

My heart pounded as I fought back, but something sharp pricked into my side, and I winced in pain. He had a knife at my back, and he would use it if he had to. The fight drained out of me, and my body felt heavy as I went limp in his arms.

He held me in place as he removed his hand from my mouth. He put a black bag over my head, so I couldn't see, and I felt the familiar itch of handcuffs click against my wrists. The truck's engine started as the door opened. The man lifted me and tossed me into the back of the truck, my knees knocking together hard enough to leave bruises. I fell over on my side, my head bouncing on the seat cushion. Brody yelled in the distance, but there was nothing he or any of us could do. There was nowhere to run. They outnumbered and outgunned us.

I felt the vehicle shift into drive and we lurched forward, picking up speed to merge back on the highway. My heart sank with every bump we hit. I didn't know what they would do with Brody or Aaron. If they were Opposition, there was hope that Smith would let them off without punishment, but if these men were Agency, then I wasn't sure they'd have a reason to keep them alive.

Chapter 37

The truck drove for hours until we finally stopped. They hauled me out of the back of the truck, but not before removing the handcuffs, which seemed like an odd mistake. Rough hands pushed me forward, and gravel slipped beneath the soles of my shoes. Someone gripped my shoulder, halting me, and the sound of keys in a lock made my heart race as they pushed me through a doorway. My elbow connected with something, and I winced as the door slammed shut behind me.

"Where are we?" I heard Brody's voice coming from somewhere, but I still couldn't see anything. "Where's Aaron? Is he okay?" The desperation in his voice crushed me. I knew little about bullet wounds, but if they'd hit a major artery, Aaron could be in danger.

Gravel crunched as their feet moved away from me. There was a rustling, and I wondered if Brody was putting up a fight.

Someone pulled on my arm. At first, I tried to pull away, but then I realized they had made the mistake of removing my handcuffs, so I did the only thing I could do. I reached out and grabbed the arm that held me and concentrated.

The world brightened, and I was seeing through someone else's eyes. It was a warehouse, different but similar to the building Isi had procured. This one was bigger, though. Brody stood near Aaron,

214

holding him up. They had both turned in my direction, though they were being led deeper inside the building.

The guy who held me was thinking about me just being a little girl. I sensed he wasn't worried about me and couldn't wait to get me inside and be done. He was also hungry. He wanted a cheeseburger.

I recalled the people I'd shifted into from my past and remembered a wealthy businessman who'd also been a heavyweight, golden glove boxer. I concentrated on his face and his form. The familiar prickling sensation that came with the change started at my fingertips, and I ripped my arm away from the man.

He'd only been holding loosely to me, so as soon as I got away, I reached up and pulled the hood from my head. Sunlight coming in from the skylights near the roof blinded me momentarily, and the thoughts that flooded through me from the man I shifted into made me hesitate. The man reached under his jacket. Instead of waiting to discover what it was, I balled my fist and stepped forward, putting my weight into it. I connected to his cheekbone, and a jolt quaked through my fist, trying to stop from grimacing in pain. The man dropped to his knees, and I bent over him and reached into his jacket, holding the heavy weight of the gun.

"Freeze!" Someone yelled from behind me. I turned with the gun in my hand, and the two men who were escorting Brody and Aaron now had their guns pointed at me. The one I'd punched was still on his knees, so I hauled him up by the shoulder and used him as a shield.

Brody let go of Aaron and moved toward the short, stocky guy. Sensing movement, the tall man turned just in time to witness Brody grab the stocky guy's arm, trying to get the gun from him. The tall man pointed the gun at Brody, but he was struggling with the other guy.

A thunderous crack filled the air, and I flinched, unable to keep my eyes open. When I opened my eyes, everyone stood still. I scanned Brody's body for blood but followed the direction of his eyes.

A woman stood in the center of the warehouse. Chelsea Abbott, like a white pants-suited assassin, pointed her gun at Aaron. For some reason, I hadn't expected her to be so handy with a gun.

She took a few steps closer to him. "Give it up, Meda."

She stared at Aaron. I looked at Brody, and he backed away from the other man with his hands up, not willing to risk her firing at his best friend. There was no telling what she would do. If I gave up, she might just shoot Aaron and Brody, anyway.

"Chayton is here." Her eyes traveled to me. "So is your brother."

There was no way to win in this situation. I put my hands up, letting go of the ponytail guy. His weight must have been resting on me because first, he fell forward, and then he got up to his feet, brushing off his knees.

"Let them cuff you." She continued to stare at me.

"Don't do it," Brody said. "Run, Meda. She won't shoot you."

She walked over to Brody, her heels crunching across the gravel like a hammer on glass, and she put the gun at his temple. "I might not, but I have no reason not to shoot you."

"Please!" I took two steps closer. "Don't do it." I put my hands out. "Go ahead," I said to the ponytail guy.

He looked at Abbott, and she nodded. He walked over and slid the cuffs into place. The familiar stinging started at my wrists, and I felt pins and needles as my knees went weak. Everything faded to black.

I awoke, strapped down to a table. I lifted my head just enough to recognize the silver straps that held me down. Smart. Any other way and I would be able to shift into someone else to maneuver out of the position I was in. Still, I tried to lift my hands. The weight of something cold and heavy hung from my right wrist.

"Aha, I was beginning to think you wouldn't wake up," came a familiar voice.

I jerked my head, which proved to be a mistake as colors bloomed in my eyes like roses. My head was still spinning as I looked up. Chelsea Abbott stood over me.

"What's going on? What do you want?" I croaked out. My throat felt like sandpaper. We were in an unfamiliar room now. There were no vehicles parked in here, but it still had the same high ceilings.

"Well, I wanted access to that database. What I found out from our person inside was that instead of planting the device to give us access, you fried the server and destroyed it." Her eyes were a deep brown, and her blond hair was pulled back in an elegant updo. But as she turned her head, I thought I saw a hint of green in her eyes.

"So, I thought we'd spend a little time together and figure out how things are going to go down from now on." Her eyes searched my face. "You see, Meda, this whole spy business was never really your thing, was it?" She smiled down at me as if she were saying something kind. I glared and tried to wiggle free again. The cold metal only bit into my wrists with each movement until I stopped the useless effort.

"Where are Brody and Aaron?" I asked. "Where's Chayton?"

"Brody and Aaron are over there." She pointed over her shoulder, and I tilted my head, getting a sideways view of them sitting on the floor. The short guy had his gun on them, but Brody was whispering to Aaron, who looked pale, no doubt from the loss of blood. Abbott continued, "This would be easier if you agreed to cooperate. Then we'd release you from this contraption." She motioned at the table.

I looked around the room, and I realized it actually looked

familiar. There were other tables, but they remained empty. "What is this place?" I tried to tilt my head to get a better view.

A smile crept across her face. "You don't remember? This was where you were first processed when you joined the Agency. This is where we bring all our new recruits."

I looked around, vaguely remembering those few days when they'd run all kinds of tests on me. I'd almost forgotten after everything that had happened.

"I'd planned on filling these tables." She looked around the room. "But plans change, I guess." She waved at someone off in the distance. I turned my head but couldn't see what she was looking at. "Oh, sorry," Chelsea said to someone. "Bring them closer."

Elan, Briar, and Bly were being held by men with guns. Chayton walked behind them with his head down.

"No," I said. "Don't do this. Take me." I struggled against my restraints. "Let them go and take me."

"You're damaged goods. You'll never be able to do what we need you to do." Her face was stone as she spoke, but there was something underneath her words. I couldn't make sense of it, but it didn't seem like she was telling the truth.

I gritted my teeth, attempting to fight the rage that was building inside. After all we'd been through, it couldn't end this way. "How can you use people? How can you be so awful?" My words were venom.

Chayton moved to Chelsea's side. "She's right, Chelsea. Meda's our best bet. She's already trained. She'll be compliant because of her family." I stared at him, trying to figure out his angle. He seemed comfortable sacrificing me.

Abbott spoke to Chayton but watched me. "So, we get rid of those two?" She motioned toward Brody and Aaron. "Because I know they'll keep sniffing around." I held my breath, glancing over to where Brody and Aaron were. "And what about Elan? He'll be compliant because of his girlfriend and her brother. And you know what? Who knows? They just might like the job."

Chayton glanced at Elan, and I wondered again why he was trying so hard to save him. I just wished he'd tried that hard for me. "We only need Meda. She's special."

"Shut up," I said between clenched teeth. Chayton looked down at me. His eyes were cold. I couldn't believe he was about to tell Abbott my secret.

"Oh, brother," Abbott said in an uncharacteristically informal vernacular. "And I mean oh, brother." His eyes traveled back to her. "Meda, I know what you think. You think I talk the talk but don't walk the walk?" She turned to Chayton. "For being so smart, you really have been an idiot." Chayton's eyes turned to slits as he tried to decipher her words.

Abbott reached back and pulled the clip out of her hair, letting it drop to her shoulders, but the color was changing from blond to a dark brown, with silver and gray highlights. Her porcelain skin darkened to a sun-kissed tan. Abbott was a mimic.

I glanced at Chayton as his mouth opened, and recognition washed down his face.

"Meda?" he asked. I glanced at him, but he wasn't looking at me. He was looking at the woman.

"You mean, Mae? Wasn't that always your cute nickname for me, little brother?" The woman moved closer to Chayton, her green eyes bright in the sunlight.

Chayton's eyes widened. This was his sister. My namesake. So many questions swirled in my head. Had she been Chelsea Abbott the entire time? Who else knew about this? What was she doing here? Why was she revealing herself now?

"But, I don't understand?" Chayton said. I'd never seen him look so confused. He was always in control of every situation, but in this case, I took little pleasure in his discomfort. "Why would you do this, Mae?" Chayton's eyes pleaded with his sister.

"Why would I do what, little bro?" Mae stared at him. "You know. It's the same reason you do it. It's the same reason that Isi over there does it. When the only one you have is yourself, you see everyone else as a competitor. Yes, brother, I wish we could have been like brother and sister. But mom and dad put all the stock in you and sold me to slavery."

Chayton shook his head. "What are you talking about?" He moved closer to her, but she took a step back.

"Oh, Chayton. You were their boy. Always smarter and stronger. What hope did they have for me? Our parents looked at us as a profit. They could make money off me if they sold me to the highest bidder. I was nothing more than a toy. But you were the real deal, ready to move up in the ranks." I watched Mae as she spoke. She sounded just like my mother, like Ava. It was true. The men always had the advantage.

"I never saw you that way. You know that." Chayton reached out to her, and she stared at him, a look of disgust on her face. "Mae, you can't do this to our people." He looked at me and said, "They don't have to end up like us. They don't have to make the choices we did."

Mae's hand tightened into a fist. She slammed it on the table by my head. "Why not, Chayton? Why shouldn't they go through every damn thing we had to? It's only fair. I didn't deserve to be sold off at sixteen, and neither did you."

"But, can't you understand that making them relive our tragedies doesn't right the injustices that occurred to us? It only perpetuates them."

"I'd heard you'd gotten soft. I'm sure it's her doing." Mae nodded her head in my direction. "Now that the database is gone, we're going to have to be stingy with our mimics."

She nodded at the man at the door. He moved over to Elan and grabbed him by the shoulder. Elan tried to shrug the man off and raised his fist to punch him, but the other man already had Briar in silver cuffs. Her eyes were far off, and she looked like she might pass out. Elan rushed to her to catch her.

Chapter 38

A lull settled after the commotion. I focused on the area over my heart, trying not to panic. What would she do with us? Would she let me go if I wasn't needed? Would Chayton bargain for me if he couldn't get Elan's freedom? What would happen to Brody and Aaron?

Chayton cleared his throat. "If you let Meda and her friends go, you won't hear from them again. They won't work for the Opposition. They won't come after the Agency. Right, Meda?"

I looked at him, trying to figure out where this abrupt turnaround came from. "I won't work for them again." I nodded my head in agreement.

"That's what I thought." He forced a smile, but it wasn't believable.

Mae looked at both of us and shook her head. "Brother, I didn't get to where I am by being stupid. In fact, I've been heading up this division for so long, and yet you had no clue who I was. What? Are you going to make Meda cross her heart and hope to die? There are no guarantees in this game. You know that more than anyone." Her words were sharp, but there was something in her voice. It was like she was delivering lines from a script.

Chayton stared at her, shifting from foot to foot. Anger and frustration simmered just below the surface.

Something caught my eye just behind him. I hadn't seen the side door before. It was now open a crack, and a black head of hair and squinty green eyes glared at me from just outside the door. It was Isi. When we made eye contact, the corner of her mouth drew up, and she flashed the gun she held in her hand. I looked away, not wanting to give away her position in case anyone was watching me.

Once again, I had to hand it to Isi. She was good at this stuff. I thought she'd run away from it all, but here she was again. And I was grateful for her. I didn't know if she was doing it for me or to secure her place at the Agency, but either way, I was happy to see her. I didn't have to wait long to find out what she had planned.

The sound of rapid gunfire striking the metal and brick walls at the front of the building interrupted. All heads turned to look toward the earsplitting noise, and three of the men — not the ones who'd brought us here — ran to the front of the building, while the ponytail guy stood by Mae's side protectively.

Then came an enormous blast, and the ground that the table was bolted to shuddered. Metal folded on metal as the front of the building collapsed in on itself in a shrieking cry of destruction. Dust and debris clouded the air. My first thought was that it had been bombed. I couldn't determine where everyone was in the room because of the straps still holding me to the table. I imagined the whole place coming down, myself buried in the rubble.

The air settled, revealing poles, metal, and glass scattered across the floor. A man in military fatigues walked through the rubble and stepped into my line of sight, and though he had a helmet on, I recognized the age-wizened eyes of Zane.

Before anyone reacted, he lifted his gun and shot the man closest to me, the guy with the ponytail. I flinched. The ponytail guy grabbed his shoulder and then dove behind the table where Zane wouldn't be able to get a clear shot.

Chayton leaned forward and released the latch on my straps. I rolled off the table and crouched behind it, away from any gunfire. I wasn't sure why he'd helped me. I wasn't sure of anything anymore.

I looked around the side of the table, and Brody dragged Aaron back from the chaos. Over his shoulder, I noticed the door that Isi had peeked through. I wasn't sure where it led to, but I thought I could make it.

I felt someone grab my wrist and yank on it. It was a woman I didn't recognize, and I pulled back, twisting my arm to get away.

"Meda, it's me! Come on! We don't have much time!" And I knew it was Isi. She couldn't wear her own face if she wanted to return to the Agency. I let her pull me toward Brody and Aaron, and we ran in a crouch to avoid gunfire.

We got to them, and Isi took Aaron's other arm, ran, and opened the door. I looked back to see Chayton observing us. "What about the rest of them?" I asked. Elan was shielding Briar, and Bly was standing with his mouth open, unsure of what to do. If we left them, Mae could still force Elan, Briar, and Bly to work for the Agency.

"Let's go!" Isi yelled. Another explosion went off at the side of the building, and Bly crashed to the floor, blasted by the impact. There was more gunfire, and I wasn't sure if it was Zane or someone else firing back.

Brody and Isi pulled Aaron through the doorway, and though I didn't want to, I shook my head and followed them through the door. I let it swing shut behind me, and an open padlock rattled against the metal door. I latched it in place, locking it behind us. Not that it would keep anyone with guns from shooting through the door, but it might buy us time.

Chapter 39

We followed Isi down the alley. Aaron gasped for breath, trying to keep up with us but struggling. Brody pulled Aaron along, but the look in his eyes told me he was concerned. Aaron had already lost a lot of blood.

We stopped at a road, and Isi looked both ways, tucking the gun in the pocket of her jacket. I grabbed her shoulder. "What about Chayton? Elan?"

"What about them?" She stepped into the street as I followed.

"We left them." I gasped for breath.

She held up her hand as a car approached, and the woman behind the wheel glared at us but didn't honk her horn. "Chayton will protect them," Isi said. "They'll be fine. They might have to do some jobs, but they'll live."

I still didn't like it. "What about Zane? What was with all those explosions?"

Isi smiled at me with her teeth bared and her eyes wild. "Don't worry about it. We got it covered. Zane has an exit strategy. Once the last bomb goes off, he'll run. We have to get to *that* building." She pointed to a church spire in the distance. "That's where we're meeting Zane. He has a vehicle parked behind the next building and is taking a different route."

Aaron was panting hard and covered with sweat, but he was moving on his own now. "What if Zane doesn't make it? What if something happens to him?" Zane had risked his life for us, complete strangers, and it was almost too much to bear.

"He'll be fine, and if not, he knows the risks." Isi turned back and motioned to the rest of us. "Let's go." She moved down the sidewalk, navigating the winding city blocks that led to the church.

Aaron and I exchanged a worried look, but we couldn't argue with that. Zane seemed totally devoted to Isi, and I wondered what she'd saved him from.

We ran up the street at a brisk pace, checking for police cars every few seconds. There were none. As we reached the intersection, I heard shouting behind us, and Aaron cursed loudly when he fell to one knee.

"Aaron!" I shouted and reached down, gripping him by the shoulder. Brody was on his other side, pulling him up.

"I can do it," he said through clenched teeth. "Just… help me up. I don't have time for this!" He tried to push himself up but stopped suddenly when a group of five police cars rounded the corner, sirens blaring.

We all froze, hoping they wouldn't notice us, and they didn't, passing by in a whirl. They were heading in the direction we'd just come from. I looked back to see smoke billowing from the warehouse. I pulled Aaron up to his feet, and he limped along.

"That was a close one."

Isi waved us along. "We have to keep moving." I glanced back at the approaching cars. "Now!" Isi pushed us into the street, and we kept going.

We were almost at the next intersection when I heard Aaron curse again, his breaths coming in hoarse gasps. He went down hard on one knee and grabbed his leg as he tried to get up. "Aaron!" I yelled, dropping to my knees beside him.

"It's the bullet wound," he said through gritted teeth. "It hurts, but I can go on."

"You're in no state to go anywhere," Isi told him.

He tried standing again, and again he fell back onto the ground, his face twisted with pain. He was breathing hard, holding pressure on his leg. "Just leave me here," he said between breaths.

Isi shook her head and grabbed him under the arm, dragging him along. He was heavy for a such a skinny guy, but she pulled him forward, anyway. She moved him with ease, and I wondered if she was drawing on some of the strength of one of the people she had shifted into. I'd heard that type of thing was possible.

The sirens were getting closer. "Stop," I told her. She shook her head.

"We can talk later, but now we run!" We ran down the street, pulling Aaron as fast as he could move, and across another intersection before turning a corner.

"Come on, this is our stop." She started walking across the street as traffic roared past. The sidewalk ended, and we made our way along the side of the road. Cars honked at us and flew past, swerving around us, but Isi never broke her stride.

I watched each vehicle rush past, waiting for an opportunity to step down into the grassy median strip in the middle of the road. A lull came, and I dashed across the street, but a car suddenly pulled up and stopped in front of me with its horn blaring right in my face. I leaped out of the way in time, landing in the grass inches from being run over. I hit my elbow hard, and it started screaming in pain.

Brody pulled me up as Aaron limped ahead. "You okay?" he asked.

I glanced at my elbow and looked back to the road. "Yeah, I think so." My sleeve was ripped, and I had a deep gash on my elbow. "It's just banged up," I said. "Come on, it'll be fine." He wrapped his arm around me, and we hobbled together after Isi and Aaron.

There was an earthshaking thud, and Isi looked back. "That's the signal. Hurry! We don't want Zane to wait. They could follow him."

We all started running, trying to get to the church as fast as we could. Aaron was moving on his own, and it had to be the adrenaline pushing him.

"How is Zane going to get out?" I asked. "There are people everywhere."

Isi glanced behind her and caught her breath for a moment while she ran. "Zane's going to slip out when everyone else is distracted. He'll disappear into a crowd, and the police will lose him."

I didn't like that idea. "What if he gets caught? They'll shoot him for sure."

"Zane's a crafty guy. He's been living on the streets since he was a kid. He's a survivor." I saw a gleam in Isi's eye. There was pride there. And once again, Isi's emotions rose to the surface in unsettled waters. I was positive I didn't know her at all.

We ran through an alley, and Aaron was finally keeping up, though his brow was glistening with sweat, and his jaw clenched with each jolt of pain. We were gaining distance from the warehouse while sirens echoed through the city streets.

As we turned a corner, I could see the church spire. We were almost there. I only hoped Zane could make it out alive. Even so, I didn't know where we would go after this.

"Almost there," Isi said. I nodded, and we picked up our pace.

As we ran to the church, a black SUV rounded the corner and skidded to a halt in front of the majestic building. The windows of the vehicle were dark, and I couldn't see inside until the doors opened. Zane opened the door and stepped out, waving us to him. He had dark circles under his eyes and a cut on the back of his hand that had stopped bleeding but still showed a dried red line.

"What happened?" Isi asked, looking at his arm as arm as we approached. "Are you okay?"

"I'm fine," he said as Isi ran to him and gave him a tight hug before waving us to the vehicle.

"Come on!" she called. "Get in!"

Isi ran around to the passenger side while the rest of us piled into the back seat. Isi got in first, and Zane climbed behind the wheel. Before putting the vehicle into drive, he looked back to make sure we were all inside.

He pulled out onto the street and turned to Isi. "Everyone okay?" His voice was gruff but concerned.

"We're good." Isi looked out the rearview mirror and kept turning and looking out the back window. "We lost them, for now anyway," she said. "Until we find out someone has a tracker on them."

Zane nodded, and we drove in silence for a few minutes until I spoke up. "Where are we going?"

Isi looked at Zane. "We're going back to the compound. We'll lie low there for a few days until things cool off. Then we'll figure out what's next."

"What will we do about our families?" I asked.

Isi looked me in the eye. "We're not doing anything about them, Meda." She said my name like I was supposed to know what that meant. Her voice was harsh, and I felt like she had slapped me.

"But we can't just leave them. No one is safe."

Isi didn't acknowledge my words, but Brody's hand found mine, and he gave it a squeeze. "We'll figure it out," he whispered in my ear.

I turned and looked out the window, trying not to let the tears that were blurring my vision fall. Smoke billowed in the sky, a remnant of our recent battlefield.

"Hey!" Zane called. "I think we have company." We looked back to see a black sedan following us.

As we drove, the sedan stayed close behind. Zane tried to lose it by making a few turns down various side streets, but the sedan was always there, lurking like a shark in the water.

Chapter 40

When the car got close enough, I saw it was Chayton behind the wheel. Of course, he'd escaped. And he was alone in the car, which meant he'd left Elan and everyone else in the hands of Mae. I wasn't sure if he was coming for us as the Agency or as our father?

Zane continued to weave through the city streets, trying to lose our tail. Isi glanced back, and I knew she realized it was Chayton.

"We can't let him follow us back," Brody said, but Isi continued to look ahead.

"Do you think he knows anything about your place?" I asked, uncertain.

"If he knows, we'll figure something out," Zane said easily. "I have places of my own." Isi studied Zane's face, and I wondered if he was like her father figure.

"He won't turn us in," she said. "He doesn't have to. I'll go willingly." She looked back at me.

I couldn't contain my surprise. "You're not done after all this?" I asked. Brody squeezed my hand as he sensed the anger in my voice.

"This is it for me. This is all I have," she said. "Plus, us destroying the database was just the beginning." Under her breath, she said, "These things take time."

"What do you mean?" I asked. "So, you just want to give up?" I was getting irritated.

"No," she said as we drove away from the city center, with Chayton behind us. We weaved through city streets to the cracked alleyways and dim overpasses. "We'll see what his offer is."

I turned to Brody. Aaron, whose eyes were closed, leaned against the window. I leaned closer to Brody. "We can't go back to the cabin," I whispered to him, sadness breaking through my words.

"No, we can't," Brody said. He grabbed my hand and leaned over to whisper in my ear. "We could find our own place, a place where nobody knows our location."

"I'll never see my dad again. Or my sisters." My voice caught as I spoke. "I just don't know what to do." I fought the tears that bloomed in the corners of my eyes.

"We'll figure it all out when we get there," Brody said. In that one sentence, Brody gave me hope that everything would be okay — that I wouldn't be forced to choose between my family and love. "But we'll have each other. And you'll be free. And maybe, given time, we'd be able to contact them."

"It's not the right thing to do. I know that now. If I can help people, I need to."

"You helped, by destroying the database. I'm not going to lie… I doubted you. But you did what was right. You need to help your family, Meda. You have a right to see them. Nobody can take that away from you. And no one should make you lose sight of what matters."

Aaron's breathing was heavy, and I realized he must've passed out.

I looked into Brody's eyes and surrendered to the fact that I would never understand his life before me. And that was okay because I realized his life before didn't matter. He had been someone else; he was not that person anymore. I spoke so only he could hear me, "The Agency is everywhere — we can't run forever. It's time I face up to what I am and who I'm going to be."

Brody squeezed my hand in his. "And I'll be here whenever you need me."

We drove in silence, our minds racing with the possibilities of what Chayton's offer would be. Would he want to turn us in? Or was he here for something else?

As we drove, I felt a new resolve form in me. Whatever Chayton's offer was, I knew I would have to face it head-on. We couldn't keep running. It was time to fight for what was right. For my family. For Brody. For us.

We made our way back to Isi's empty building. Chayton pulled in behind us, and we all piled out of the vehicle. Aaron looked a little better after his nap in the car, but he hobbled on his wounded leg. Brody stayed by his side as Zane led them into the building. Isi and I waited for our father.

I watched him approach and again noticed the dark circles under his eyes. His hair was messed up, and his suit was smudged. He looked exhausted. "You're all safe," he said.

"How did you get out of there?" I asked.

"What's going on?" Isi asked, glaring at Chayton.

He paused for a second, looking at Isi. There was something in his eyes. He reached out to place his hand on her shoulder, but she ducked it. He let it fall to his side. "Good job, girl." He stared at her, awaiting her response.

Isi lifted her chin at him as he turned his attention to me.

"So, I just get to go now?" I asked Chayton.

"Well, you know it's not quite that simple, Meda. They'll never just let you go. You'll have to be wiped. You'll need to go in deep, always looking over your shoulder." He looked at Isi.

I moved closer to him. "What's the alternative?"

"Well, they'll hold tight to me and Elan and you if they can. Now that we've erased all their research, it's us, Isi, and maybe a few other mimics. The other mimics are loyal, and the Agency can persuade Isi. They will do anything they can to keep their assets."

"So, we need to destroy the whole damn Agency?"

"We're not going to do that on our own." Chayton shook his head. "Plus, I can't. It's my sister."

I scoffed at him. "Maybe we should all just stop lying to each other," I said before glancing at Isi. "Maybe we should confess all of our sins and get it on the table. You and your sister. What other children are you hiding — or *protecting*, as you like to call it?"

Chayton shook his head. "You've got to stop taking this all so personally."

"The hell if I do," I said. "They've toyed with me and jerked me around so much I have whiplash. It is personal."

He looked at me for a minute and then sighed. "Okay, Meda. You're right. I'm sorry. We all are. But we need to focus on what's important now."

"Which is?" I asked.

"Getting rid of the Agency. For good." Chayton crossed his arms.

"Come on," Isi said. "Let's talk inside." She turned her back and led the way into what I assumed was our new headquarters. The Resistance.

When we walked in, Aaron sat in a chair, and Brody stood in front of us, waiting to hear what Chayton had to say. Zane stood back, not a part of the conversation.

"So, what's the plan?" Brody asked.

"We need to get rid of the Agency," Chayton said.

"How?" Aaron lifted his head, disbelief clouding his eyes. The Agency had always been untouchable. But Chayton was suggesting we take them down.

"We need to get the entire Agency," Chayton continued. "And we need to do it before they can find us."

There was doubt in everyone's eyes, but especially in Aaron's. We had always been the underdogs. The ones who fought for what was right but never won. The Agency had always been too strong.

"We need to hit them where it hurts," Chayton said. "Where they're the most vulnerable."

"And what's that?" I asked.

Chayton looked at me and then at Isi. "Their assets."

"What do you mean?" I asked.

"We need to take out their financial resources," Chayton said. "Destroy their bank accounts, get rid of their investments. Cut off their funding."

The plan took shape in everyone's minds. The Agency was too strong, but maybe this was our chance. Maybe we could take them down. "When do we start?" I asked.

Chayton grinned at me. "Now."

Chapter 41

Chayton and Isi wanted to chat about what they could do from inside the Agency to help move things along. It was obvious that this plan was a new idea, barely formed or thought out. Brody waved at me to follow him upstairs to the bedroom we'd shared the last time we were here. Once we were safely behind closed doors, he motioned for me to sit on the edge of the mattress and joined me.

I sat down next to him and reached up to twist my earring, but I found nothing but earlobe. I closed my eyes and inhaled. In a few weeks, I'd discovered my entire life had been a lie. Even more, I had this ability to read minds that would forever make me hunted.

Brody wrapped his arm around my shoulder, and I rested my head on his. "Do you know what I'm thinking right now?" he asked. And I realized that even though he touched me, it did not catapult me into his head like with the others. Maybe I was gaining control.

I lifted my head and turned to face him, taking both of his hands. "I'm sorry I didn't tell you right away about it." I looked back down, studying his firm hands and touching the thickness of his fingers.

"It's hard to get your head around this." I looked up into Brody's face. "I'm not mad at you for hiding anything from me. It just hurts that you thought you couldn't tell me. Like I haven't accepted everything about you."

My throat closed up as he let that sink in.

Brody let go of my hand and cupped my cheek like he was going to kiss me. But his lips met my forehead, and he pulled away quickly. My skin burned where he'd touched me. "I'm sorry," he whispered. "I just don't know how to deal with this."

"Brody, it's okay." I scooted closer and wrapped my arms around him. He leaned into me, and we just sat there for a few minutes. My eyelids grew heavy, and Brody pulled up my chin to look at my face.

"You're exhausted," he said. "We'll talk more in the morning."

I yawned and nodded, letting him help me get comfortable on the mattress. I stayed in my dirty and bloodied clothes, too exhausted to worry about cleanliness. Brody crawled in next to me and spooned me from behind, his hand coming up to rest on my stomach.

"I'm here," he whispered. "I'm not going anywhere."

I drifted off with the warmth of him at my back.

"Meda…" The voice was a whisper, a quiet echo in my head. I looked to see if someone had entered the room, but there was no one. The voice called again. It was coming from inside my head.

I turned to Brody, but he was fast asleep. I realized then that it was my voice, calling to me from inside my mind. I closed my eyes and concentrated, trying to reach out to the voice. But it was like trying to grab a shadow. I couldn't hold onto it.

"Who are you?" I whispered, but there was no answer. Brody stirred next to me, so I turned over, careful not to jostle the mattress. I pushed myself up to standing, and my legs were jelly as I walked over to the door. I placed my ear up to it, listening for voices. But it was silent.

"Meda, do you have the ring?" The voice was stronger now, more solid. There was a presence, like someone was standing right next to me.

I closed my eyes and tried to focus. The image of the ring popped into my head, and I reached into the bottom of my pocket, having forgotten about it. My hand closed around the then cool metal, and I opened my eyes.

The presence was closer now, and I could make out a shadowy figure. I stepped back, but the figure didn't move. "Who are you?" I asked again, my voice trembling. A chill ran down my spine, and I took another step back. "What do you want?"

"Twist the ring and lock it into place." I couldn't make out the face of the figure, but I knew they couldn't really be there. No one was in the room. The shadowy image flickered like it had poor reception.

"What'll it do?" I asked.

"It'll signal me so I can come and get you." I held the ring up and stared at it. "Don't worry. It only sends a signal when you decide to turn it on."

"Why would I do that?" I asked, feeling stupid for whispering to myself.

"So you can come with me, and I can show you how to control your new powers."

"Moira?" I asked. I thought back to the shifter in the Agency building. How was she doing this?

"I can show you," the voice said again. Suddenly, the room around me flickered, and I was back in the office with her at the Agency. "None of it was real. I projected on you."

I moved to the corner of the room, far away from Brody, so he wouldn't hear me talking to myself. "I thought this didn't work on other mimics."

"No. Mimics have many walls up in their brains, compartmentalizing the knowledge of all the marks, but with practice, we can communicate with each other. Come with me, and I can show you. I can train you."

"Who are you?" I asked.

"My mother is the head of TAC. You met her as someone else. She was pretending. I'm your cousin."

Realization splashed down like a bucket of cold water. Moira was Mae's daughter. I was tempted to throw the ring across the room.

"Don't, Meda. Don't stay with Chayton. You can't trust him. The Agency was always a feeder program for TAC, so that we could find and help mimics. Chayton turned it into a political money-making scheme. My mother allowed him to do what he wanted as long as we could help others."

"Your mother just strapped me down to a table and threatened me."

"That was a show. She was doing that for Chayton's sake. She's not Abbott. She's only pretending to be Abbott to gain access to the Agency." So many more questions erupted. Who was the *real* Abbott, and what had happened to her that Mae could take over her life?

Brody shifted around on the mattress, rubbing his feet together. I put the ring back in my pocket as I turned away.

"Come with me," Moira pleaded with me.

"What about Brody? Aaron?"

"They can come with you. We can train them as handlers. We wouldn't dare split you from your friends. That's not who we are."

I closed my eyes, rubbing the ring through the fabric. It sounded too good to be true.

"I'm only asking you now. This is your last chance before you get in too deep with Chayton, and we can't trust you anymore."

I stared at Brody, sleeping in his bed.

"You wouldn't need to run anymore. We have a safe place for you to stay."

"How do I know that you're telling the truth? How can I trust you?" Before the word even left my mouth, an image flashed in my mind. It looked like a village in the tropics. People ran about, and homes dotted the coastline of the island. Moira stood on the beach, her feet in the water. She smiled and waved at me. I could even smell the ocean. I blinked, trying to clear my eyes of the image that was forced into my brain.

"You can't. I understand that. But trust me, Meda. I'm your family."

I thought about the ring and the signal it would send. If I turned it on, it would be like I was giving myself up to her. But if I didn't turn it on, I had to worry about betrayal from Chayton and Isi. Plus, the Opposition was bound to come after us.

"What about Isi? I can't just leave her here after everything."

"Isi can't come. We can't trust her."

I thought about Isi. Moira was right in saying she couldn't be trusted, but she had risked her life to help us. I felt like I was beginning to understand her, to crack her façade. But maybe, if I went now, I could convince Moira later that Isi would be better off with us.

"Okay," I said finally. "I'll come with you." I held the ring up and pinched it between both thumbs and pointer fingers. It surprised me when it gave way to two half circles. I locked it back in place. "What next?" I asked.

"Get Brody and Aaron, and meet me a block east."

"How am I going to do that?" I asked, but my head was empty. Moira was gone.

I ran over to Brody and knelt down by the bed. He was snoring lightly, his mouth ajar. I shook his shoulder gently. "Brody," I whispered.

"Mmm?" he muttered, his eyes still closed.

"We have to go." I pushed on his shoulder again.

He sat up quickly. "What? Where?"

"I can't tell you. You just have to trust me." I grabbed his arm and pulled him to his feet. He followed me to the door and down the hallway. Aaron was in the next room, and as we entered, Brody went to his side and put his hand over Aaron's mouth as he nudged him.

Aaron's eyes shot wide open but regained their normal size when he saw Brody. They had their own system of nonverbal communication. Brody shook his head and put one finger to his mouth before pointing at me standing by the door. Aaron nodded, and Brody helped him up as Aaron fought the groan that threatened to escape his throat.

We crept down the stairwell and into the main room. Zane was snoring on the mattress in the middle of the room, but I didn't see Isi or Chayton. They had to be somewhere in one of the side rooms, but there was no way of telling whether they were asleep or awake. I heard a low thunder from outside, and I motioned for the boys to follow me to the side door.

We slipped out the door and into the empty nighttime streets. The only sound was the rain that pattered against the asphalt. Brody helped Aaron, who hobbled at a jog.

"Which way is east?" I asked, and Brody pointed. The noise in the sky was growing louder, and as I looked up, there were lights in the distance. "That must be her," I said to myself. She was picking us up in a helicopter.

"Come on," I picked up the pace. The boys followed as best they could as the sound of the helicopter's approach grew louder. If Isi and Chayton weren't awake before, they definitely were now.

We turned the corner, and I saw the helicopter. It was hovering one hundred feet away, with spotlights shining down on us. The noise was so loud it was making my teeth hurt. "Hurry!" I yelled and ran. The boys ran in front of me, leading the way, but someone tackled me from behind, and I hit the ground hard.

My head snapped back, and for a moment, I saw stars. I struggled to get up, but someone's foot was on my chest, holding me down. I looked up, and Isi stood, glowering down at me. "What are you doing?" I asked.

"Helping you," she said. "You're coming with me." If she thought she was helping me by keeping me from Moira, this was a strange way to do it.

"Let me go." I grimaced, but Isi pushed down harder. I reached up and grabbed her toe and heel and twisted. Her leg buckled as she grimaced in pain. I attempted to stand, but she grabbed onto my leg. I kicked at her, trying to shake her loose.

"Let her go!" Brody yelled back at us. He and Aaron were at the helicopter, and Moira was in the pilot's seat, watching us fight. She motioned for Brody and Aaron to get on, and the two clambered into the back of the helicopter.

"No!" I yelled, trying to get to my feet.

Isi pulled me back down and punched me in the face. The lights faded, and I knew I was going to pass out. A gunshot rang out through the night. I vaguely thought that we were drawing a lot of attention to this new hiding spot. Isi let out a grunt, and when I looked up, a figure in black tactical gear approached me. It was Moira. Her powerful hands gripped me by the armpits and began dragging me. Isi was a lump near my feet.

"Is she okay?" I asked in dazed confusion before blacking out.

When I woke up, the sound of the helicopter blades filled my ears, and I tried to sit up, but Brody was next to me, his head against my shoulder. Aaron was across from us, with his eyes closed and his head leaned back against the wall.

I sat up, looking out the window. We were flying east, and the sun was coming up. "Where are we going?" I asked, but no one answered me. I thought about Isi and hoped she was okay.

Chapter 42

We dropped altitude somewhere along the coast. I could see the ocean from the helicopter's window. I had no clue where we were or where Moira was taking us, but I hoped it would be a better place than we'd left. The old doubt crept in, making me wonder if I'd made the right choice not only for me, but for Brody and Aaron too. I felt responsible for them now. No matter who else came out of the woodwork, these two were my family.

When the helicopter landed, Brody stirred, lifting his head from my shoulder and blinking groggily. He looked at me, and I knew what he was thinking. "What's going on?"

I shrugged at him and glanced at Aaron, who also shifted in his spot, wincing as he propped himself up.

The mechanisms of the helicopter slowed to a stop as Moira turned to us. "We're just refueling before we head out." I had so many questions to ask Moira, and I wasn't even sure if I could trust her yet.

She exited the helicopter, ducking as she hustled across the bare tarmac. I looked around us, and we seemed to be at a small airport, but it had to be private. It was empty except for a few smaller planes.

"What are you guys thinking?" Brody asked, speaking loud enough for Aaron to hear.

"I think I feel like shit." Aaron groaned.

I crawled over to his side, examining his wound. "It's not bleeding anymore, but we need to get you to a doctor and get that cleaned up."

He tipped his head in my direction, and I knew he wanted to say, "Duh," but he kept it to himself.

"I agree." Moira spoke from behind us, making me jump slightly.

I hadn't heard her approach. She leaned in the helicopter's side as the fuel truck pulled up next to us and two men got out, pulling a hose with them and climbing the ladder on the side of the truck. I turned to her, and she gave a tight smile.

"As soon as we get to the island, we'll have our doctors take care of him."

"Wait, where are we going?" I asked, now ignoring the men.

"I showed you. We're going to TAC Island." She reached over, grabbing Aaron's leg to examine it. He grimaced but didn't pull away. It was something about Moira's straightforward nature and directness that made her trustworthy.

"Is that what it's called? TAC Island? Really?" I asked as she pulled back, satisfied with the wound for the moment.

"I mean, that's what *we* call it. It's just a remote island in the Atlantic Ocean." She turned back to Aaron. "Are you sure you'll be okay until we get there? The wound looks clean." Aaron nodded back at her.

I continued my questioning. "And who lives there?" The men in the truck had finished and were packing up the hose and getting back in the truck.

"All the TAC agents and their families. It's a safe place."

I wasn't sure what to make of that, and I didn't want to ask what it was safe from. "Wait, you guys own it? Who owns it?"

"Well, a shell company owns it. We're a group of scientists

documenting the migratory patterns of seabirds and marine activity."

"Do you actually do that?" I asked, surprised that she was even answering my questions.

"No clue." Moira peered out across the tarmac as if waiting for someone to show up. "That's what they told us when we took residency. I think it's mostly a cover." She slapped the floor. "We better lift off," she said before closing the side door.

I wanted to ask about Isi — if she was okay. But Moira continued to the front and slid back into place, firing up the aircraft.

We continued to the island in silence. I was trying to take it all in and figure out what it meant. The pulsing whir of the helicopter and the glistening vastness of the ocean put me in a sort of daze until I saw an island ahead. I squinted. It wasn't a large island, and I could see how they might choose this location. Then again, if anything went down, they'd be trapped. I glanced at Brody, who was not sharing my fears, and his eyes were wide as he watched our approach.

Moira lined us up and set us down on a helicopter landing pad that was just off the beach. As we hovered to land, I could see people approaching, as though welcoming a group of tourists to an exotic resort.

After shutting down the machine, Moira came back to help. I crawled back over to Aaron to help lift him as Brody continued to his other side. Moira stood outside the helicopter, extending her arm for Aaron to take.

"Don't worry, Aaron," she said as we exited the helicopter. "We'll get you some help."

The three of us exchanged glances but said nothing and followed her. As we walked just outside the landing pad, a group of people were waiting for us. I examined them, wondering if they were all

TAC agents, but then I noticed kids running along the beach and dogs playing in the sand. It looked like a normal family scene. But I recognized that it was anything but.

When the group parted, a tall, slender woman walked forward. It was Mae, not hidden behind the face of Chelsea Abbott anymore. Moira approached her mother, and they embraced. A sudden jab prodded my heart at seeing the connection they had.

Mae came forward to greet us. "Welcome to TAC," she said. "I'm so glad you're here."

"Thanks." I tried to keep my emotions in check. I was overwhelmed and didn't know what to expect.

"I know you have a lot of questions," she said, "and I'm sorry about the ugly business back at the warehouse, but we need to get moving. We're already behind schedule." I opened my mouth to speak, but Mae held up her hand for silence and gave us all a weary smile. "Let's go inside, and I'll explain everything."

She paused, pointing at Aaron. "Moira, can you get this young man some medical attention?" Aaron still looked pale and drained, but relief washed down his face, knowing they were going to help him. "Brody can come with us," Mae said. Brody looked unsure about splitting up with Aaron, but I grabbed his hand, giving it a squeeze.

We followed Mae into the house. It was a typical family home, with a kitchen, living room, and bedrooms. But there were also workstations set up in each room and video monitors everywhere.

"This is our headquarters," Mae said. "All of our communications and operations are handled from here."

I tried to take it all in. Mae led us down the hallway to what I assumed was a private office. As we entered, I noticed the backs of two glossy-haired heads seated in front of the desk. My eyes darted to Mae before one head turned to face us.

"Meda?" a voice asked.

"Briar?" I said in return.

Briar stood, her eyes big. The person next to her turned. Bly yelled, "Meda!" and jumped up to give me a hug. I stumbled back, surprised by his enthusiasm.

"What are you doing here?" I tried to keep the disbelief out of my voice. Briar got up and hugged me tightly. They were still dirty and bloody from the fight. "Where's Elan?" I asked.

"He's safe," Mae said, and we all turned to face her. "He's with the Agency."

I let out a breath I hadn't realized I was holding. "Thank God," I said.

"We'll explain everything later."

Mae cut off whatever Bly was about to say. "Right now, we need to get moving. Chayton is making plans to take us down. And we're going to stop him."

CHRISTINA HAGMANN is an award-winning author of young adult fantasy, horror, and suspense novels. She writes fictional page-turners that entertain and leave readers wanting more. Christina continues to lead a not-so-secret double life as an author and an English teacher. She lives in Wisconsin with her husband and their basement full of arcade games.

Acknowledgement

First and foremost, I'd like to thank my family — my husband and son — for believing in me even when I wasn't doing much writing. I'd also like to thank my mom, dad, and sisters who've supported me along the way. Our nomadic, pinecone-picking upbringing is a big part of my creativity. I wouldn't trade it for anything.

Thanks to everyone on the Orange Hat team who helped me so much. Special thanks to Shannon Ishizaki, who makes Orange Hat so welcoming, and Lauren Blue, who helped me with the first Stratagem book. Thanks to Team Resistance — Jenna, Josh, and Kaeley, who worked tirelessly to make this book a reality — and Kim Suhr from Red Oak Writing, who provided valuable feedback.

I'd like to thank my friends, author friends, and readers. Along this journey, I've met so many like-minded book lovers who have supported and inspired my writing, from my wonderful teaching friends and librarians who are always searching for great books to get into young readers' hands, to my Askew friends and my Insta and BookTok readers and writers. Thank you for your insight and great book recommendations.

Last but not least, I'm thankful for everyone who read the first book and asked for a second book of what I originally thought would be a standalone. I, too, wasn't ready to leave these characters. I hope you enjoyed the Resistance.